EGYPTIAN
MOTHERLODE

BOOKS BY DAVID SANDNER
& JACOB WEISMAN

DAVID SANDNER

Fiction
His Unburned Heart

Non-fiction
*The Fantastic Sublime: Romanticism and
Transcendence in Nineteenth-century
Children's Fantasy Literature*
Critical Discourses of the Fantastic, 1712-1831

As Editor
The Afterlife of Frankenstein
Fantastic Literature: A Critical Reader
The Treasury of the Fantastic
(co-edited with Jacob Weisman)
Philip K. Dick: Essays of the Here and Now

JACOB WEISMAN

As Editor
The Sword & Sorcery Anthology
(co-edited with David G. Hartwell)
The Treasury of the Fantastic
(co-edited with David Sandner)
*Invaders: 22 Stories From the Outer
Limits of Literature*
The New Voices of Fantasy
(co-edited with Peter S, Beagle)
The Unicorn Anthology
(co-edited with Peter S, Beagle)
The New Voices of Science Fiction
(co-edited with Hannu Rajaniemi)

Praise for
EGYPTIAN MOTHERLODE

"In its wildest moments, *Egyptian Motherlode* reads like an apocalyptic mixup of Tananarive Due and Robert Anton Wilson. The research is impeccable, and the clear-eyed, revisionist view of the sixties is most welcome."
    —Lewis Shiner, author *Outside the Gates of Eden*

"*Egyptian Motherlode* is beautiful and loud. Psychedelic and surreal. It flows through the landscape of twentieth century music like the river of the dead, summoning ancient gods and chasing down lost volumes of occult knowledge, until every note is perfect, and we're all singing along at full volume. This book has *soul*."
    —Josh Rountree, author of *The Legend of Charlie Fish*

"*Egyptian Motherlode* is a psychedelic trip through musical history, where reality twists itself to the lives and dreams of the musicians who wove blues, jazz, rock, and funk into our world's fabric."
    —Jason Sanford, author of *Plague Birds*

"With *Egyptian Motherlode*, Sandner and Weisman lay out a mosaic that is two parts music, three parts magic and one part charming mythological romp across time. Fans of literary, musical fantasy will be delighted."
    —Ken Scholes, author of the Psalms of Isaak series

"David Sandner & Jacob Weisman blend their voices beautifully into an organic whole that reminds me of the tonality of John Kessel or Karen Joy Fowler."
    —*Locus Magazine*

EGYPTIAN

MOTHERLODE

DAVID SANDNER
JACOB WEISMAN

FAIRWOOD PRESS
Bonney Lake, WA

For George Clinton and Sun Ra,
celestial travelers.

1
EGYPTIAN
MOTHERLODE

California, 1993

I STOOD OFF-STAGE WITH ERIC AND MY BROTHER A.J. watching The Prophet. My brother and I were half a rap group, Crushed Ice, which was supposed to have been on stage an hour and a half ago, except Egyptian Motherlode wouldn't get off, their dance numbers extending through chorus after chorus, and now The Prophet droned on unintelligibly. Suddenly straightening the microphone, The Prophet's voice became clear in a harsh, amplified whisper.

"The Time has come to speak of something far more deeply interfused," The Prophet said. "A Funk Sublime—a motion and a spirit that impels and rolls through all things—where every groove belonging to me as good belongs to you."

My brother groaned and shook his head. Toward the back of the club patrons were starting to get up and walk away.

"The time has come," The Prophet said, "to speak of all unspoken things—why the darkness is boiling hot and whether pigs have wings."

He vocalized low, pulsing hums, sometimes crying out, sometimes falling silent. I could see Rat, part of the other half of Crushed Ice, at the back of the club, outlined in the doorway, trying to chase customers back to their seats. I had known him only about a week and a half. Our agent back in Oakland, Bobby Times, had put my brother and me with Rat and Desmond just for the tour. None of us was happy about it. Now, opening night, by the time we got up on stage at all, there wouldn't be anybody left to play to. I didn't know where Desmond was, probably talking to the manager, trying to make sure we got paid whether we played or not, whether there were customers or not.

The Prophet made a low hum or growl that made the hair on the back of my neck stand up.

"Funk is the sweet voice—Funk the luminous cloud—all melodies the echoes of that voice—all colors a suffusion of that light."

"Tell it like it is," Eric shouted. Although the way he said it, dull and flat, I could tell his heart wasn't in it. When I talked to Eric before the show he'd been in awe of The Prophet. Now he didn't seem so sure.

"Nobody wants to hear this shit anymore," Desmond said, coming up behind us. "Get him off the stage. It's embarrassing."

I didn't like his tone. He was desperate. A bead of sweat ran down his temple. He wore a black beret, a tan button-down shirt, green fatigues, and black boots. He towered over Eric and me.

"Look, man, people are leaving. The manager isn't going to pay us if everybody leaves."

I looked out at the audience. A minute ago there had been around twenty people, now there were six. Rat joined us. He had his hair tied up into stubby tails of red and green rubber bands. He put his hand on Desmond's shoulder. Desmond's face was red. He was blinking rapidly and his hands wouldn't stop shaking.

"This is our shot," Desmond said. "This is it."

"Shit," Rat said.

"I have touched the fire flowering from the sun," The Prophet said, sitting up "and felt the Martian darkening wave pass beneath my feet—and I have swum the gaseous sea of Jupiter—but it meant nothing to me—for I have been where Alph, the sacred river ran down to a sunless sea—where gardens bright with sinuous rills blossom many an incense-bearing tree—and seen the Red King asleep and dreaming of me."

The room burst with white glare and we had to shut our eyes. When we opened them again The Prophet stood there on the stage, the microphone limp in his hands. He let the mike drop to the floor and walked off-stage in our direction.

Desmond stepped in front of him as he passed. Eric grabbed Desmond's wrist but he shook him off. Rat and A.J. had to hold Desmond back. I stood between them and The Prophet, my hands up, warding, wondering what I would do if Desmond got loose. He was the biggest of us and right now the veins in his neck stretched out in long purple tracks from the top of his chin to below the line of his shirt. A.J. whispered, harsh and quick, in Desmond's ear, but he shook his head, no.

"Let him go," said The Prophet. We all turned in surprise as if we'd forgotten he was there. Rat and A.J. loosened their grip and Desmond leaned forward, menacing. The Prophet touched his hand. Desmond started as if shocked by static electricity. His face, first surprised, drooped.

"It's my fault," The Prophet said. "We played too long."

"This is our shot," Desmond said. "All we get."

The Prophet turned and walked off, followed by the guitarist in the wedding dress, and then Eric. I let out a breath I didn't know I was holding.

"All we get," Desmond repeated, more to himself than to any of us. A.J. nodded, but Desmond didn't look up. He put his face in his hands and started to cry.

That night I dreamed I crouched beside a man laid out on a table. I thought at first it was a hospital and the man an etherized patient, but he was dead and the table was made of stone. The white-haired man was laid out in ceremony with silver pitchers full of amber fluid and gold platters piled up with molding bread. I dreamed of a river, a great black river, slow-moving and inexorable, overflowing the banks of my imagination.

After last night's disaster, we'd been on the road all day. Driving under gray skies, not talking at all, Desmond and A.J. taking turns at the wheel. I was still too young to drive and Rat seemed too tired. I slouched in the back seat reading a faded, tattered copy of Richard Leakey's *Origins Reconsidered*. The back cover showed the paleoanthropologist sitting at his desk in a shirt and tie, his sleeves rolled up, examining a skull with a protractor as he scribbled notes onto a piece of paper.

Rat and Desmond teased me about the book, until I told them it was about dinosaurs. The two of them exchanged knowing glances. I had, after all, just turned fourteen. But the book wasn't about dinosaurs at all. It was more a rambling discussion of the evolution of human thought based upon evidence supported by the fossil record. Richard Leaky, I was discovering, was more a philosopher than an anthropologist. He was more concerned with what it all *meant*—the evolution of mankind and the confluence behind the origin of intelligent thought—than with the digging up of rare bones.

I was fascinated by the book. And in the silence, I felt compelled to devote my full attention to it, afraid to risk looking at anyone too closely. The dark sky pressed in, seeming about a foot above the roof, making me slouch deeper into my seat. My neck hurt.

Rat slept beside me on the back seat, drooling. He wore oversized jeans and a black T-shirt. His face, even asleep, looked worried. Sometimes he put his head on my shoulder, his arms crossed on his chest. Sometimes he snored, his mouth open, and his eyelids fluttering. As we pulled up to the theater in Eve Falls for a two-night run, the sky opened up at last, all at once, and it began to pour. Water filled the streets, running along the gutters, splashing beneath the tread of our tires.

The theater had a long row of scuffed, black-painted doors up front. One was propped open. A small ticket window to the right had a black curtain pulled down. Fronting the second story, in dirty green plastic letters on a field of dirty white plastic, the theater's sign spelled out:

EGYPTIAN MOTHERLODE
w/ CRUSHED ICE

"Oh, man," Desmond said, slapping the dashboard. "Our names should be on top. We're headlining. Bobby promised."

The Motherlode bus was parked down the street. The hood was up and smoke filtered out into the rain. Eric and a couple of the other band members stood on the sidewalk seeking shelter beneath the roof of a dilapidated building.

"Look at that old fossil," Desmond said, laughing.

The bus had been painted in haphazard smears of yellow-green-purple—some flowers, some moons, but mostly just a smear of color.

"Hey, Michael," Desmond said, turning back to me, "we found you a new dinosaur—check out Funkasaurus."

He waved his hand out toward the bus. I didn't say anything. Desmond frowned and turned around.

"Let's call Bobby," he said. "I'm tired of this shit."

Desmond and A.J. got out and headed for the open door. I rolled down my window when A.J. stopped at the door and turned around. "Don't go anywhere," he ordered, pointing at me, before turning back and going inside.

Eric, one hand in the pocket of his trench coat, the other holding a newspaper over his head, his collar turned up against the rain, walked briskly down the street to me.

"How's it going," he said.

"Not much," I said. "I mean, fine."

He reached into an inside pocket and pulled out a small, thin book.

"The Prophet said to give this to you."

"I don't even know The Prophet."

"He said you might enjoy it."

I took the book and wiped water drops from the cover. It was a tiny Xeroxed pamphlet. In cursive, the title read: Interpretations of the Egyptian Book of the Dead. Below that was written Motherlode Connection. There was also a drawing of a pyramid with an eye at the top, like on a dollar bill.

"I don't know, Eric."

"No, man, keep it. Check it out."

I flipped open the book. A neat handwriting covered the pages, next to sketches of mythological figures and hieroglyphs.

Rat had woken up on the seat behind me. He rubbed his face. Seeing Eric, he sat up and glared, finally getting out of the car and heading into the theater out of the rain.

"I better take off," Eric said, standing under the awning of the theater long enough to shake out his newspaper. "I'll see you tonight at the show."

He trotted off toward the bus.

*

I sat backstage, my arms across the back of metal folding chair, staring at my reflection in the splintered surface of the dressing room mirror. A large crack ran from the top to the bottom directly in front of me so that I looked like I had two faces: a small shriveled face on the left, and on the right, a face more recognizably my own, only older and haggard, already tired of living out of suitcases piled in the back of Desmonds' Oldsmobile.

"It'll get better," Rat said. "At least we'll get to play tonight." He paused. "We'd better."

Desmond sat in the corner, lifting dumbbells, his veins rising deep purple. He wore tight jeans, top button undone, and a tan tank top. He grunted with each repetition.

The Motherlode tested the acoustics of the new theater. Muted sounds, a sharp, gritty guitar riff, the beat of drums, the feminine voices of backup singers, filtered into the tiny room. Rain tapped at a high window left open. Water trickled down the wall from the window into cracks of the concrete floor. Cold air touched the back of our necks and turned our breath to mist. A.J. had gone for a walk.

"Keep your head up," Rat advised me. Desmond rolled his eyes at the ceiling and walked away from the stage, making his way toward a water fountain at the front of the theater.

"Sure," I said.

I wiggled my head side to side, watching my head change shape in the mirror or kaleidoscope into multiple images.

Most of the time, Rat's eyes were dull, a calm, inappropriate blue. He would appear preoccupied, as though he monitored events occurring far away behind his eyes. Other times, his presence in a room was full. Right now, his concentration was directly focused.

I looked away, unwilling to meet his stare.

"The Prophet says he's been to Venus," I said, changing the subject.

"The Prophet," Rat told me, "is crazy." Perhaps The Prophet was the wrong subject. Rat turned away.

"Rat," I said. "Don't worry about me. I'll be fine."

He didn't turn around, just looked at the door. In the mirror, his eyes were closed and I could tell he was concentrating.

"Stay away from Eric," he said at last. My mouth dropped open. I felt betrayed somehow, but I remained silent.

"He's my friend."

"I mean it. He's in The Prophet's back pocket," Rat said. "You can't trust him. You can't trust any of them."

"Look," I began, but he must have heard the hurt in my voice, the bewilderment. Here I was, supposedly on my own, just me and my brother, away from home for the first time and already I was being ordered about, told who I could and could not associate with.

"Just be careful," he warned me. "That's all. These guys were into all kinds of things back in the '70s. Ask Eric about The Prophet's brother, Lamond Henderson, some time . . . why he doesn't tour with the Motherlode anymore."

"I don't know anything about that."

"I know," he said. "Just be careful."

We finally got our chance to perform later that night. The Motherlode ran through a short set and yielded the stage to us almost before we were ready.

We stormed the stage at once. Rat and Desmond clapped their hands together to get the crowd going as my brother set up the turntable. "Hey, Eve Falls, all right," Rat shouted into the microphone. The crowd cheered. Then the bass kicked in, vibrating the entire stage. The lights faded out and we were engulfed by a swarm of swirling, saucer-shaped, red and green lights.

"Let's do it," Desmond yelled. A pair of jazz horns blared through the heavy bass, plaintive and enticing. Then Desmond ripped off a scream as we all did turns doing push-ups around each other—a game of human three-card monte. At last, Desmond started to rap.

I'm blacker-meaner-keener.

I'm an unbeliever.

I'll rip your heart out.

He was really into it tonight, flashing anger, sweat streaming down his face. He circled the stage like a wounded tiger. He seemed to believe every word he said.

I'm meaner-leaner-keener.
I'm a savage deceiver.
You'll never see me coming.

I spotted Eric sitting with The Prophet at a side table, looking mildly amused. They had their elbows firmly planted against the table top.

I'm the midnight walker.
The back-alley stalker.
The last sight you'll ever see.

The Prophet ignored a large, dark purple drink in front of him, his hands spinning as he attempted to convey something complicated to Eric. In a loose circle around them, a woman in a red jumpsuit sat making something—a giraffe?—out of play-dough, and a couple kissed in a tangle of red and black robes and dreadlocks. A man in a Dr. Seuss hat leaned in, nodding at every word The Prophet said.

Rat and I danced over each other, back to back, arms locked, pulling each other over and over faster until I felt dizzy. Desmond ended his song bent into the mic and shouting.

I'm the last sight you'll ever see.
What you needed me to be.
You'll never see me coming.

Rat introduced me next. I wasn't ready. My first number, a dinosaur rap, "Brontosaurus on Main Street," just didn't work, not after Desmond. It hadn't seemed so jarring, and stupid, in rehearsal. I felt wrong, foolish and exposed, and that made things worse. I cut my set short and everything felt half-finished. Rat picked up though, doing an extended set to fill out the show, ending with his jazz-inspired "Variations on Langston Hughes, or a Raisin in the Microwave," which I liked a lot. Desmond and I traded off improvising some strong dance moves to end it, A.J. laying down some deep grooves, definitely influenced by the bass of Egyptian Motherlode, not that he'd admit to it.

When the lights came up, though, Eric and The Prophet were gone. I looked for Eric backstage but couldn't find him anywhere.

After the show, A.J. and I took a $15 room at a rundown mo-tel. Desmond and Rat slept in the car. I called home. My mother

asked if I felt homesick. I didn't say yes, I said "sometimes." Big
mistake. She said, why not take the next bus, she'd pay for it and
pick me up at the station. I couldn't stand it. I listened, flushed,
embarrassed. Then she got A.J. on the phone and yelled at him.

"Oh, Mom," he said.

He said we'd be back in the Bay Area, in Oakland, in two
weeks and even said she could come to the show. He hated that.

"Yes, I'm watching out for him."

"No, nothing like that, I promise."

"OK."

"Goodnight, Momma."

"Goodnight, Momma."

"Goodnight, Momma."

After he hung up, A.J. paced around the room for a while,
clearly, by the expression on his face, not wanting to talk to me.
Finally, he did some push-ups and went to bed. I sat up late in
bed, reading the book The Prophet had given me until I fell asleep.

I awoke to someone speaking.

"What?"

"There is a certain way to walk this place. You must walk right
foot lifted, knee bent under, foot turned out just so . . . forward
only a half-step . . . head turned in . . . shoulders up so."

I sat up in bed. My nightshirt had twisted in my sleep, binding my right arm, choking me. I pulled at the collar, I coughed.
The room felt warm, smothering. Smoke haze burned my eyes. I
squinted. An ember glow backlit a figure by the door, tall, gaunt,
moving slowly as if swimming the shadows. I felt ill, my ears
buzzing, the put of my stomach opening on nothing.

"Always this direction."

The scarecrow silhouette moved clockwise around the bed in
a strange herky-jerky dance. "This is the direction of the wind
around the world, of the beetles' dance at the Creation. This is the
direction of the living returning from the land of the dead."

"Who is it?"

The figure bent forward into the light, hands reaching out to
me. I screamed. His body, his hands, were human, but his head
was too large with fur bristling along his muzzle. He had fangs,

and his eyes, his large, cold eyes, were inky night.

A.J. shook me and I fell back on the bed. Everything was quiet except a buzzing in my ears. There had been drumming, I realized, loud drumming, but now it was gone.

"That's the third time tonight," A.J. said, his voice thick and angry, and rolled back to sleep.

I sat back in bed, not wanting to sleep, not believing I would ever sleep again. I was asleep almost immediately.

The next day, at breakfast, A.J had creamy bags under his eyes. I asked how many times I had woken him. This had been the second night in a row I'd kept him up most of the night. Sometime last night he had stopped trying to wake me when I screamed. He didn't look at me while he ate, just kept his head down the whole time. When he finished, he said that if I couldn't handle it maybe I should go home. I went for a walk instead. The day was overcast and dark.

I found Egyptian Motherlode's bus parked behind the theater. Eric came out to talk to me, and sat on the bottom step of the bus. Nobody else was around.

I asked him about Lamond Henderson.

He looked me up and down as if seeing me for the first time.

"Lamond was the Motherlode's first bass player, and The Prophet's brother," he told me. "Drugs played a big part in those years. I wasn't there, you understand." He looked uncomfortable.

"What happened to him?" I asked.

"Strange things can happen in your mind, things that are unbelievable. There are no words to articulate them, only the experience. It's like in dreams, only now it's all real."

I told him I wasn't sure I understood, but I was afraid I understood all too well.

"Back then nobody knew what the stuff could do," he said. "After gigs, the band members would play dare games with a salad bowl full of various drugs—acid, speed, all kinds of things. Nobody ever knew what was in there. That night Florence, a back-up singer, still with the band, took what might have been about three tabs of acid. She told me the story, Star Baby took four and some other things; The Prophet took more. Lamond took nearly a whole handful of stuff, enough to kill somebody.

"Florence spit hers out. Lamond, though, swallowed all of his. He started hallucinating. The Prophet tried to calm him down, but Lamond wouldn't have any of it. The hair on his body was standing up as if he'd received an electric shock. He called out for his father, and turned away from The Prophet. By this time, he was hallucinating so badly that many people who were there claim they shared the illusion with him, even ones who hadn't taken anything. They said they could make out an open coffin in which an elderly, white-haired man lay.

"'I'm sorry,' Lamond yelled, over and over again until his voice gave out. Finally, somebody called security and they took him away. They had to leave him there in Montreal. He doesn't play for anybody now."

"I didn't know," I said.

"It's all right. I'm just glad you asked me and not somebody else."

I didn't know what to say. It all seemed too horrible, almost as if I'd been there myself.

"Tell Rat to watch his mouth," he said.

"There's something else," I said. "I want to talk to The Prophet." Eric didn't answer, just sat there waiting for me to say more.

"It's about that book. I saw . . . I don't know what I saw—a man . . ." I didn't know how to describe the dreams. All I knew was that there were some pictures in the book that reminded me vaguely of the experience, of the way it felt. ". . . a wolf's head. Teaching me a dance."

Eric looked at me for a long time.

"I'll go get The Prophet," he said.

He motioned me on and pointed to the back of the bus where The Prophet stayed. The Prophet's bed, covered in a Guatemalan blanket, was suspended from the wall and ceiling, next to a table with incense and candles, and below that shelves of books.

I thumbed through the books, reading passages of Ptolemy's *Almageste*, an astronomy text; the *Radix*, a 19th-century astrology journal; Alexander Hislip's *Two Babylons*; Walt Whitman's *Leaves of Grass*; skimming past books on etymology, hieroglyphics, color therapy, African-American folklore, ex-slaves' writings; thumbing through the theosophical works of Madame Blavatsky, a spiritually channeled book called the *Book of Oahspe*; the selected poetry of Samuel Taylor Coleridge; *The Urantia Book*, a spiritual account of the history and nature of the universe; Lewis Carroll's *Alice in Wonderland*; the Bible, and accounts of the origins of the Rosicrucians.

Eric didn't come back. I left to go find A.J. He'd be wondering where I was. Besides, we had rehearsal in the afternoon, and while I had waited the sun had come out.

I headed back to the room. I felt weak from lack of sleep and needed to splash some water on my face.

A.J. wasn't in the room, but I heard a noise in the bathroom. I walked in on Desmond. He was naked, on his knees in the shower. I started to apologize, backing up—then I noticed the syringe in his hand. My stomach dropped and my mouth suddenly felt as dry as if it were stuffed with cotton.

"It's nothing serious," Desmond said between tight lips and clenched teeth. "Not drugs. Steroids." Fear flickered in his eyes now. He stood up, placed the syringe filled with amber fluid on the sink and turned to face me. His stare was cold. I wasn't sure he recognized me. He seemed to look right through me.

He leaned over and brushed some lint off my shirt. His other hand was clenched. Muscles bulged with angry veins across his shoulders. He seemed to be waiting to see what I was going to do. I met his gaze, briefly, then turned my back to him and walked out.

I no longer needed to splash water on my face. I felt more alert than I'd been in over a week. Jesus. What was going on?

Desmond didn't show up at rehearsal, and no one saw him until just before showtime. We sounded terrible. Desmond wouldn't look at me, and he had no edge. Rat had no energy, like he didn't want to be there. Only A.J. seemed to be into it, spinning groove after groove.

The Motherlode, on the other hand, were starting to come together. They had the feel of their instruments again, and played like they meant it. Hardly anybody came to the show, though I saw The Prophet walking around backstage after the show, talking to anyone who would listen, clearly excited, but I felt too shaken about Desmond to talk to anyone about anything. I avoided him by hiding in the bathroom until everyone had gone.

That night, the dreams were worse than ever.

I told Rat about Desmond's yellow syringe the next day, but he already knew. "It helps him perform. Gets him angry," he told me. "Besides, if he doesn't take it he'll get stomach cramps. His skin will itch and he might throw up. He'll be all right." I wasn't convinced.

Now that I knew about the steroids, I began to see some of the other side effects Rat hadn't told me about. Desmond's hair had begun to thin. His back was streaked by a swath of red and purple acne sores. His face was smooth and bloated while the rest of his body was lined by a multitude of purple veins. There were other, deadlier side effects to watch out for as well. God only knows if his testicles had shrunk. I wasn't about to ask.

In my dream, I stood looking at myself in a mirror, cracked down the middle, dividing me in half, one half me and the other half unrecognizable, a distorted shadow or apparition. It was as if I was there and somewhere else, too, both at the same time. I could hardly stand up because of the heat. My throat was too dry to speak. Incense and smoke choked me and made my eyes water and blink. Behind me, I could see in the mirror, the silhouette of the wolf-dancer. I moved in rhythm to his movements, jerking like a string puppet. I coughed, my lungs searing, my vision smearing dark. I pleaded incoherently with him to stop. I was crying. I don't remember what happened next.

I awoke every morning bathed in sweat, my throat sore. I began to dream during the day, dozing in the car or napping backstage before the show. Dark bags sagged under my eyes and the skin of my face and neck looked blotchy. A.J. looked wiped out, too, and he stopped talking to me except to tell me to stay in the car or get out of the room during the day so he could sleep.

The car rides became like trips to a morgue. Desmond hardly

slept at all the whole tour, and kept Rat awake. Everyone sat in sullen silence or fell into deep, stiff-necked sleep, everyone except Desmond. Desmond did all the driving now. He was the only one who had any energy, but he was manic. During one gas station stop, when Rat and A.J. were out of the car, I watched him flip a hammer he'd found somewhere end over end from hand to hand, his muscles taut, his neck bulging. He flipped the hammer from the moment he stepped out of the car without stopping until it was time to drive again, then shot out into traffic. The attendant had watched Desmond's antics with horror and forgotten to charge us. I spent the next couple of miles looking over my shoulder, searching for a police car that never materialized.

Most of the time, Desmond wasn't so bad, except when he played chicken with the other cars on the highway dividers, laughing when we yelled at him. The other cars always swerved out of the way at the last moment. He never stopped talking while we drove, often telling us how important the tour was, how we had to get it together.

Once, when no one else was around, Desmond offered me something to give me some energy. I declined, but I had to talk to The Prophet soon. Rat and A.J. had begun to wake me up in the car to keep me from talking in my sleep. They wouldn't tell me what I'd said.

Whenever I looked for The Prophet, though, he was nowhere to be found. Even Eric seemed to be avoiding me. I saw him down at the end of a long street once, but he turned aside and by the time I got to the corner he was gone.

In Mud Creek, I slipped out of practice early to search The Prophet out. Egyptian Motherlode's dressing rooms were on the far side of the theater. I walked down a long, dim passage under the stage to get there. Someone in green fatigues came out of the darkness behind me, through a door I hadn't seen.

"Hey," he said. "Hey, hey, hey."

I started to run. Fleeing through a series of black curtains into a back room, I bumped into two large purple-robed men with star-spangled turbans and long beards shot with gray. They were part of the Motherlode, but didn't play any instruments, none that

I ever saw. Bodyguards? I smelled the sickly sweet odor of pot, and something else I couldn't identify. In a far corner, a woman in loose, colorful pants sat on the floor doodling chords on an electric guitar. One of the men clasped my shoulder.

"Rock should not walk in the evening," he said, his smile widening into a grin. He nodded in agreement with himself.

"The Prophet," I said.

The man pointed. The Prophet sat alone, half out of sight behind a pillar, cross-legged on a large paisley-patterned pillow. I approached him. The Prophet wore red-tinted sunglasses, a kilt with spandex biker shorts underneath, and a white mesh tank top. He had on dirty red socks, sandals off and next to the pillow. As I came close, I saw the man in green fatigues kneeling beside him. He had been hidden by the pillar. It was Eric. He looked up at me, his eyes wide and staring; he was sweating. He reminded me of Desmond, only older. He moved away quickly out of sight into the darkness.

"Ah," The Prophet said, with regret. "You're lost."

I sat cross-legged before him, my hands held out, but he spoke first.

"I have had a roomful of people out on the floor," The Prophet said, "listening to the drum hours at a time. No twitching, fidgeting, just straight into dream, just from the beat of the drum."

He reached out and pulled me close by the elbow. With his other hand, he tapped on my chest, two fingers thumping a beat.

"Like this. Like a heartbeat, life itself. The shamans knew. All the world knew once."

The steady thumping on my chest startled me. I thought, first, that it hurt, but it didn't. He tapped harder. Each beat made me start, each like the flash of a strobe. I felt the presence of the dancer, the wolf-head dancer, behind me. I sat up, afraid, the sudden heat overwhelming. The smell of incense, burned and pungent. A voice explaining. There was another figure there, too, something large, stony, and olive-brown. Its eyes glared fiercely as it observed the ritual.

"Then with arms above, supplicate to the sky, step to the edge of the circle, drop the hand into the river . . ."

The new figure dropped down on all fours. It had short, scaled arms and a hooked nose. It seemed to be looking past The

Prophet, past me, searching for something, its head tilted upward as if it were trying to catch a glimpse of something just beyond the range of its vision. I grabbed The Prophet's hand. He had been speaking. Was it the same words as the dancer behind me? I could see the room again, the pillar at my side. But I felt calm now, sure of The Prophet.

"My first time was like an awakening," The Prophet said. "I could see the energy in my hand, moving in the grass, Celtic knots, mandalas of light. But wait awhile, you're young. Drugs can be too seductive, too much, too powerful all at once. My brother—"

"I know about your brother," I interrupted. I had to speak. "Did you think I wanted drugs?"

"I thought you were like the other one."

"Desmond?"

"Rat. He hasn't come for a few days. I thought he sent you."

My mouth dropped open. Rat?

"Ah," he said, "you're the dreamer, I remember. I was told you were coming."

"By who?"

"By Eric. Who did you think?"

I told him everything in a rush, everything about the dream, the dancer, even what I felt when he drummed on my chest, everything but the strange, stone figure. The Prophet seemed uninterested, distracted. He nodded when I finished. He stood up, straightening his kilt, slipping on his sandals.

"What should I do?"

"This dream is a Dream, capital D Dream," he said. He began to move past me.

"What does that mean? Tell me. Why is this happening to me?"

"Wrong question. Let the dream complete itself. We will meet my brother in Oakland for the final show."

"I'm afraid to sleep."

The Prophet turned to me. I grabbed his hand, relieved. "You look tired," he said. "I can help."

*

When I awoke, The Prophet, everyone, was gone. I didn't remember falling asleep. The Prophet had touched my forehead. My sleep was dreamless. I felt better. I could hear the Motherlode playing, The Prophet wailing, vocalizing high-pitched trills echoed and reverberated through a sound box. A.J. must be looking for me, frantic by now. I stood up, uncertain, rubbed my face and headed for the front of the theater. Rat found me first.

"I need to talk to you," I said.

"No time. After," he said. He grabbed my arm.

"After," I said, and let him lead me back to the dressing room.

I confronted Rat backstage when my brother and Desmond went to get our money.

"What are you doing with The Prophet?"

"What? Nothing. Who told you that? Not The Prophet, some of the other guys."

"You told me to stay away from them."

"I needed something for Desmond, something to keep him down, something to make him sleep. He doesn't sleep anymore."

"This whole tour is a mess," I told him. "I can't go on like this. Desmond can't go on like this. He's going to hurt somebody. We need to make him stop."

"Yes, but not now. He'll pull through. We need to make the act work, at least by Oakland, or we'll have thrown everything away. The steroids keep Desmond going, but they're laced with amphetamines. We just have to accept it and concentrate on the act. Make it work. We can help Desmond later—if he wants our help."

I nodded, defeated.

"Bobby said some producers might be there."

Amphetamines, Jesus. Desmond might pull through all right, if he didn't have a heart attack first.

The next day I found Eric in front of the deli across the street from the theater, sitting on a lawn chair, smoking a cigarette, and eating a chili dog.

"What happened with The Prophet?" I asked. "Why have you been avoiding me?"

He looked up with a tired expression, motioned for me to sit at the foot of the chair, but I stood my ground. At last, reluctantly, he stood. His face was pinched around his eyes and he looked pained by what he was about to tell me.

"When I was in high school," he said, "I bought a single by a group called the Pathfinders. That's what The Prophet called his group back then. This was when Motown was at its height and the Beatles were still together and here's this record . . . this record about the quest for immortality in ancient Egypt, about black people being from Venus. There was nothing else like it I'd ever heard. I've been playing Funk ever since."

I nodded, not sure where this was going.

"When I got the chance, when The Prophet brought the band back together, I had to be a part of it, a part of those old 45s and what they used to mean to me. I've been with The Prophet for three years now, he's shown me all his books and helped me along as much as he's been able to, but I can't do it.

"Sometimes, when I take the drugs, I hear the drumming, but I never saw a wolf's head."

Not a wolf's head, I wanted to tell him, but a man's body. A man's body with a wolf's head. Not a mask, but the head of a wolf. And something else, too. A figure that looked for all the world like a tortoise.

"I'm sorry," I said lamely.

"Don't be. It's no blessing. It eats at The Prophet until he's not himself anymore, until he can barely function."

Eric walked back into the deli to pay for his lunch. I thought about following him inside. But what could I do besides apologize again? Nobody saw the dream but me and The Prophet. What did it mean?

I headed back to the theater, my head down.

The next night in Modesto, at the Junior College, we had our best set of the tour so far. Desmond didn't seem as manic. Perhaps Rat had found something to calm him down, after all. My brother added some samples from the Motherlode's horn section. And

Rat sang with intensity all night long.

But Desmond disappeared after the show, taking the arm of a young woman in a red halter top, and wasn't around the next morning. We waited in the car in the sun for over an hour and were just getting ready to leave when he finally showed up. His shirt was torn in two places and his eyes were a bit glazed, but otherwise he looked OK. It was getting harder to tell with Desmond, what was up and what was down? He nodded in no particular direction as he slipped into the back seat.

That was it. No explanation, no words. It had been so long since he'd said anything to anybody that I wasn't sure that he still functioned on that level. His manic energy had all but dissipated and left him empty.

After we'd been driving for an hour or so, Desmond took off his shirt, balled it up, and placed it against the side window to use as a pillow. He was asleep almost immediately. The first time he'd slept in days.

I could *feel* the river before I saw it. It rushed by smooth and dark behind the stage, winding out of a vague immensity, a darkness pierced by points of light, perhaps stars. Nobody took any notice of it, or seemed at all surprised. The river gurgled as it passed and lapped at the back of the stage, pooling behind the drummer. I smelled the sharp, cold smell of it.

The Motherlode was deep into their set, oblivious. The Prophet stopped singing and handed the mic to Star Baby. Star Baby wore thigh-high black leather boots, dark sunglasses, a propeller beanie, a large diaper, and gold chains. He wasn't singing, just talking in a deep, rolling voice, explaining the power of Funk to move and heal and give visions, exhorting everyone to get up and join the dance of Creation, laughing often, sometimes breaking into chorus just long enough to get the crowd singing out loud while he spoke. Everybody was on their feet, arms waving and weaving, heads nodding to the beat, eyes sometimes closed to feel the vibrations moving up through their feet, into the pits of their stomachs, up their spines.

The nights on the road had all run together in a quick blur and here we were at last, in Oakland, playing at Crazy Eight's

House of Rock—the big show. Desmond had called a meeting with Bobby Times, but nobody was really interested in whether or not I was there, so I skipped out to see the Motherlode play their set. A.J. had nodded, looking relieved, and reminded me to see Momma. I stopped by at her table in the back to say hello as quickly as I could before heading for the front of the stage.

The place had been packed early. The Motherlode had started loud and gotten louder; the crowd, indifferent at first, had begun to shout out and whistle, and then to dance. The heat of the place had become stifling. The music, though, brought a kind of joy, a nervousness released by the dancing and the beat, but it only teased, making the crowd hungry for something else. They were waiting for the Motherlode to take things another step further, to the next level—if they could.

The beat, never wavering, only slowed, imperceptibly at first, as the night went on. While Star Baby spoke, The Prophet walked along the edge of the stage, eyeing the crowd, sometimes offering his hand and drawing someone up on stage—women in ripped jeans and teased hair; men in metallic shirts; a transvestite in full drag, a red feather boa around her neck; an old man in tie-dye who cried and hugged The Prophet. The Prophet had them dance in a large circle around Star Baby, joining many of the Motherlode who already danced—the purple-robed men in star-spangled turbans, some of the guitar players in mini-skirts and gold lame, the backup singers holding remote microphones—everyone on stage except for the drummer, the keyboards, Eric, Star Baby and The Prophet. The Prophet wore a yellow and brown dashiki, a wraparound hula skirt with cheap green plastic strands hanging down that didn't reach all the way around his pot belly, a three-pointed jester's hat, dark sunglasses, and pointed shoes that curled up at the end. Sweat dripped from his bare arms and scruffy, graying beard, and flew off his dreads when he shook his head.

The Prophet smiled when he saw me, a big smile, and I couldn't help smiling back. He put his hand out to me and hauled me up onto the stage easily, with surprising strength.

"Michael, Michael," he said, "oh, yeah, Michael."

He put his arm around my shoulder, gripping me tightly, urgently. He led me up to one of the dancers, a heavy-set man, his face expressionless, his movements stilted and mechanical. The man wore a white suit, with a white bow tie, gloves and a top hat. He resembled The Prophet, only worn out and used up.

"This is my brother, Lamond," he said to me, patting Lamond on the back. He leaned in to his brother and shouted, "Lamond, this is Michael, he's going to help us go home."

"Home?" Lamond asked.

Beyond the other dancers as they ducked and whirled, I could see Desmond off-stage, his arms folded, waiting to make sure the Motherlode finished in time. I already knew they wouldn't. The Prophet seemed to be just getting things rolling, everything still rising toward some unknown release, a crescendo.

"The dance, show me the dance. Show us all the dance."

Suddenly, for the first time that night, I felt uncomfortable, even a little frightened. The Prophet must have seen the look on my face.

"It's all right," he said. "Take it easy."

He took off his sunglasses and I could see his eyes, bloodshot with bags underneath. When had he last slept?

"Michael, are you all right?" he asked. "I need you to concentrate. Now." His glare was intense, stern.

Behind him I saw the ponderous, round shape of the tortoise climb out of the river and onto the stage. "He's here," I said.

"What? Who?" The Prophet looked toward the river, surprised. He didn't see anyone.

"The tortoise."

"Tortoise?" He turned back to me. "No, that must be your guide, your helper. Help me find the other one, the wolf. Show us . . . show me the dance."

The tortoise stood awkwardly on two legs, water dripping off his back and his white and yellow belly, his stumpy arms hanging loose at his sides. He cocked his head at me, then nodded.

I wasn't sure I could remember the complicated movements. I had never performed it alone, only with the dancer in half-remembered dreams.

Star Baby had stopped singing and The Prophet handed me the microphone. I hesitated for a moment, then stepped into line with the other dancers.

"There is a certain way to walk this place," I said at last, "right foot lifted, turned in just so, arms out . . ."

All the dancers turned to me, watching. Their movements, awkward at first, became more certain, as if they'd known the steps all along and needed only to be reminded. I repeated everything I'd learned. I repeated it twice. I dipped my hand in the rising river and poured my cupped water over my head. The dancers followed my lead.

The Prophet took the microphone, vocalizing a long trill, then whispering, "yes, yes, yes," stepped back into the center of the dance, his arms raised, his head tilted back. "The time has come," he said, "to speak of something far more deeply interfused. A Funk Sublime—a motion and a spirit that impels and rolls through all things—where every groove belonging to me as good belongs to you."

Eric put his hand on my shoulder, grinning, caught up in the excitement. He had handed his bass off to someone else so he could dance in the circle. He wore his brown trench coat, Bermuda shorts, and bright blue sandals.

"I hear it," he said, "the drum, it's talking. I hear it."

"Come to the river," I said.

"River?" His face drooped a moment, then he smiled wanly. He looked around. He couldn't see it. He danced faster, moving past me in the circle.

The Prophet growled and shook himself.

"Funk is the sweet voice—Funk the luminous cloud—all melodies an echo of that voice—all colors a suffusion from that light."

Stars shimmered in the distance. I saw what seemed like planets, the hot gas clouds of Venus, red dusty Mars.

Then I saw the dancer. He sailed down the river in a flatbed boat with stylized eyes painted on the prow. I saw his silhouette first as he polled before yellow-white Jupiter, winding downriver toward us. He wore a white wrap around his waist, silver armbands, and a kind of coronet on his head. His arms and chest were powerful. His skin was dark and hairless, except for the wolf's hair beginning at the shoulders.

He seemed a long time coming. Everyone seemed to be waiting for him. I could hear only the drummer, the bass, and the back-up singers still singing, wailing long cries that never died.

The dancer poled into the reeds I had not seen rise up along the shore, behind the stage. His lupine eyes fixed on me. I faltered in the dance and fell out of the circle.

"Death is different than we had supposed," The Prophet said, "and luckier—that's what the poet said once—there is no death, only more life, and more life."

Looking up, I could see Desmond on-stage now, heading toward The Prophet. He was dressed all in black. A T-shirt tight over his muscled chest, sharp, creased pants, and unlaced combat boots. He shoved away one of the dancers who tried to pull him into the circle. She stumbled and fell. He pushed The Prophet from behind.

"Get off the stage, old man."

Desmond's face was contorted with frustration. The Prophet turned and reached out for him. The two men in star-spangled robes and turbans pushed out of the dancers. Eric followed them, his arms out. Rat came onto the stage.

"No," The Prophet said to Eric and the turbaned men. "No," The Prophet said to Rat. No one moved.

"It's time to go," The Prophet said to his brother. "It's time to go home."

The Prophet boarded the boat, leading his brother by the hand. He didn't even turn to say goodbye to me, taking his place at the prow. Others, some of the dancers, began to board the boat. I wanted to go with them; the feeling was overwhelming, the river promised longing fulfilled, an ease, a forgetting, but also an oblivion. Many had got on but there was still room. I stepped forward. Someone touched me on my shoulder. I turned to find the tortoise beside me. I reached out to him. The pads of his feet were surprisingly soft. His eyes, beneath a fierce gaze, were surprisingly sad.

"No," he said, "not you, not yet."

When I looked back, the boat had pushed off from the shore. Already, the river seemed indistinct, the stars receding. I saw Eric in the back of the boat, smiling at me and nodding. I passed through the back of the stage, through the river that was now fading away. Desmond knelt on the stage. Clearly, he could see everything. Rat, bent over beside him, tried to get Desmond to his feet, but he wouldn't move.

I exited through the back door into open streets, where I wandered off by myself into the cool night air, from time to time looking up at the perfect silence of the stars.

*

Crushed Ice never played again. I haven't seen Rat since. I saw Desmond only last week, nearly six years since the tour. He was on a street corner, dressed in a tight blue suit and a bow tie, handing out Black Muslim literature. He looked good, still intense but more at peace. He smiled as I shook his hand. I asked him about Rat. He said Rat produced local bands now. We agreed he was always the most talented of us. Desmond asked me about A.J. I told him he was traveling around the country on a motorcycle trying to get himself together. Desmond said he could understand that.

I told him I was on full scholarship at UCLA, as an anthropology major. I was only in Oakland for a couple weeks before going on a dig, my second, down in South America. Some Mayan ruins had turtle temples, not exactly tortoises but they would do. Of course, when I had the opportunity and money, I planned to go to Egypt. My studies focused especially on the religion and culture of Ancient Egypt. I know now the name of the dancer. Sometimes I even guess at the name of the river.

I look for the tortoise always, but I haven't seen him since that night. I long to see the river again, and sometimes think my life since that night has been only a waiting for it. The Prophet waited a long time. I can wait a while.

I talked to Desmond for half an hour on the street corner, but he never mentioned what happened to him the last night of the tour. I don't talk about it much either. Who would understand? But I think about it all the time. For others there is only the present, only themselves. For me, I know, even if the people are long dead, the dreams of a culture live on, perhaps only knowable to us changed and interpreted by our dreams, but undeniable and with purposes we can never guess, promises for which we can only long and wait.

In the meantime, I study my anthropology. When I next encounter the river, I want to be ready. Not just for the river, but for what lies beyond as well.

2
MINGUS FINGERS

San Francisco, 1952

I SAT ON AN OLD, BATTERED PLYWOOD STOOL in the shed behind the house, playing trumpet along with Erskine Hawkins' new record, "Tuxedo Junction." One of the legs of the stool was too short; every time I tapped my foot, keeping time, the stool tapped counterpoint. I had gotten used to it.

My sister's son, Kenny, ran about the yard chasing rabbits. A copse of trees abutted the backyard. Beyond the trees lay a warren, a large pile of rocks, or a small hill, mazed with burrows. There must have been fifty, maybe a hundred rabbits back there. I had long ago given up gardening, or even trying to fence them out, and had learned to ignore them—the easy hopping always at the edge of my vision, the sudden scattering when I came upon them unawares. Kenny had been trying catch one all afternoon. He would creep up in front of one, trying not to startle it. The rabbit would lift its head from the grass, watch Kenny until he got too close, then bolt to safety through the copse of trees. Kenny would follow, but not nearly quick enough. I should have found the whole thing impossibly funny, but Kenny looked too much like my sister to make anything funny. He had her wide-set eyes and high cheekbones. I missed her. I'd tried to get her to move up to San Francisco with me, to get away from that husband of hers, but that hadn't worked.

I'd had only had Kenny for about two weeks, ever since my sister's house had burned down in Los Angeles. Kathleen was staying with our mother back in Louisiana until things got settled with the insurance company. Meanwhile, Mom had asked me to look after Kenny. She didn't like Richard any more than I did and wasn't about to put up with him in her house. She'd taken Kenny's older brother, Lamond, but she's felt Kenny needed to grow up with a real man around the house. I would have to do. Kenny seemed like a good kid, although a bit on the quiet side. He was only six, and things were tough for him right now. Just the other night I'd caught him crying in bed after lights out. I didn't know what to say to him. I didn't know if I'd ever get the hang of this father thing. And already it had made the music thing that much harder. I wished I could have said no to my mother. My life, a jazz musician's life, barely brought in enough money for me, and it wasn't a very good life for a kid. But it took too much effort to refuse. "Only for a little while," my mother had said.

Kenny was getting tired now, and sweat was running down his cheeks as he dashed about the yard. He sat down in the middle of the yard. The rabbits, as always, emerged from the trees to eat the grass whenever Kenny was still, inviting him to try to chase them again.

Distracted, I trailed off my own playing and listened to Hawkins' record, nodding along, the stool tapping a beat. Like a lot of material I'd played over the years, it was rhythm and blues disguised in a jazz idiom. Nice, but not very difficult. The trick came in Hawkins' mellow groove and soft tones; the ease with which he played that was difficult to emulate. I had to get up to turn the record over on the turntable, so Kenny surprised me when he spoke. He had come up beside me.

"Someone here to see you," he said.

I looked at him. He had a rabbit cradled in his arms. How had he done that? For a moment, I thought Kenny wanted me to speak to the rabbit. Then I wondered if Kenny should be holding it. It was a wild animal, if only a rabbit. But before I could speak, a man stood at my door. Kenny had backed away, and stood outside petting the rabbit and watching the man warily. And for good reason: a white man who'd evidently squeezed through the hole in the fence of our front yard after not finding anybody home was quite an anomaly.

The man took off his hat and extended his hand. I placed my

trumpet back in its case. I hadn't put the needle down on the record yet, and just let the turntable slowly spin. The man introduced himself as Karl Radcliff.

"You've been a hard man to find," he said grinning. It was a grin that came easy to him, and meant exactly nothing. He seemed friendly enough for the moment, but I didn't trust him. I'd seen his kind before, both working in jazz clubs and in my former profession, boxing. I could tell by his damaged nose and fingers he was here about the boxing.

"I was down at your gym a couple of days ago, but nobody had seen you in months."

I waited for him to continue, but he seemed to want some sort of explanation.

"I don't fight anymore, Mr. Radcliff," I told him.

"I hope that's not true," he said. He grinned wider. "I saw your last fight, against Bratton. You gave him a real battle."

I remembered the fight all right. I didn't think anybody had ever hit me so hard before, punches I'd have expected from a heavyweight, crushing blows that splintered my ribs and left me seeing double for months after the fight. Certainly not the punches of a welterweight. As I'd circled around him, trying to stay out of reach of his jab, not wanting to let him hurt me again with another combination, I realized for the first time that there was another level to the sport that I had never before encountered. Within two years, in 1951, Bratton would win the National Boxing Association title by beating the Italian, Charley Fusari, in a fifteen-round decision. But I didn't know that then.

"He was a tough one," I said. "What can I do for you?"

"I represent Kid Galviston," he told me handing me a card that I put in my wallet. "You stood up to Bratton so well, we figure you'd be a good test for the Kid, see how good he really is."

I knew of Kid Galviston, and nobody needed to see how good he really was. The champ wouldn't fight him, and nobody else wanted to either. Bratton had been strong, but his big baby face and a gentle smile let you know that none of the damage he was inflicting on you was personal. By contrast, the Kid was a monster. He was a bulldog who wouldn't stop pounding away at your body until you got tired and dropped your head. Then he'd go for the kill with a vicious uppercut. No way did I want a piece of him, but the potential pay day made it tempting. I looked out the door for Kenny, but he and the rabbit were gone.

"I'll give you a call if I change my mind," I told him. "I'd need to start training again. When would you need an answer?"

After I'd let him through the house and out the front door, I sat down in the living room, trying to think of a way I could make the same amount of money by not fighting. The music paid a little, in fits and spurts, but not as much as a steady gig with a championship contender. And if I did well and the Kid didn't put me in the hospital, I would probably also get another good paying fight after that. I knew enough already to know that there was no way I could expect to win the fight. One more fight, I told myself, just to get through the summer. Then I can retire. Again.

I went to the kitchen and got myself some lemonade. I stood drinking the lemonade from the pitcher before the open door of the refrigerator. I thought about calling Liza to see what she would think. I knew what she would say; she'd be worried about me, but she'd also be excited about the money. Perhaps I just wanted someone to talk me into taking the fight. I felt I needed to stop worrying about myself so much and just do what I knew I had to do. When I went to the phone, I remembered Kenny out back, and the Hawkins record still spinning in the shed.

I looked out the kitchen window and saw Kenny sitting cross-legged in the middle of the yard, surrounded by rabbits, one in his lap, another putting two paws on his chest to sniff at his face, a dozen others all around. Butterflies flew in and out of the trees this time of the year, and they had come into the yard in numbers, thirty or forty, and fluttered close around Kenny's head. What the hell? I stood dumbfounded. What was with this kid? What was I getting into? Suddenly, I laughed, loud and long.

The Nighthawk was a dump. It was old, dank, and smelled of beer and cigarettes. The tables were tiny and surrounded by too many chairs. It was a wonder that the patrons could find room to fit their drinks on the tables. But somehow the summer fog that washed through San Francisco every night muted all the dirt and grime until all that was left was the music. I loved the place.

I sat on stage waiting to play, trumpet lowered, but still pressed to my lips. Kenny sat at the back of the club with Liza. They had a special section for underage patrons, a fenced off area way in the back that made you feel that you were watching an exhibit at the zoo rather than a live performance by human beings. Liza hated sitting back there. Kenny loved the Nighthawk. Maybe he just wanted to get closer to me, but if so, it worked. I took him here most every night I played, and many other nights as well, enough nights that I began to feel guilty about it. He'd made friends with Helen, the owner's wife who worked the cash register at the front door. She'd let Kenny eat or drink anything he wanted and wouldn't charge us a thing. And watching Kenny happy, bobbing his head along with the music, slapping the beat on a table top, was a relief from the Kenny I had to live with the rest of the time. He was so quiet that I'd almost forget that he was there and then he'd turn up all of a sudden, right under foot. The club brought us both relief. But I'd decided I'd make an effort to be a real parent, and keeping Kenny up late at night seemed to be one of the things I was going to have to stop doing. Just not tonight.

Tonight, the after hours session was really cooking. If it hadn't happened to me before, I don't know what I would have done. Instead when the bass players' appearance began to change, I merely squinted my eyes in an effort to pretend everything was normal. It wasn't, though. The groove he was laying down was too smooth, too pure. I even knew enough to expect the change when the music was that good. His skin began to blotch and his neck began to stretch until I was looking at a giraffe in a tuxedo. Nobody else noticed, nobody else ever did.

The first time it had happened I was just out of high school, playing in a band back in New Orleans in a club on the corner of Eighth and Franklin. Two other bands were waiting to play and were about to move us off when our Creole piano player, Isidore Washington, began banging on the keys. It was a sound of jubilation, unlike anything I'd ever heard. When I looked up at him, he wore a sickly smile and looked for all the world like a hyena. We played the rest of the evening. Nobody was going to move us off that night.

Only a few months ago a local group, the Dave Brubeck trio, had made a name for themselves at the Nighthawk, recorded a couple of albums and moved on. Now there was a new group fronting the club. Red Norvo, the xylophone player who had made some recordings with Benny Goodman, had his own trio featuring Tal Farlow on guitar and Charles Mingus, the giraffe, on bass. I had heard about him, but none of it did him justice.

Norvo and Farlow were fine players, but Mingus was fascinating, his deft long hands gliding effortlessly across the strings. His eyes would scrunch tightly and his face would twist into a grimace as if he were frustrated that he couldn't shut out the world and just be left alone to play his music without the benefit of an audience or backing musicians. Mingus had played with everybody I admired: Louis Armstrong, Dinah Washington, Lionel Hampton, and Duke Ellington, staying only long enough for a cup of coffee with each one before moving on. In the end, though, he must have been too defiant, too much his own man. Tonight? Well tonight was something special. He'd surpassed himself and altered himself in a way I didn't quite understand. What would it feel like, I wondered, to play at that level? When I'd fought Bratton, he'd had something of that intensity, too. But he hadn't changed. If he had, he probably would have killed me. Only the music brought the change.

Mingus—the giraffe—opened his eyes. He looked out at the club, then straight at me. I realized I hadn't played a note yet. I had been mesmerized by his playing. I thought he was going to yell at me about it, but he just nodded toward the back of the club.

"That's your boy, isn't it?" he said loud enough for me to hear.

I looked out at Kenny, not quite understanding the question. My boy? It didn't seem quite right.

"My son? No," I said. "My sister . . ."

Mingus dropped right back into playing. He turned away from me. And then, impossibly, he took his playing up to a whole other level. One maybe I didn't know existed. One I didn't want to know existed. The giraffe tilted his long head back and began to croon, his neck undulating at the effort. The weird keening thrilled me like an electric shock, a shiver running up my spine. I started to play. Smooth and deep. This was what it was all about. Not those endless nights out on the road. Not the endless hours practicing, hoping to be able to record a record nobody would ever listen to anyway. None of that mattered, just to be in the moment. I never changed, though. I waited for it, but it never came.

After the show, when everybody else had gone home, Mingus sat at the piano on the stage, Kenny standing beside him looking up into his face while Mingus played, explaining how chords went together, how the music went together to make music out of noise. Mingus was a man again, a young man with a sharp, hurt look in his eyes. He leaned back and half-turned to me as I came up. He put one hand on Kenny's shoulder.

"You have to teach him to play," Mingus told me.

I nodded. "He likes Count Basie, a lot," I said. "He's crazy about Billie Holiday and Louis Jordan."

"He knows the good stuff already, now he just needs to know the bad. Then he can play in the soul." I wasn't sure what Mingus was talking about anymore, but I nodded anyway as if it all made perfect sense. "He's got to know the agents and their cut, the club owners and their cut, the people never letting you be, the women." He leered when he said women. "Then he can play just for himself, and everything will come out like morning dew—like the first day."

Kenny looked at me as if asking my permission. Did he want to become a jazz player? My mother would never forgive me.

"Is that what you want?" Mingus asked him.

Mingus didn't slur like a drunk, but there was a rambling quality, a headiness to his speaking that made him seem distracted, even as he stood right in front of you and looked you in the eye.

"We've got to go, Mingus."

"You come back to play, tomorrow."

"I'll be here." But I wasn't sure that I would. The vision of Mingus as a giraffe, the impossible music, and his ramblings had left me a bit unnerved now that the thrill of playing had passed.

"And bring the kid. Teach him so he learns right. All that bad stuff, he'll learn on his own. You teach him the good stuff. You teach him the underground."

I nodded. I already knew that was Mingus's language for the place he went when the music was everything and he didn't have to think at all, the underground. Every musician called it something.

Kenny and I hardly spoke on the way home. In truth, I didn't know what to say. "So," I felt like asking, "do you want to be a trumpet player like your Uncle?" But Kenny had fallen asleep on the back seat.

I dropped Liza off at her mother's where she lived. I hadn't invited her over since Kenny's arrival. She didn't like that any better than having to sit at the back of the club behind the fence. As I thought, she had liked the fight idea, though. I think she thought I was better than I was—than I would ever be. She kissed me quick and got out without a word. I couldn't blame her. I didn't have much to offer her lately. She was twenty-two, working in a shirt factory. She lived for the nights at the club, for dressing up in tight dresses, listening to the music, and talking to the musicians. I was losing her fast. And I couldn't blame her at all. I watched her walk up the step, unlock her door and go inside without looking back.

I had to carry Kenny up to his room when we arrived home. When I turned to leave the room, I caught Kenny looking at me in the mirror on his dresser. When I turned back at the doorway, he had closed his eyes again and pretended to be asleep.

I heard a tap at the window. A butterfly outside fluttered against the pane. Soon there were two, then five, tapping softly like light rain. Kenny pretended not to hear. Later, when I checked on him on the way the bathroom, I found the window open and seven or eight butterflies nestled around Kenny as he lay curled up on his side. In the morning, they were gone.

The first punch hit me like a sledge hammer, pushing through my jaw, trying to get into my head. I shook it off and approached my sparring partner from the left, trying to keep him off me with a series of quick jabs. I hadn't boxed in what seemed like ages and it was coming back to me slowly. Not the timing, but the drive and willingness to absorb the pain.

I took another shot, this time in the ribs, that took all the air out of my stomach. I was going to have to get much sharper if I was going to box again, lose fifteen pounds or so. The foot speed just wasn't there yet.

I got in close and grabbed the back of his shoulder with my glove, clinching him in tight, not letting him throw another punch until I'd gained back my wind. I hit him on the arms a few times with a combination that didn't do any damage, but gave me a chance to back away.

Hal, my trainer, rang the bell. He looked up at me from the floor below ringside and just shook his head.

"What are you doing in there?" I didn't want to talk to him. All I wanted to do was sit down, curl up in a ball and go to sleep for a million years.

"Too slow?" I asked.

"Too slow, too stiff, too stupid." It was Hal's job to inspire me.

"I'll be okay."

"Sure you will. Come back tomorrow and we'll work on it some more."

"Two more rounds," I pleaded.

"If you get hurt now, I don't get paid. Come back tomorrow."

Warming up that night, I had trouble blowing my trumpet. My lips hurt and the whole left side of my face felt heavy. I had a nice shiner starting to form. The other musicians kept their distance, nodding at me knowingly, wondering what back street alley I'd stepped into.

My trumpet was flat and so was my spirit. Kenny was eating what looked like two or three slices of pizza at his table, listening to music, but looking a little preoccupied. He hadn't liked it when I'd come back home with my face looking like raw sausage. He'd insisted on touching the side of my face and running his hand along the long, sinewy bruise that ran from my eye down to my jaw. It had taken all of my strength not to flinch.

"You're paying your dues." Mingus. I looked up. "That's cool. Really."

"Mingus . . ."

"No, I mean it. You're a fighter, right? A what-do-you-call-it, pugilist?"

"I don't . . ."

"Larry over there," Mingus motioned behind him with the back of his thumb, "he washes cars. In the summertime he's out there every day without his shirt on over on Columbus, washing away. Tony, the light skinned clarinetist, he once fronted a klezmer band. Barney drives a cab, maybe he'll even give you a lift home one of these nights." I didn't question Mingus on how he knew any of this. Sometimes he seemed oblivious, as if there was nothing but his music. Other times, he seemed to know everything about everyone.

"Me, I've played in every big band you could name. I play a backbeat all night long, every night. Maybe I get a solo or two when nobody's listening. I might as well be playing that rhythm and blues crap. Might as well play in some lounge or at one of those Bar-mitzvahs. It pays the rent, don't it? Then we can come out here and jam. Only you're selling a bit more of yourself than the rest of us, one piece at a time. A nose here, a shoulder there. Tonight, it was your lip. You got to be ready to give it up before it takes the one thing you got, before you lose your chops for good. Then every night will be tonight."

I started to say something, I wasn't sure what, but he just put his hand up.

"You'll know when the time is right. Something will let you know."

Nobody likes being called a whore. But when you're called a whore and told that it's okay to be one, it leaves you angry but also a little ashamed. It took a lot of nerve, though, for Mingus to say something like that to someone like me, someone who he knew could do a lot of damage when he wasn't made to wear a pair of gloves. I struggled for an answer, the blood rushed to my head and into my injured cheek, where it burned, throbbing in rhythm with my pulse.

Mingus left before I could form any sort of reply.

"Kenny," I heard him call as he passed by me.

"Charlie!" Kenny ran up to Mingus. Charlie?

Mingus caught him with both hands under Kenny's armpits and lifted him in the air.

"You had spots and a long neck," Kenny said, as Mingus lifted him onto a wide shoulder. "You had a large spot right here." Kenny drew a circle around the side of Mingus's neck.

This couldn't be happening. Nobody ever saw any of it but me. Mingus nodded.

"When you get underground, it'll happen to you."

I sat dumbfounded. I didn't get a chance to talk to Mingus before we started playing. Once during the set, Mingus just laughed at me, at the expression I couldn't wipe off my face. Shock. That's what it's like when a private madness becomes something casually spoken about by others. Impossible. My world had mother-may-I taken two giant steps to the left.

Right in the middle of the set, Mingus leaned in to me and whispered something I couldn't quite hear.

Then he turned away. Mingus knew all about it. Maybe that would change everything, help me understand. And Kenny? Before the set finished, all hell broke loose.

I saw the gun flash, even in the smoke. Chairs pushed back, some people screamed, more cried out "gun!" as people crouched down. An argument in one corner had turned ugly, five or six men standing, bumping chests, becoming a brawl, then the gun waved. It didn't even fire. I jumped off the stage and headed for Kenny. Some guy, not even involved in the fight, tried to jump me. He didn't last long. I hoped I didn't break his jaw, but I didn't have time to take it easy. When I got to Kenny, Liza had him by the hand and was crouching behind a table. He looked wide-eyed, but calm, quiet. He knew not to be conspicuous when trouble started.

I moved Kenny and Liza up by the stage, rules be damned. I was glad I did. After a few minutes, we tried to play again. But the mood in the Nighthawk had turned bad. People milled about, eyeing each other, waiting for trouble, cursing, knocking bottles to the floor or pushing at one another. Then there was gun fire outside—two shots. Then order through a bull horn. The police had gotten involved. No one wanted that. In a colored neighborhood, at night, nobody wanted that. The place cleared out, people pushing out like they had all done something wrong. Like being at the scene was a crime itself.

I left with Mingus, Liza, Kenny and the other musicians out the stage door. We stuck together, piling in Barney's large Ford, Kenny on my lap and Liza squeezed in beside me, and he drove us to our own cars in turn.

Later we learned, in the same way we got all our news, through word of mouth, that the guy the police had shot out front wasn't even involved in the fight inside. He was standing out by the curb, drunk, in the wrong place when trouble was happening. He wasn't armed. They shot him twice.

The next night, I was back playing music, but I left Kenny at home. And Mingus had taken the night off. Everything sounded off and I hadn't any heart for it.

*

Red Norvo's gig with the Nighthawk ended the following week, and he and Mingus moved on. Kenny asked me about Mingus a couple of times and I didn't know what to tell him. Finally, I told him Mingus had gone away for a while, but in all honesty, I had no idea if he'd ever be back this way again. People were always coming and going from my life.

I started training again that week, running a route that took me through the Fillmore and Mission Districts and then up to the top of Potrero Hill. I'd use my last reserve of energy to sprint up the dirt roads until I got to the top and you could see the bedrock jutting out of the earth. I'd find a spot in the sun overlooking the Bay and sit and eat my lunch, fending away the goats. Somedays, when I didn't feel like going home and practicing my music, I'd walk down to the water and follow the piers along the Embarcadero, stroll through the Presidio, and walk out to the ocean before making my way home.

It was hard that first week. I'd gotten soft around the middle and I could feel my lungs burning for air even as I started out. But as time went on it got easier.

I circled around my opponent, jabbing, keeping him at arms distance. My sparring partner this afternoon was Lawrence D'Antoni, a burly Italian bruiser who'd once had a shot at the title but had more recently gone to seed. Fat rippled his middle and he had a hard time breathing as he moved about the ring. He was still dangerous, though. One blow and I could easily wind up on the canvas, wondering what day of the week it was.

All of the fighters Hal hired to help me train were big men with quick hands and a knock-out punch, like the Kid. Many of them belonged in higher weight classifications, all of them had reach on me, some by as much as half a foot. If I was going to be prepared for Kid Galviston, I'd need to be ready for the punishment his long, spindly arms could deliver.

D'Antoni was being patient, not rushing in to get inside my jab. Slowly he crept after me, closing ground. If I let him get me into a corner, as washed up as D'Antoni was, I might not get out before he'd done enough damage to keep my ears ringing for a few days. I wanted him to come inside, to duck my jab and leave himself wide open. So far he wasn't taking the bait.

I circled back the other way. D'Antoni threw a jab of his own. When I pushed it aside, he threw a right that I could hear as it parted the air beside my head. I ducked. Standing up, I threw everything I had into an uppercut to the body. The smack was deafening, but D'Antoni seemed unfazed. At last the bell rang.

Hal ran up, wiped my face with a rag and gave me some water. My arms ached and my feet were blistered from all the running, but it was hard not to smile. I still wasn't fluid, my thinking in the ring a bit mechanical, but I'd come a long way in just a few weeks. For the first time, I began to suspect I might have something for the Kid, after all.

I was playing a set at the Tin Angel when I next ran into Mingus. The Tin Angel was a converted warehouse on the waterfront that was cluttered with all kinds of trinkets that the Angel's owner, Peggy Tolk Watkins, had collected. She called them found objects.

They played mostly Dixieland at the Angel. Not usually my cup of tea, but Kid Ory was fronting a band there and I wouldn't have missed it for the world. When I was a kid, growing up in New Orleans in the Garden district, I'd see Ory all the time, carrying his big trombone case late at night, rushing off to work. I'd snuck into his backyard once to hear him practice. Ory had always had the best trumpet players in his band, and to play alongside him, now that I was older, was as close to being Louis Armstrong as I would ever get.

Dixieland can sound mechanical when it's played by people who've only heard it on record, but tonight we had a good group and the music was swinging hard. It all seemed to be led by a bouncing baseline. I turned around to see who was playing bass and Mingus winked at me.

"How's Kenny," he asked me when we'd finished. "I hoped he'd be here." He hoped Kenny would be here?

I thought about trying to explain to Mingus that I was just being a good parent, but the whole situation was just too absurd.

Had Mingus really known that I would be here? I didn't believe it, maybe deep down, maybe, but not on the surface where I expected everything to make sense.

"I'm going south, to Los Angeles. I'll be back through in a month. I wasn't planning on it, but I will now."

I nodded. Kenny had something. I hadn't heard him play anything, but I knew. Mingus knew it, too. I never would. And it was clear that more would be open to him, things I didn't know about, couldn't even dream of.

All you had to do was look around. Jackie Robinson, Roy Campanella, Monte Irvin, Willie Mays and a host of other black baseball players were tearing up the big leagues. It was only a matter of time before the same thing happened and our music came crashing through the ghetto that had held it for so long.

I was a good jazz player. I was a good boxer supporting himself as a musician. But I wasn't great. I didn't have it. Kenny did.

I bought Kenny a set of bongo drums the next day. They were cheap and it seemed as good a place to start as any.

His face lit up when he saw the drums and he hugged me hard around the knees. I promised myself I wouldn't push Kenny, that a jazz musicians' life shouldn't be pushed on anybody. But the joyous glint in his eye when he saw the drums for the first time shattered my resolve and I knew I would do whatever it took to help him on his way.

I stayed inside all day making love to Liza. I didn't have many more chances. She seemed to know it, too. Our lives were drifting apart, and there just wasn't much to hold us together. Afterwards, we smoked a cigarette between us, lounging on the bed, enjoying whatever time was left. I had fifteen years on her. She enjoyed things the way they had been. I could understand that. But something had to change for me. Whether I liked it or not, I could feel it coming.

Kenny was out back, tapping on his bongos. He wasn't too bad, for a kid, and Liza and I joked about how long it would be before he could sit in with me. When the tapping finally stopped,

I thought it was time that I'd better check on him. He'd been out there alone for hours. I left Liza the cigarette and pulled my shirt on, leaving it unbuttoned over my white undershirt. I slipped my shoes on without bothering with socks.

I found Kenny out by the rabbit warren, surrounded, as usual, by a crowd of rabbits, lazily hopping and chewing grass. The butterflies were there again, too, circling his head and landing on his shoulders. Even some birds seemed to have hopped to the branches closest to Kenny. It didn't look strange anymore. Funny how you could get used to things.

"What are you, Dr. Doolittle?" I laughed. Only Kenny seemed able to make me laugh lately.

Kenny had turned his bongos over and was dropping dirt inside. Not the way you treat your instrument, but I had just left him alone for hours and was feeling guilty about it, so I let it go.

"I don't want you to fight," he said.

Kenny didn't even look up at me. He had grass stains on his white and orange striped shirt and on his jeans. I knelt down beside him. The rabbits hardly moved, hopping languidly. Guess they'd gotten used to me, too. I could have touched one. I could have had it for dinner.

"I already promised," I said. I knew Kenny didn't like the injuries I came home with, but this was the first time he'd said anything so blankly. "You know," I said, "too many of your friends are rabbits. You need to get back with your brother, have some kids your own age around."

Kenny nodded. "I know. Not yet," he said. "Soon." What did that mean? Kenny looked at me with his wide brown eyes. "I have to see Charlie again."

Have to? Kenny could be so matter of fact it was disconcerting, even when he was loading dirt in his bongos like any other kid. Why did he have to see Mingus? I was almost afraid to ask, somehow. Mingus wanted to see him, too, though I didn't say that. Jealous, maybe.

"He'll be around soon, maybe after the fight."

"You might get hurt bad this time."

"I can take care of myself."

"No, this is different."

Again, so certain of things, so serious.

"How do you know that?"

"Charlie."

What was this? Was Mingus scaring Kenny? I was starting to get angry.

Kenny just looked at me. That egged me on in some way.

"Look," I told him. "I'm your Uncle. Mingus has no right to scare you like that." Even as I said it, I knew it was something more. I could see it in Kenny's face. He wasn't talking about boxing this time, he meant the next fight in particular.

"It could be really bad this time," he said. What had I gotten myself into?

How could Kenny be so certain of things? More than whatever it was Kenny had, more than knowing that Kenny would probably make the change someday, would know what that felt like, I envied him his certainty. I had drifted into music, into boxing and out again. How could he know things so young? Had I known once and forgotten?

I wandered inside. Liza was in the kitchen, her long flowered dress rebuttoned wrong, rummaging in the refrigerator.

"How's Kenny?"

"He's fine."

No, I was the one in trouble. I could feel something cold in the pit of my stomach. I had no idea what was coming. But no more drifting. I was going to face it head on.

I was back in the shed, fooling around with a riff I'd come up with from listening to an old Jimmie Lunceford recording, when Mingus showed up next. The record had long since run out, but I left it spinning and the static emanating from the speakers made my playing sound as if it were a recording.

"That's nice," Mingus said. Kenny sat in the crook of Mingus' arm. "I heard a little Kenny Dorham in there, too. Nice." Mingus had his bass held steady in his other hand. He put Kenny down. "Let's play," he said.

I wanted to be angry with Mingus. I didn't have much time left to train for the fight. It had been nice to just relax and play, but I didn't have time for much more. I laid the trumpet aside, wiping it with a rag and putting it back in its case.

"Mingus," I said. "Why don't we go into the house. Can I get you something to drink?" It was a hot day for San Francisco. There were few clouds in the sky and the sun had managed to hold the fog at bay for several days.

As we crossed the yard, Kenny's hand in Mingus', a crowd of rabbits followed at a respectable distance.

"Hippity-hop, man," Mingus said, turning to Kenny and making a face. Kenny laughed. Mingus was in a good mood, soaking up the sun and radiating it out. Even I was starting to feel better, starting to realize just how tense I'd been lately.

I grabbed a couple of beers from the icebox, handed one to Mingus and introduced him to Liza who shook his hand. I gave the other beer to Liza and poured two glasses of water from the faucet for Kenny and me. Kenny, back in the doorway, looked doubtful about his place among so many adults until Mingus waved him in.

Mingus looked about the room until he found Kenny's bongos on the floor by the couch. He motioned to Kenny. *Yours?* Kenny nodded. "Want to play something for me?" Mingus asked.

Kenny looked at me, unsure. I was about to say something, tell Kenny he didn't have to if he didn't want to. "Come on," Mingus said, turning to me, "let's show the kid what we've got. Let's go play something."

I shrugged. Why not? Mingus was not to be denied, not today.

It was crowded in the shed with Mingus and Kenny. I had to unplug the turntable and push the stool back against the wall. Liza came out to watch and stood in the doorway. She had to shy away from the butterflies that also waited in the doorway.

"The bass," Mingus told Kenny, "is a lot like playing drums. A really good drummer is judged not on the music he plays but on how much better he can make the other musicians."

Mingus started us off with a couple of slow blues numbers from the Mississippi Delta. Mingus would play the part of the guitar, very simple, very sparse, I'd play the vocals on my trumpet. Soft, pleading numbers.

Each note Mingus played reverberated as strings snapped against wood, eschewing virtuosity in favor of raw emotion. We played this way for a while, my trumpet echoing the voices of Muddy Waters, Elmore James, Brownie McGee, and Mississippi

John Hurt. Every once in a while, I'd strike a more modern lick and Mingus would make a face. "That sounds like Art Farmer," he'd say. "Where did Hank Mobley come from." Mingus squinted his eyes and looked around the room.

Mingus was goading me to play in a style of my own. Over the years I'd gotten comfortable borrowing a phrase here and another phrase there, relying on a common language to express an idea. Mingus wouldn't let me do that. At first, I felt restrained playing this way. As we began to play more modern compositions, though, I began to see what Mingus was after.

Playing with Mingus was certainly more challenging than anything I was used to, like walking a tightrope without a safety net. I was used to imitating other musicians to make a wry comment about the music, but this was special, joyful, if I didn't fall flat on my face.

But I didn't. I found myself playing better than I ever expected I could play. The notes just seemed to happen. I'd think a thought and the sound would come out effortlessly, as if my lips and hands were extensions of the sound and not the other way around.

Mingus spoke while he played, leading me onward, saying "That's it" over and over, almost to himself but to me, too, or, with a wry chuckle, "what's that you have to say?"

I knew Mingus was pushing me to my limits, knew that if we went any farther, or if I thought about what I was doing too much, I'd falter and wouldn't be able to continue.

A sweat broke out all over my body, making me run hot and cold, flushed and then shivering with excitement. I must have closed my eyes because when I opened them the room was darker, as if a cloud had covered the sun. But that wasn't it. Underground, I thought. But that wasn't it either. I was startled, but I stayed with the music. Mingus was still there. Kenny was there, his head down, bowed into his bongos, playing, staying with the beat as if he couldn't stop. It kind of scared me to see his intensity. What he played was simple, but pure. How did he do that?

My heart felt steady but beat way too strong, pounding against my chest. I glanced out the doorway of the shed trying to see what had happened to the light. Was I going blind?

The doorway wasn't there. We weren't in the shed.

As my eyes adjusted, I saw there were windows looking out

on a moonlight bayou. It was night here. I had seen swamp like
that only in Louisiana where my family, and Kenny's father, came
from. Maybe it was somewhere else, though. Maybe it was nowhere at all. Had Mingus created it all, or been drawn to it?

I looked at Mingus. He had changed, his impossible spotted
neck bent almost to breaking as he loomed over us, his long face
noble and calm.

Mingus moved his hooves along the strings, shaking his long
head in time. Had I changed? I couldn't tell. I looked down at
myself and I didn't seem any different.

The shed's four walls seemed to close in on us from a long
way away. The world seemed to unravel in a spiral, as if Mingus
was putting all the toys he'd taken out to play with back in a box,
one by one. Liza clapped as we finished, my horn sounding one
long last wail. I hadn't seen if Kenny had changed. But I knew he
would someday. And I never would. Mingus had taken me there.

Mingus leaned forward.

"Now you know," he said. And I knew the whole show had
been for Kenny, not me.

Mingus walked over to Kenny and tousled his hair. "I've got to
go and I don't know when I'll be back. But now you know the way."

I was surprised to find it was evening outside. There was a
cool breeze blowing in from the ocean, thin wisps of fog floating
through back yard. How much time had passed? It didn't seem
that we had played so long. Kenny was exhausted and went right
to sleep as soon as Mingus left.

That night Liza and I made love, the window open and the
cold air touching us whenever we parted. After, I laid back holding her, smoking, staring at the ceiling, thinking about what happened in the shed. Would it be enough to have been there once? I
wasn't going to get to go back. I felt that to be true. Some only see
through the doors others will walk through on their way somewhere else. I had a lot to think about, a lot to try to unravel about
the music and what I had heard and what it meant. It was more
than most. It was enough. It had to be.

The fight was at Harry Fine's Gym in Oakland. The fight
might have been a high-profile fight, at least for me, but we were

still a long way from Yankee Stadium or Madison Square Garden where Joe Louis often fought. Hell, it wasn't even the Civic Center Auditorium in San Francisco.

But it was home. Most of my early fights had been there as the undercard to bigger fights. Pasted along the dark mahogany wall panels, hundreds upon hundreds of posters, all displaying earnest fist-cocked men, promoted countless fights from bygone eras. A few of them, no doubt, bore my name.

Finally, the bout before mine ended in a split decision and my name was announced. I slapped my gloves together to get my blood moving and walked out of the dressing room. My adrenaline caught with the restrained roar of the crowd and I jogged into the ring.

Bratton, the man who had beaten me into an early retirement, stepped over to my corner to wish me luck. I acknowledged him by tapping my glove to my forehead.

There was a loud rumble among the stands. Kid Galviston stepped out of the other locker room and walked slowly down toward the ring as if he didn't have a care in the world, as if he was mildly annoyed that he'd had to show up.

Young fighters climbing into the ring often appear dazed, even a bit glassy-eyed. The handshake is the social event before the rumble. The referee will grab you and tell you how he wants a clean fight. Your opponent may even wish you luck. Galviston seemed completely at ease.

His face wasn't pretty. It was long and drawn and riddled with acne scars below the neck. His hair was cut close to the top of his head, leaving only a thin layer of kinky hair. But his arms were what drew my attention. They were amazingly long and powerful. If he held them at his side and did a squat, they would touch the floor.

I was still wondering how I'd be able get inside of his long reach without getting clobbered myself when we touched gloves.

Galviston sneered as he came out of his corner. He closed in quickly. I hit him with a jab and moved quickly to my right. I didn't want to stay in one place too long. We circled around each other a couple of times. He jabbed and I ducked and the blow sailed harmlessly over my head. Then he caught me with an uppercut, a glancing blow along my temple.

My vision blackened around the edges and a chill swept through my body. He followed with a savage combination. I felt, rather than saw, three blows land across my body. Two somewhat low on my chest and another, that sucked my breath away, on my side. A fourth just missed my face, the sweat—my sweat—flying off his gloves and spattering my cheek.

Time to wake up.

Galviston came at me again. I threw another jab. Galviston parried it easily with his right, momentarily exposing his chin. I was too far away, though, to do anything about the opening. It was clear he didn't think I could touch him if he didn't want me to. Not with those long arms.

I threw another jab just to be sure. Again, I could see his chin. Then the bell rung.

I sat down heavily. Hal wiped my face off with a towel and poked me a bit to make sure I was all right. He was silent and methodical in his treatment.

I took another blow to the head in the third round and two more in the fourth. I was able shake them off, retreat, and re-group, a little wobbly but intact. As long as I stayed conservative I'd survive the fight, but I was falling behind on points. If I lost another couple of rounds my only chance of winning would be to knock him out.

Coming out of my corner to start the fifth round, Galviston caught me with a jab that smacked off my forehead. The crowd roared as Galviston charged in, punching with both hands and driving me back to the ropes. I managed, somehow, to keep both hands up in front of me and caught most of his punches on my arms and gloves. Galviston paused, slowed his assault, and then paused again. I pushed him back toward the center of the ring with two hands.

Galviston started forward again. I caught him with a jab, jabbed again. He deflected the second jab, once more exposing his chin. This time I leaped forward and caught him with a short right hook which snapped his head back in a spray of sweat. I followed with a left uppercut which drove him back several steps.

The crowd roared.

I pressed on. I could see his eyes getting real small and his balance begin to falter. Inside his reach, I drove a combination to his body. He stumbled back to the ropes. I chased after him, caught him flush with a left to the chin, then several more shots to the body. Then I felt his weight on my back as he grabbed me and held me tight. He was so strong that I couldn't move.

Galviston held on until the referee came in to break us up. I circled cautiously around him as he tried to keep me away with a series of jabs, using his long arms to keep me out of reach. The bell rang.

I was tired. I'd taken a lot of punches and thrown much of what I had into the last round. Still, Galviston seemed to be worse off. A cut had begun to form along the bridge of nose and there were bloodstains on his shorts.

Hal slapped me hard on the back and poured water over my brow. He was beginning to feel that maybe, just maybe, I could win this fight.

I had abandoned everything we'd worked on in practice. I'd stood toe to toe with the Kid and slugged it out and I was still standing.

Maybe, I thought, as the bell rung to start the sixth round, maybe boxing wasn't that different than music. I'd always been a good boxer but never a great one. In the same way, I'd never been a great trumpet player. But I'd reached something special inside myself playing with Mingus out in the shed. I'd abandoned my set phrases and gone out on my own. Perhaps I could do the same thing as a boxer.

Galviston crept in cautiously. I could see by the way his right arm bobbled that he was looking for my jab. I jabbed anyway. Galviston covered up, no longer exposing his chin. I threw a punch that must have looked as if I were swinging at his chin. Instead, I waited for him to raise his glove and put everything I had into a blow that landed squarely on the inside of his right shoulder. Maybe I could take some of the punch out of him that way at least.

Galviston's face contorted in rage. Tiny drops of blood stood out along his white mouthpiece. He moved in, caught me with a jab, and threw a wild combination that was a flurry of motion but left me unscathed. When he was finished, I popped him on the shoulder again.

I was feeling good now. My nerves were calm and my motion fluid. I shuffled my feet as Galviston came after me again. I felt like a well-oiled car easing into third gear. I'd never felt this comfortable in the ring.

Everything he did seemed to be in slow motion. I could read what he was about to do by the way the muscles flexed along his forearms or by the way he clenched his jaw or furled his brow. I could see it all before it happened. After every series of punches he threw, I'd hit him with a single clean, solid blow, either on his shoulder or where I'd opened a cut on his forehead the round before.

Nothing had ever been so easy. Then I felt the change. The muscles on my back pulled out, unfolded. The hair on arms and back began to thicken. Feathers? Wings? I looked down at my hands, expecting to see large talons, but saw only boxing gloves. Dark, black feather lined my arms.

Galviston must have hit me then, because suddenly the canvas reared up and struck my face. Then blackness.

I left for Europe not long after the fight. I stayed for a few months until my mother called Kenny home to reunite him with his brother. I told Liza I was going on tour. I never came back. I stayed in Paris awhile, where the people loved Jazz, and mostly my color didn't matter. I went to London and Berlin, just passing through. A lot of bombed-out buildings remained from the war, but new ones were going up everywhere. Sometimes the people seemed a bit dazed, frantic to make things better after looking down into a dark, dark place. They replaced the past a building at a time.

After a while, I didn't want to be on the beaten track anymore. I went down into Spain and fell in love with its bright and open countrysides. The civil war had ended badly, but it didn't have any effect on me. I found a small village away from everything else. I married a local woman who thought I knew some secret of life from America which I embedded in my music. I thought she was like sweet wine. I wanted to hold and savor her, slowly, a lifetime's worth.

I toured sometimes, sitting in with whomever came through from the US circuit. It was enough. I thought a lot about the change and the music, the meaning of it like poetry, but I never could have said what it meant to me. I thought about Mingus and Kenny from time to time. I never saw Mingus again, and didn't see Kenny for a long time. I didn't envy Kenny anymore. I knew his ability would take him far beyond anywhere I ever went, but I was at peace. You can ask for more, I suppose. I certainly had. But I learned better. Mingus would spend time in an asylum after the death of his friend Eric Dolphy. He stopped playing for a few years after that, but he eventually reemerged on the scene, beginning a second career as a composer. And Kenny, when he did come through and see me, years later, touring with his own band, well, the living hadn't been easy for him either. We didn't talk about Mingus, hardly talked at all. Kenny seemed to be somewhere else most of the time. Of the three of us, Mingus, Kenny, and me, I thought I was the lucky one.

3
HELLHOUNDS

Morgan Creek, California, 1959

W HEN PEOPLE TALK ABOUT MY BROTHER IT'S AS
if he was born with the knowledge of cabalism and escha-
tology. They believe all that crap he spouts in his songs about not
being from this planet, how he arrived here as a traveler from a
distant galaxy, a black man sent to return his people to their na-
tive land.

One of my first memories is of Kenny's birth. Mom and Dad
lived in a hovel by the train tracks in Louisiana. I remember
women yelling, the windows steamed from water boiling, and the
train's low whistle screaming as it hurtled past. He certainly didn't
mention being from the Oort Cloud then, or of taking us up to
the space station orbiting Jupiter to rendezvous with the mothership. He was like any other newborn kid. He was tiny, no more
than six pounds, with a red, angry face squashed like a football.

When I first realized that Kenny was special, truly special,
was the summer of 1959, right after my junior year in high school,
my last year in school. By then, Mom had sent Kenny and me to
live in California with Aunt Lydia for a while. It was the summer
I formed my first band and played real gigs around town. It was
also the summer I almost lost my brother.

Kenny shook my shoulder again. I pulled the bed sheet to
my chin and turned to face the mattress. I knew I should get up

and see what he wanted. But I just wanted to sleep a little longer through the hot afternoon. I had been dreaming of a cool fog off the San Francisco Bay.

"Go away, Kenny." My voice sounded throaty, like it wasn't mine. I tried to clear it.

Kenny shook me again. He said nothing. He didn't like to talk much.

"What?" I said, loudly. But he had won already, and I pushed myself out of the bed to stand unsteadily in the unfamiliar, dark wood-paneled spare bedroom of my Aunt's house. I pushed Kenny, but not hard.

I parted the white, frilled curtains and looked out the window.

At first, I didn't see anything but the old road disappearing over the rise, lined by scrub and sand. Nobody there. I was about to pound Kenny. Then I saw a dust cloud approaching from the other side of the rise. A battered pickup truck bounced down the old dirt road. White dust spun off the rear tires, billowing out behind it like a parachute, as the old truck pulled up to my Aunt Lydia's house. The sun shone yellow amid a high California sky. All the dust floated up and out toward the sun. For a moment, I thought the truck might dissipate in a cloud of dust, a thick cough of exhaust spreading up and away, thinning into nothing.

What happened was something more surprising than that, though.

Two white men in their late forties climbed out of the truck, their legs stiff and bowlegged from many hours of riding. The shorter man craned his neck to look back at the road while the taller man checked something he'd written down in a spiral-bound notepad.

Kenny tapped me gently on the shoulder and we walked out toward the truck. I put my feet into my unlaced boots and re-clasped the belt on my old jeans before we hit the porch. I looked out through the partly open screen door. Kenny peeked out from behind my elbow.

"Are you lost?" I asked.

The smaller of the two, wearing jeans and cowboy boots, slunk back toward the truck, but the other man smiled and tipped his cap, a blue Kansas City Athletics baseball cap that had faded long ago.

"Does Ernest Walker live near here?" he asked.

"Not anymore," I said.

Ernest Walker had been a field hand at the Hudson Farm. He had lived in a shack about two miles down the road, back in among the trees. Kenny had led me to the place about a week after we arrived in the County. Walker had been a blues musician. Kenny really dug that sort of thing. The Blues. I did, too. A little bit, anyway, although I didn't like to admit it. I was into the street corner sounds of doo-wop. I liked the way the girls faces would light up when I'd come in with that big bass voice of mine when we covered songs by the Dells or The Spaniels. Blues was an older form of music, rustic, uncouth, and not as popular with the ladies, particularly the young ones. Even then, I knew Kenny was going to make us famous. He sang all of Frankie Lyman's songs and the covers we did of the Cadillacs and El Dorados. But we'd played around a couple of times with Walker. Mostly I'd been humoring Kenny. Walker wasn't around anymore though, not for about a month.

"Used to," I said, trying to say it so they'd understand. "He's down at Mendal House."

The taller man started to ask directions.

"It's the colored hospital," I told him. The way I said it, I hoped I'd made it clear. Ernest Walker had a better shot at surviving a life sentence at San Quentin Penitentiary than ever returning from where he was now.

"Can you take us? We've come a long way. We could pay you."

Before I could reply, the shorter man nudged his companion and pointed behind me.

At the mention of Walker, Kenny had pushed his way out under my arm and onto the porch. Butterflies had come to him, fluttering cascades of yellow and white and blue.

"How about that," the shorter man said, dumbfounded. I looked at Kenny. He stared intensely at me. He nodded imperceptibly. He wanted to see Walker again. At least that's what I made of his stare. I looked back at the tall man. "All right," I said, "we'll show you the way."

So much for driving a hard bargain. But I didn't feel like I had much choice. And the butterflies, still arriving in larger numbers, were starting to unnerve me anyway. It was time to move.

"The guitars," Kenny said calmly. "We'll need to get Walker's guitars." They must have been the first words he'd spoken in days.

Both men looked surprised, like they thought Kenny couldn't talk, or maybe just that this black kid sounded as if he'd come out of some sort of snooty, big city prep school. The short man didn't seem too pleased with the whole business, but the other man smiled and held out his hand. His name, he told us, was Milo Johnson. His friend was Aaron Silvers. Kenny, a swirl of butterflies in his wake, jumped into the back of the truck.

"Further down the road," I told Mr. Johnson, "that's where Walker lived."

"O.K.," he said, motioning Mr. Silvers into the bed of the pickup. "Let's go."

I pushed through eddies of wings and shadow-flickering light. The butterflies happened to Kenny a lot, during summer months.

"What's with that?" I asked Kenny once.

"Souls," he said, "broken, incomplete, waiting for their return."

I didn't understand and didn't push it. I just ignored it, like so much about my brother.

I climbed in the cab of the truck so that I could give directions. Silvers rode in the back with Kenny. They had equipment under tarps in the back, electronic stuff of some kind. Kenny looked a little sick. It was hard to relax in the back of the pickup. The wind whipped across his face as the truck bounced up and down on the dirt road. Mr. Silvers didn't look comfortable, either. His outside hand held a rigid death grip on the edge of the truck. At least we quickly left the butterflies far behind.

The Hudson farm, as far as I knew, didn't have any other field hands besides Walker. During harvest season, migrant farm workers were brought in by the dozens in old, dilapidated school buses.

Sand and scrub gave way all at once to sweeps of irrigated green fields as we neared the farm.

We drove down winding paths that made the dirt road we'd come down earlier seem like a superhighway. Finally, we turned off-road past a line of trees, pulling up just fifty yards later in front of a tiny shack at the edge of a small field.

We piled out of the truck and the two men exchanged silent looks. Kenny pushed the shack's door open and peered inside.

An elderly white woman in a wood-paneled truck pulled in behind us. Mrs. Hudson was tall and upright, her back stiff as a washboard as she walked up to us. Her two dogs growled softly at us from where they were tied down in the back of the pickup truck. A pair of rifles lay across the rack in the back window.

She scowled and walked past me to talk to our companions.

"What do you want with these two?" she asked.

Mr. Silvers began to stammer a reply.

"It better not be something dirty." A pair of black teenagers accompanied by two middle aged white men wasn't an everyday occurrence in Morgan Creek. We were a long way, both spiritually and in miles, from San Francisco.

"We're looking for Ernest Walker," Mr. Johnson said. He kept his voice soft, but there was a slight strain in his speech that I wouldn't have noticed if we hadn't talked earlier. "These two boys were kind enough to help. They said he lived here."

"He's not here."

"They're going to show us the way to Mendal House."

Kenny walked out with two guitars in his hands and a shoebox under his arm that I knew had Walker's photographs, some of them decades old.

"You going to take his stuff to him?" Mrs. Hudson asked. "I need to clean out his room."

"He'd want these," Kenny said to me.

"We're taking him everything that matters," I told Mrs. Hudson.

"Well, you just be sure to get those things to him," she snapped.

We drove away without looking back.

Mendal House stood between a pair of vacant lots on the corner of Second Avenue and Pine Street, in what passed for downtown in Morgan Creek. I'd never been inside before. The ancient wood-frame structure had been built over 100 years ago, back when the train had carried miners north to gold rush territory. It was easy to see your future in the weathered building. I had an uncle who had died there. Someday, if I stayed close to home, I would too. I wasn't going to stay close.

The nurse on duty wasn't going to let us in at all, but Mr. Johnson told her he worked for a record company looking to tape some of the great old bluesman before they died. Walker was one of the ones they had tracked down. It had taken them months. Mr. Johnson also paid out some money. So the equipment in the back of the truck was recording equipment. Kenny and I carried the guitars and the shoebox.

We found Walker in a closed in room at the back of the building. He looked emaciated and he had dark splotches on his face I hadn't seen before. His hair had turned all gray from the salt-and-pepper of just a couple of months ago. His sad brown eyes had sunk even further into his head. Walker had on a dirty white gown open at the back. He had trouble breathing; Kenny had to help him to a sitting position on the bed. He had nothing in his room besides his bed and a bedstand, not even a roommate. The other bed sat empty, unmade except for a single white sheet. The floors were made of cracked tile, green flecked with white and black. The walls had spiderwebs in the plaster and his one window wouldn't open anymore. Mr. Johnson and Mr. Silvers introduced themselves. Walker nodded at them, but smiled at Kenny. He took the shoebox, and we all sat quietly while Kenny and Walker looked at the pictures. He named places in the pictures that he had played twenty, thirty, fifty years before.

Eventually, Walker had Kenny get the guitars and sit by him. The two began to play. Mr. Silvers started the machine they'd brought, which hissed softly as it turned. Walker had to stop to stretch his fingers. He had arthritis. But he played on. This might be his last performance. He and Kenny traded some licks.

Walker's voice, when he began to sing, sounded badly worn. Mr. Silvers brought him a glass of water from a tap in the backroom and after that Walker's voice filled out. The rasping quality was still there, but now it sounded as if it came from experience, from too many nights spent away from home, playing in bars and nightclubs, drinking whiskey. Sometimes he broke from singing to make jokes or tell a story. It was sad and great and full. I wanted to be him so bad right then. It was my curse, of course, to always want the limelight and never be able to step into it myself. It was waiting for Kenny.

They stopped when Mr. Silvers ran out of tape.

"Just a minute," he said, "and you can start up again."

Kenny had been accompanying Walker, playing a steady rhythm while Walker showed off his skills on the guitar. But as they started up again Kenny became more assertive in his playing. And when they started up in to "Diving Duck Blues," Kenny took the vocals.

> *If the river was whiskey, Mama,*
> *Then I was a diving duck.*
> *I would dive to the bottom.*
> *Lord, I'd never come up.*

I was startled that Kenny would cut in on Walker's session like that. But more shocking still was the way he sang. Kenny's high, youthful voice had terrific range. But as he sang now his voice sounded modulated, like an older man singing falsetto. It was chilling in the same way as a performance by Peetie Wheatstraw or Skip James could be, two musicians who were rumored, along with Robert Johnson, to have sold their souls to the devil in exchange for their blues talents.

Walker turned his head and looked for a while at Kenny, just stared into his face, the veins of his neck twisting beneath the loose skin as he leaned forward. Then, apparently reassured, he leaned back and strummed a few notes as he tuned his guitar.

He started to sing a song I'd never heard before. More of a chant than a blues tune. His guitar playing was soft, yet piercing, as he used a bottle neck to bend the high notes.

> *Two angels came from heaven*
> *And rolled my stone away*
> *The Lord'll bear my spirit home*
> *After I've passed my time away*
>
> *If I had wings like a dove*
> *I would fly*
> *But I was born to die*
> *And lay this body down*
> *When my trembling spirit flies*
> *Unto a world unknown*

His rage clearly simmering, Walker stared defiantly at Kenny the whole way through the song. The mood of the recording session had unraveled completely.

When he finished at last, Kenny stood up, pushing his chair away.

"If that's the way you feel, old man," he said. "I'll go. I thought you'd be happy to see me again." And with the guitar still in his hands, he walked out.

Horrified, I started to apologize, to Walker, to everybody, when I heard an engine turn over and the pickup truck we'd ridden in earlier pull away. By the time I reached the front door, there was no sign of Kenny or the truck.

Mr. Johnson owned the truck Kenny drove off in. Luckily, Mr. Silvers was able to rent a beat up, blue four-door Chevy Impala from a nearby auto shop. It took the better part of an hour to find the car and finish haggling with the shop's owner. Mr. Johnson, Mr. Silvers, and I searched all over town for Kenny with no luck. I had them drive me out to a few places that I thought Kenny might have gone to simmer down, but the evening wind kicked up and the setting sun forced me home to tell Aunt Lydia.

When I arrived, she was in the kitchen cooking up some food, just beans and rice with Creole spices. My mouth watered. Aunt Lydia was a nurse in the hospital the next town over, and was gone from first light to last. She always told us she didn't have time to cook for us and clean for us and we had to make do-and we did all right for ourselves-but she always tried to take care of us like Momma would, leaving us rice and sausages wrapped up in paper in the icebox, or wiping Kenny's dirty face with the corner of a wet cloth. She had taken us in for the summer as a favor to Momma, and I hated to have to tell her Kenny had run off. She didn't need more worries.

Aunt Lydia had changed out of her nurse's uniform into a light summer dress, orange and white, a dress from some other time in her life than now. Some other place than her lonely house. She had absent-mindedly left her hair up in a nurse's tight, efficient bun. Sweat stuck the dress to her back as she stirred over the hot stove. I let the screen door slam as I stepped in to the smell of Louisiana spices, my stomach constricting with fear and hunger both. She hummed, turning to me, stopping when she saw my face.

I told her everything, my lower lip trembling. Well, I didn't tell her everything-I told her about meeting Mr. Johnson and Mr. Silvers and going to Mendal House and Kenny playing with Old Man Walker and that Kenny had gotten mad, left and driven off before anyone could stop him. I left out the part about the strange voice Kenny used and what passed between Kenny and Walker. I couldn't explain that anyway, not even to myself.

Aunt Lydia hugged me hard. She cried, but had a look on her face like she'd seen herself through things before. She only said, "Kenny," once, sadly, and "what will I tell Kat?" Kathleen. Her sister. My mother. Kenny's and mine. When Aunt Lydia went outside to talk to Mr. Johnson and Mr. Silvers, I ate my fill of rice and beans. I was hungry, but I couldn't taste a thing.

On the phone that first night we lost Kenny, Momma had been hysterical but then preternaturally calm. "You find him," she said in a voice I'd never heard her use before. "I'm counting on you." After that, I would have walked into hell itself. Almost did, as it turned out. "I'll be on the next bus out," she said, "but you've got to do for him until then."

Momma didn't arrive until almost a full week later. By then, it was all over anyway.

The police found Mr. Johnson's pickup truck two days later, parked in a ditch just outside of Munsonville, a small town fifty miles down the road. The passenger side window had been broken out and a headlight busted, a small trickle of blood across the dashboard, just enough blood to set the police looking for Kenny, even if he was just a colored runaway. But that lasted only about a day. They'd stopped looking for him by the time I rode out with Mr. Johnson and Mr. Silvers in the Impala to pick up the truck.

I planned to head into Munsonville and find Kenny myself. Aunt Lydia wanted to forbid me to go, not wanting to lose both of us, but I was getting too old to stop that way. Mr. Johnson and Mr.

Silvers had driven me all around the County looking for Kenny the first few days. They felt bad, especially Mr. Johnson, but it wasn't their fault and eventually they had to move on. Mr. Johnson had offered to take me into Munsonville and get me situated before he left.

I waited in the cold while Mr. Johnson stepped into the cab of the pickup, tried the ignition, and gave a small wave back to Mr. Silvers when the truck started up. Mr. Silvers drove off before I had even climbed in beside Mr. Johnson.

Before leaving Morgan Creek, I'd visited Mendal House a few times to see if Kenny had returned there to finish whatever it was that had started between him and Ernest Walker. It was as good as any lead I had, but it didn't seem like Kenny had been there. Walker was asleep mostly when I saw him, but one time I found him awake. He lay rigid, seemingly smaller than before, like he was shrinking away. His face was slack, his mouth open and dry, lips cracked and crusted. His eyes were glazed, as if his vision was fixed on something that hovered in the middle of the room. He didn't notice me at first. His breathing labored and seemed to take all his concentration. It was like he was listening to something intently, trying to hear distant music. Finally, he seemed to notice me and looked up suddenly.

He said something I couldn't quite make out and motioned for water. I filled his half-empty glass in the back room and handed it to him. He sipped loudly, his hand shaking.

"I never did like him all that much," he said.

"Kenny?"

"No. The other one. He snored. Kept me awake nights. I was glad to see him go."

"Have you seen Kenny?" I asked, although I knew it was hopeless. Walker was going downhill fast. But the nurses hadn't seen Kenny either so he must not have come back.

"I'm sorry," Walker said, though whether to the ceiling, to me, or somebody else, I couldn't tell.

Before Mr. Johnson and I had driven half a mile toward Munsonville, it began to sprinkle and then to snow. Big fat white flakes that melted before they hit the ground. Snow in coastal California may not be as rare as a cold day in hell, but it's close. I felt cursed, like I carried a mark of shame, like there was something I should have done for Kenny to have stopped him, stopped everything from happening. But all I could do about it was pull my coat in tighter around my neck and blow ineffectually on my hands, trying to feel something. And I had to admit—the snow was beautiful. Cold as death, but beautiful.

The Impala had had a good heater, I missed it as the wind whistled softly through the broken window of the truck. Munsonville turned out to be just lonely buildings scattered at a crossroads. The north-south road ran long and straight before curving around a hillside. The east-west road didn't look like it went anywhere, though I knew it ran straight into the ocean in one direction and deep into impenetrable mountains in the other. Munsonville was the kind of dilapidated backwater my father used to tell me about as a child when he told me anything about growing up in Louisiana. In my father's stories it was at crossroads like this that people would come to sell their souls to the devil in exchange for a better life.

At first, I thought finding Kenny was going to prove ridiculously easy after all. Munsonville seemed so small that you could walk across it from one side to the other in minutes. A motel, a decrepit movie house, a grocery store, and a saloon made up the main drag.

I checked the grocery store first and then the movie house. I wasn't allowed into the saloon, but Mr. Johnson checked it and found it empty. Next, I paid for a room in the motel, a large boarding house really, owned by a freckle-faced, dark skinned woman, Mrs. Gunnerstand. If she had any reservations about renting a room to black youth without any baggage of any kind, she didn't show it. Maybe it helped that Mr. Johnson waited until I got the room before he left.

"Maybe I should stay," he said after I got the key.

"No, go on. It's not your problem," I told him.

He bit his lip, wanting to leave, I could tell, but wanting everything to be all right, too.

"You sure you're all right?"

"No. But I'm sure you can't do anything more about it that I couldn't do myself."

He nodded and looked at his feet.

"Aaron and I are going to do some more recording not too far from here tomorrow. I'll be back to find you after that, here or in Morgan Creek. If-when everything works out. Maybe we'll get on with that recording with Walker. A couple of those tracks were really special."

He shook my hand, then left, looking back more than once.

I started canvassing the streets the next morning. Unfortunately, Munsonville turned out to be larger than it looked at first, parts of it hidden behind hills or veiled by dark copses of trees. I lost myself walking down long, winding streets that led nowhere. I no longer knew what I was looking for. Did I really expect Kenny to appear in the middle of a cow pasture or on a porch of farm workers?

I found my way back to the motel for lunch. Mrs. Gunnerstand made me a big lunch and I started out again. I had tried to ask Mrs. Gunnerstand if there had been anyone new in town, a kid, but like the few other people I met, she didn't want to talk. This time I set out toward a part of town I'd previously overlooked, with its vast stretches of farmland separated by shacks and barns. It wasn't as cold as it had been the day before, but as the day waned the cold crept through me and into my bones. Where would I go next if I couldn't find Kenny, I wondered? On to the next town, perhaps. And after that? Would I have to make the long trek back home empty handed? I thought I might rather die of cold.

I was at the lowest point I'd been since Kenny had run away when I thought I heard the faint sound of a guitar. It sounded like a rhythm line, a faint echo of a train engine. Following the sound, I cut through a yard and crept between houses and came out behind a rustic shack that must have been a speakeasy before prohibition. The still was set up inside a barnyard door, in full view.

Inside the woodsy, redwood-paneled house, a small figure sat hunched over a harmonica performing before a few solitary customers seated at a few tiny tables. There was one man dancing, swaying, with his right arm bent over an imaginary partner, even though the music wasn't something you could dance to easily.

I knew at once that the harmonica player wasn't Kenny. The hands that folded over the tiny instrument were much too big.

By the time I got to the doorway I spotted Kenny seated behind the other player, guitar in hand.

He looked older. Older than me. His face was drawn, almost gaunt. Gone were the soft lines of childhood. Even his eyes seemed smaller and his eyelids drooped as if he was ready to nod off at any moment.

He looked up at me as I entered but there was no recognition in his jaded stare.

Something felt wrong. It was cold in here. Almost like a meat locker. Colder even than it was outside.

The cold seemed to be inside me, starting in my lower back and shivering up my spine. It was darker in here than outside, too. Even with a few bare electric bulbs dangling from the ceiling. The sun was setting, so the sky outside had faded to a deep twilight, a mix of blue still behind the black, but in here it was night. The shadows seemed to push out from the corners and claim the room. What the hell was going on? I sat at one of the tables, leaning over it nervously, unwilling to leave without Kenny but unnerved, unsure how to talk to him.

Then I noticed the man dancing again. Tears ran slowly down his cheeks and he smiled, a big happy smile. "Maggie," he whispered, sobbing, "Maggie, Maggie." Around the room the other customers sat rapt, looking into corners or at wisps of smoke like they all saw something, each something different. I wanted to grab Kenny and run out of there as quickly as possible, before something I couldn't see came after me. But I knew it wasn't going to be that easy.

When the players finished their set and Kenny made his way to the kitchen, presumably to ask for food, I followed in case he decided to leave through a side door. I wasn't going to lose him now.

He slipped around a corner. When I followed, I felt something hit me from behind, then an arm gripped tightly around my throat and the sharp edge of a knife blade.

"Who are you?" Kenny hissed. The tip of a large kitchen knife rested against the bottom of my chin, pressing upward into the soft flesh.

"Lamond," I croaked. "Your brother." He swung me around violently to face him, keeping the knife between us. He looked me up and down.

"Sit down," he said, pointing to a back room with a dark-stained table and chairs.

"I'd rather we left this place," I said.

He shrugged.

"It's cold outside. This will do. No one will bother us."

There were people working in the kitchen, but they wouldn't look at us. And I could feel it, too, what they felt. Like they had done something wrong. Like something was wrong and they didn't want anyone to know, so no one moved or looked at each other but just did their work and hoped the feeling would let them be-the fear of being caught, found out somehow, I don't know by what. But whatever it was, Kenny somehow was, or somehow embodied, that thing that they feared.

He walked behind me, still carrying the knife, as we made our way to the back room.

He put the knife down on the table and pulled a chair out to sit down. His guard down, I felt the urge to . . . do what? Push by him and run out the door. Escape? Or try to overpower him before he could pick up the knife. And then what? Drag him home?

I sat down on the other side of the table.

"Say what you got to say," Kenny prompted. He was hunched over with his chin resting on his arms which were crossed across the table.

"I came to bring you home," I said.

"Home?" He spat. "What makes you think I want to go home?"

"We miss you."

"Who?"

"Me. Aunt Lydia. Mom's worried sick."

"Man, don't you listen, I don't know you. I'm not your brother. My name's Jones."

"Jones?"

"Emanuel Jones."

I shook my head. Nothing made any sense.

"Never heard of me, have you?"

I shook my head dumbly.

"You'd have to be about ten years older. I'd been in Mendal House almost that long, unable to play." He looked at his hands and they twitched slightly, playing imaginary strings and frets.

He smiled. A quick, darting smile, a smile meant for a guitar but not for me. He seemed fascinated by the way his hands moved.

"You're dead, aren't you?"

"You're not as stupid as you look, but you still bug the shit out of me."

"You've got to let Kenny go." I put my hand out to plead, but Kenny pushed away from the table, out of reach like I was attacking him.

"I didn't have anything to do with this. I was fine, more than fine, where I was. Starting over as a snot-nose kid isn't my idea. They laughed at me here, until I started playing. And I can't smoke; I hacked out a lung trying. And don't start me on women. Shit, I did all this already, and I don't want it. Not anymore. I'm tired."

"What are you going to do?" I said miserably.

"I don't know, but you see what happens wherever I go. Weird shit, people seeing the dead come back to life. And the cold. I can never get warm. It gets worse when I play. But that's the only thing I know how to do."

"You need to come back with me," I said firmly, mustering as much resolve into my voice as I could. "You've got nowhere else to go, am I right? And I know Kenny, maybe we can find a way to bring him back." I didn't have a plan just then. My family was from Louisiana, maybe somebody knew some kind of voodoo thing I'd never heard about. There were rumors about some of my family practicing, in older days. No one I had ever met. That's how everyone explained Kenny—" runs in the family," they'd say, whenever something strange happened. It didn't seem very plausible, not even to me then, but it was all I had to hold on to.

Kenny thought, rubbing his chin, years he didn't have registering in the weary look he gave me.

"All right, he said. "But keep your Mom and Aunt away from me. I don't think I could take it. I'm too old to be anybody's child."

We left through the back.

Out front, the man who had been shadow dancing was sitting in the middle of the road, his head in his hands, crying like he'd lost everything all over again. I think he had. We walked on in silence. Every shadow I saw had teeth.

*

A farmer gave us a ride back toward Morgan Creek the next morning, early. It was windy but at least the sun had come out again, though distant and with little heat. Kenny sat tuning his guitar while we drove, but I didn't want him to play.

"Don't play," I shouted to him above the wind. "Wait."

"I didn't ask for any of this," Kenny said.

He scrunched his mouth up like a sour old man.

"I think maybe I know a way out, though," he said, with a sly grin.

"What's that?" I asked.

"I should be dead. Maybe I should just go back."

"What do you mean?" I didn't like the way his eyes seemed to recede into some distant place.

"I could just throw myself over the edge, on to the road, and just die."

The road unrolled below us fast. He moved to rise but I jumped on top of him, holding him down.

"Kenny," I shouted.

"I'm not Kenny," he hissed.

"Don't do it."

"You're right," he said, his body relaxing under mine, smirking at me. "You're right. I'm younger than I remember. I'd probably live. Just hurt a lot."

The farmer had glanced back when we knocked around, and now his truck rolled to a stop.

"Get out," he said. "I don't need fighting back there."

I let Kenny up and we climbed out.

The farmer looked more rattled than he should just from having a couple of boys rolling around in back. What had he seen when Kenny played?

Kenny sneered at me as the truck rattled away.

"Day was, when I could have kicked your ass."

"We'll get another ride," I said.

"Sure," Kenny said, "or, if a car goes by too fast I can just leap in front and end this farce."

"Shut up," I said. I wanted to hit him, hard in the face. If only it wasn't my brother's face, already twisted into a parody of itself.

Kenny laughed at me and shook his head until we got another

ride back to Morgan Creek in the back of another empty farmer's truck.

Kenny started to play and sing. And I didn't have any heart left to stop him. At least he wasn't trying to die while he was singing. He sang a song I'd never heard before.

> *I no longer know my home*
> *No longer know my home*
> *Like one on a lonely road*
> *Walks in fear and dread*
> *And having once turned round*
> *Turns no more his head*
> *'Cause he knows a frightful fiend*
> *Close behind him treads.*

Only when I knocked at the truck's rear window and asked the driver if he could make up some time for us, and he sped up, did Kenny stop singing.

Our last ride into town was in a hearse, making its end run back to the funeral home from the cemetery. We rode in the now coffinless rear with our legs stretched out. It was almost impossible to make out the landscape through the darkened windows as we traveled. I could just see the dark shapes as they passed, but they proved too elusive, too far away.

We stretched gratefully as we climbed out of the back. The sun had just begun to climb over the horizon, lighting the small town like the set of a Western movie. The houses seemed incredibly clean and insubstantial in the bright, pale sunshine.

Kenny dusted off his jeans and looked around.

"It's all different," he said.

"How do you mean," I asked. I was too tired to care, but I wanted to let him talk. I was afraid if I tried to lead him away that he wouldn't follow.

"I don't mean the mortuary. I wouldn't remember that. But these buildings. And the cars are so much smaller."

I nodded. It was strange to hear Kenny talking like an old man. He *was* an old man.

"That used to be a ballfield," he said, pointing to a row of not so old yet dilapidated buildings just down the street. "We used to have a team called the Sage."

He gazed out, something lighting up his eyes from inside.

"I guess I'm young enough to play again. Didn't think of that."

He stretched his arm back and motioned straight over his head, throwing.

"Kenny," I said. "Emanuel . . . Mr. Jones." I wasn't sure what I wanted to say.

Kenny spat, an ugly look on his face. He was starting to scare me again. His moods seemed to be changing so quickly.

"We have to get back," I said. "Please. It's this way."

He turned and I led him quickly back to the hospital. We glided past the nurses—too few to really watch the door carefully. We made our way to Walker's room. He wasn't there. The beds were neatly made. The window opened to the light. His guitars sat piled in a corner, not leaning separately as a musician would leave them. Someone had just hastily put them on top of each other to get them out of the way.

"Ah, fuck," Kenny said, and sat on the bed across from Walker's.

"Mr. Walker?" I called out, not wanting to believe the obvious, as if there were somewhere for him to hide. Could he be in another room, or out somewhere?

"He's dead," Kenny said. "Sorry, kid."

I sat on Walker's bed.

We sat awhile in silence. Then Kenny started to speak without looking at me.

"This was my bed," Kenny said. "I died here."

He patted the mattress and sat down, swung his feet up and down when he realized that they didn't reach the floor.

"Walker and me," he said, "we'd known each other a long time. We had been friends, at first, a long time ago, then enemies—partly because of some things with the music—some business and some to do with, well, what we believed in—and partly, as so often happens, because of a girl. An amazing girl, I grant you. Then I'd ended up here, and Walker used to visit me sometimes, and we were, not friends, I don't know, old hands, and all the old troubles didn't matter."

Kenny shrugged and I slumped, put my hands in my pockets,

not really listening. I turned away to look out the window, but Kenny, this one, went right on talking, filling the emptiness.

"And having been dead," he grinned, "I can tell you, that was right—it doesn't matter. It really doesn't. The only thing that signifies is that we had some god-damn fun before it was over."

Kenny's old voice had been flat, emotionless, but at the last he made a low moan, almost to himself. I looked at him, his eyes bore on me.

"I died here," he said. "I waited around a while. Didn't know what else to do. Thought Walker might conk out any day and then the two of us might . . . I'm not sure what. But as the days passed, I felt myself fading away, forgetting who I was and everything I knew. And then I just floated away. The preacher growing up would have said that I went home to live with God. But it wasn't like that.

"It was like the universe was one big egg shell—with gigantic fissures running through it. I floated up and into a very small part of one of those cracks and healed it, made it whole. Or maybe it healed me. I can't remember anymore."

Kenny jumped off his bed and picked up the guitars. He dropped one on Walker's bed beside me and sat back on his old bed. All I could think of was butterflies, swarming in sunlight, souls, waiting. Kenny tuned his guitar, humming absently to himself.

"I thought you and Walker would play Kenny back," I said. "Like before, only in reverse."

"I know you did," Kenny said. "I got that." He motioned at the guitar beside me, but I let it lie.

Kenny began to play softly.

"Your brother's gone," he said. "If nothing changes, I'm going to have to go soon, and make my way, playing music, I suppose. Only thing I'm any good at."

"No," I said, but I had no heart in it.

"I'm sorry, kid, I really am. I don't want his body. He can have it back. But I don't know what to do."

I heard a familiar truck outside and went to the window. Mr. Johnson, alone, without Silvers, had pulled up and stepped out of his truck. He'd said he'd come check on things. After a time filled with Kenny's expert doodling and bending of notes, Milo

Johnson came into the room.

"Kenny," he said, smiling, "hey, all right. I was hoping it would work out."

I had sat back on the bed, my hands still in my pockets. I looked at him bleakly.

"It's not Kenny," I said.

Johnson stopped, even backed up to the doorway a half-step. He looked quizzically at Kenny, then at me, clearly not believing, but willing to see where this was going.

"My name is Emanuel Jones," Kenny said.

Johnson looked at Kenny for a long time, waiting for the punch line. It didn't come.

"'The Road to Calvary,'" Johnson finally said. A test.

Kenny leaned over his guitar, stretching his child's fingers to reach the chords, and began to play. He frowned deep in reverie and moaned low and guttural, eerie. I felt the hairs on the back of my neck stand up. The room itself seemed to darken as Kenny tapped his foot in time. He sang.

> *Walked the road to Calvary*
> *Wept beneath the cross*
> *But I didn't ask for this*
> *I just can't bear the loss,*
> *Just can't bear the loss.*
>
> *Can't stay and say I'm sorry*
> *Just can't bear the loss*
> *Can't stay in safe harbor*
> *My soul all tempest-tossed,*
> *my soul's tempest-tossed.*

Kenny croaked out the verses. In between singing he returned to his guttural humming, a sad sound of shadow-filled rooms and cigarettes and things better left unsaid. Kenny sang from old pain and sorrow. I started to cry for Kenny, for *my* Kenny. Johnson just stared with the most peculiar look on his face until Kenny finished.

Johnson started to speak, his voice failed him. He swallowed dryly.

"Stay here," he said. "I'll be back." He left to get his equipment. The nurses had come with the music, but Mr. Johnson soothed their complaints with money, explanations.

"But why can't you play somewhere else," the head nurse asked, "Can't you take these kids somewhere else to play?"

Johnson had simply handed her more money and they left us alone. Johnson quickly got a tape on the reels and got it rolling.

"Mr. Jones," he said, "please."

Kenny began to play. I fell over on my side, lying on the bed, tears drying on my cheeks, my nose running. But I kept my hands in my pockets, not even caring enough to wipe my face while Kenny was lost somewhere. Not caring while Jones played to spite the living, come back from shadows and nothingness. I stopped listening when I felt something behind my temples, then my head throbbed painfully in time to the music. I sat up without realizing it and picked up the other guitar. No, I didn't. Or, maybe I did.

It happened so fast. I couldn't tell if it was a decision I had made or if somebody else, Walker, perhaps, had reached for my body. Anyway, I thought I could feel Walker there with me, suddenly there, his deep brown eyes and lined cheeks, sallow and care-worn, staring out from beneath my brow.

In any event, something at that point rushed at me from a long distance and shoved me out of myself completely. I tumbled away into a corner of the room and looked back at myself as I started to play.

I stood, tried to right myself, to find my bearings. But I kept slipping. Without a body, my spirit was incredibly light, buoyant.

I started to float away. The world around me seemed to cease. I stood up somewhere else, somewhere first dark, then shadowed with light and fleeting shapes. There was a signpost of decayed wood. It read "Golgonooza" and was sharpened to a point on one end. I followed the sign's direction down a dusty road shrouded in mist until I saw light ahead. A two-story building hunched at a dead-end, eaves overhanging a porch. A sign swinging from the overhang was too worn to read. The place looked like a bar, a gin joint from some earlier time. Its walls were darkly stained, the wood badly warped. I could hear the walls creaking loudly, then, getting closer, I heard voices, singing, music filtering out. I could see shapes inside behind pulled shades that glowed with a soft light. The door stood ajar.

I stepped nosily across the sagging planks of the porch and pushed through the door. I hadn't known how cold I was until the heat of the crowded room blasted me. An enormous man in dark glasses, a thin mustache and a neatly tailored brown suit with a thin black tie on a white shirt nodded at me as I entered.

"Come freely," he said, smiling, "and leave something of what you bring."

He motioned me toward an open table at the edge of the circle of yellow light that dominated the center of the room. The room sweated with music, many people playing, bathed in that light, trading riffs or weaving their music in and around one another. The musicians huddled into the light but still more played in the blackness beyond it. It was impossible to tell how many people were there. I could see at least a half-dozen guitarists, an upright bass, two saxophones, a trumpet; somewhere in the darkness, a drum beat and the faint tinkling of piano keys. In the darkness, bright coals of cigarettes flickered and yellow light reflected off dark glasses like headlights glinting off the eyes of wolves just off the road.

Kenny sat in the inner circle, head fallen back in abandon, not looking while his fingers scratched angrily at the strings of his guitar; his fingers bled, his face scrunched up in a grimace, but he nodded to himself like everything was just right somehow.

I should get him out of here, I thought. But how? Where was I?

For a moment I did nothing. Something held me back, some bit of corrupted knowledge about magic that I could only articulate to myself by thinking: never wake a sleepwalker. I had found Kenny, and I didn't want to hurt him by disrupting whatever he was doing too quickly. But then I meant to sit down, and didn't. In confusion, I stumbled into the light.

"Please," I shouted, "Please, Kenny, please."

Kenny looked and held me for a time with his clear eyes, deep like stones in a river. And he sang a song whose words I cannot remember. I can still catch fragments, but not the tune. And not a single word. But it made me stop for a moment, all those wolf eyes glinting, all those firefly lights in the darkness. I should have held still, but I reached out and touched Kenny's hand. I thought of

Mom coming, and I thought of Kenny lost. But mostly I thought of me—of how I missed and needed him, how we would play together in our band and I wouldn't end up in Mendal House; we would go—he would take me—away from a life I hated, feared. I wanted something from him so much that I reached out and touched him and broke the spell he wove.

I touched him and something seemed to drop away from him. The music kept on, a bass solo stepping in where Kenny faltered. Kenny's eyes focused, seemed to see me for the first time; then he lowered his head and stopped playing.

"Hey, Charlie," Kenny said over his shoulder to the bassist, "another live one, like us."

The serious bass player with the ragged beard and deep frown didn't stop. He looked familiar, like we'd met somewhere. But I kept my attention on Kenny.

"It's good to see you, brother," Kenny said softly, eyes still lowered from me, "but you're early."

Kenny examined his fingers, bleeding darkly.

"I didn't feel a thing," Kenny said. He pressed the tips together to staunch the flow.

"Hey, William," Kenny said, standing unsteadily, "come take my place." An old white man with a great beard stepped up. He wore a loose-fitting white shirt and hand-made coarse pants, like from some period drama on tv. He took the guitar and sat in Kenny's place. "I'm going outside a moment."

Kenny took my hand. The new guitarist grinned at me beatifically. He and Kenny were the only ones not wearing dark glasses. He had green eyes that blazed, glittering like supernovae. Before we got outside, weaving through tables, the man sang of the fourfold path, of angels in trees scolding him, and of him scolding them back. Then I was outside with Kenny, my head suddenly clearing in the cold.

Kenny closed the door and turned, creaking the floorboards of the porch. He took my hand.

"What are you doing here?" Kenny asked, without enthusiasm. He looked tired. This wasn't where he belonged. I think only the dead belonged here.

I shivered with cold sweat, and felt ill, lost, fading. The shadows seemed to be taking substance, to be closing in. I wasn't even sure that the gin joint was there anymore. Was I standing in the mist, on the road? Was there even still a road?

"I need you to come back. I promised. We've got to get out of here. You need to get out of here."

I rambled. I couldn't even see Kenny clearly anymore, a fog obscuring him. But Kenny didn't let go of my hand. Still, he wouldn't look up at me.

"This is a good place," Kenny said. "Where I want to be. I'm not lost."

I panicked then. I broke down. I felt myself whirling into the shadows, my legs drifting into smoke and mist. I begged Kenny. I reached out to shake him, to make him look at me. I felt my eyes going, my vision receding as I fell into nothingness.

"Don't let go," I pleaded. "Kenny, don't let go."

I sobbed and cried hysterically and reached out madly grasping at him until I felt hands, two solid hands, holding me. And a floor solid below me. I was on my back. These were real hands and a voice.

"Calm down, child, calm," over and over. The voice spoke sternly, authoritatively. I looked into the eyes of a nurse at Mendal House. I was in Walker's room.

"What are you going on about?" The nurse asked.

As I calmed, my breath slowing, I saw Kenny—I saw what looked like Kenny sitting on Jones's bed. I lay back.

"I don't need this nonsense on my watch."

Milo Johnson was handing the woman yet more money, and grabbing his equipment up as quickly as he could. The nurse hustled us out and into the street. All I could think was that the uneasy light through the clouds made the time uncertain. When was it? Then I wondered, was it Kenny who walked quietly beside me, his head bowed? The nurse had had to help me out, and I leaned heavily against the railing out front. The nurse left us there, primly telling us we were never welcome there again. I looked at Kenny but he wouldn't look at me. Even as tired as I was, I couldn't help smiling.

Milo Johnson couldn't get away fast enough. I guess it hadn't looked so good at the end there. Despite my condition, he didn't press giving us a ride. He asked, but Kenny waved him off and the truck jerked away in a cloud of dust. He had tapes of both sessions, of course, but what good were tapes of a couple of kids pretending to be dead singers? Who would want them?

We walked home with our hands in our pockets.

Aunt Lydia actually shouted out her thanks to God. She fed us well and asked for stories, touching Kenny's cheek again and again until he shook her off. Kenny wouldn't speak. I told her things about where I traveled, but nothing of the land of shadows. She could tell—who wouldn't have?—that my story was incomplete, but she was too happy, and relieved, to press it. Momma would arrive the next day. Kenny, still not speaking, accepted Aunt Lydia's caresses and fussing a little longer, then yawned a few times and headed to bed.

I followed him.

We brushed our teeth and climbed into our narrow beds in a daze. I pulled the blankets over me, grateful to feel them against my skin, grateful to feel anything. I could feel a knot of terror in me, a knot I would never really lose, about the emptiness of the shadows in the place where I found Kenny.

I sat up suddenly.

"Kenny?" I asked. "Is it you? You haven't said a word. You're not Jones?"

The blanket fell around me. Kenny had his back turned to me. He didn't move except to sigh. He spoke in a tired voice, defeated and small, a whisper.

"It's me," he said. "I'm here."

"It was terrible there," I said. "Sad."

"No," I could barely hear him say, "it wasn't."

Though I looked at him for a long time, Kenny didn't speak further. Eventually I lay back, thinking about what he had lost. We would start our band, singing soul first, then funk, making hits. Kenny would always be distracted, looking for something. People would come to hear him sing of outer space and a future that would bring all us aliens together into One. They would call him Prophet and seek him out, even follow him. Only I would know what Kenny really lost, the true geography of his outer space, his fantasies of dream worlds where the lost chord played. Only I, too, knew the land of the shadows.

I would be Kenny's manager, my brother's keeper, building his career, our career. My eyes on the money he never cared about, on the airplay, on the fame. He would never be right, whole, again, from that day to this. But I couldn't change a thing and, to my shame, though I love him, I knew I wouldn't change things even if I could. The sets he played were like revival meetings, séances, gospel singing, all in one. He set people free, out of his loss. They needed him. I needed him.

I could see all this, our future gigs, the people coming to touch him, desperate as I had been desperate in that other place. I could see it all that night, sense it before us. I heard it in Kenny's "I'm here," spoken forlornly.

I wanted it all too much to be sorry, but I am sorry. I slept only after a long, uncomfortable, hot time of tossing, turning. My dreams were shadows, swirling.

Next day Momma arrived on the bus. She wore her traveling dress, dark blue and serious, and a frown at first. Then there were smiles and hugs and "let me look at you." Kenny got most, but I was not left out. Kenny surprised me by speaking up and telling his story. Everything. Momma and Aunt Lydia listened pensively, with pursed lips. When Kenny finished, Momma sighed.

"It runs in the family," she said.

And that was about it.

Momma and Aunt Lydia traded gossip about the family and cooked up more food than we could eat. And later, Momma made Kenny tell her everything again, as we sat sipping lemonade in the sun.

Then she said, "take it easy, will you, for a while?" to Kenny while touching his cheek.

"I will, Momma," he said, butterflies circling him with friendly waves.

"And you," she said to me, "take care of him. He needs you."

And I hoped he did. I wanted him to badly, but I doubted it—a doubt I kept tight and darkly bundled with my shame and my knotted fear in a place somewhere in my gut. I would never lose any of those things, ever.

"I will, Momma," I said.

People eat up Kenny's stories about being from somewhere behind the sun, dancing with aliens from Groove. Sometimes I think he believes it, too, somehow. But I know this isn't science fiction but some kind of ghost story. And I hear it in the music. I hear it in the beat and in his chanting growls late into the night that bring the audience to some ecstasy of sweet dreaming and patchouli oil, through marijuana and the beat, to dancing and the One. But there's more than joy there, as my brother preaches. There's terror, too, a nothingness. I know that.

I know it, even if he doesn't.

4
ELECTRIC LADYLAND

San Francisco, 1964-1967

A S THE POLICE CAME RIDING TOWARDS US, THEIR horses in a formidable line, we set up a chorus line of high-kicking splendor, the sunlight glinting on our sequined dresses, our limp boas, feathers plucked or fallen in the earlier melee, flapping lazily in response to our energetic dancing.

This memory must be from 1967. The crowd behind us had been protesting something, somebody in the 60s was always protesting something, but we—the Sun Dreamers, the Solar Children, descended from the planet, the archetypal positive of this rock and its hatreds, that circled always out of sight on the far side of the sun—we came to celebrate ourselves, to splash color on the dour on all sides, to open eyes; our group, somewhere between a band and a happening, a performance troupe and a commune, we came, men and women, in spectacular drag, the men fabulous women with beards and too-long glitter eyelashes, the women more than women in heavy purple eye shadow, rouged cheeks and impossibly large lipstick lips shaped into ruby kisses, gender a joke to us, choosing anything instead of everything a bad joke to us.

As we kicked, our Prophet, come from the sun to bring the good news, resplendent in a full length red strapless torn silk evening gown, his Afro colored red, white and blue, elevator shoes with mirrored sides shining, and a lime green boa rampant, burst into song, a wordless chant, a call to wake the living and groove the dead, to bring the aliens down upon us in a rain of silver and wide-saucer eyes. We joined him in a full-throated roar.

The protesting crowd, lost, hemmed in by the police on opposite sides, sensed something and started to gain shape and purpose, surging behind us, picking up our wordless, eerie chant, our wail, our keening. The police, on their horses, sensed something, too, and their ranks before us broke, or a space opened up, or perhaps the aliens did rain down to ray blast us out of there, who knows? Our kick-line opened up and we ran out, the crowd bursting through behind us; we ran laughing down Haight Street into Golden Gate Park. I remember sunlight steaming. Then it was night. I remember singing on the beach and a bonfire, kissing The Prophet, running in the cold surf of the Pacific, laughing, always laughing. Once, my life was like that a lot, once when I knew The Prophet, before the music became a business, with Egyptian Motherlode, the best funk band from the 70s that nobody ever heard of, before the drugs turned bad on us all, destroying the dream of San Francisco and a hippie runaway like me. It seems like several lifetimes ago now, when magic was everywhere, before the impossible became impossible again.

The Prophet was the first person I saw when I arrived in San Francisco, stepping off a greyhound bus in search of a new life in 1964. I only remembered him later because his appearance was so unusual. His head was shaved then and I noticed the way the light glinted off its rounded ridges, even though the sun was hidden behind a thick blanket of fog. I was cold and I quickly passed this unusual looking man, playing a smooth sounding saxophone, pea green beret for collecting change at his feet. I'd have left a few coins if I'd had any.

In the months that followed, I'd often see him and I began to think of him as something of a personal good luck charm.

Early in the morning I might see him walking through Golden Gate Park. He'd be whistling some Jazz tune with his dog, a wiry coated Jack Russell Terrier, walking by his side. Occasionally I'd recognize the tune he whistled, a scrap of Thelonious Monk or Sonny Rollins. But usually it was too obscure for me, or more likely, although I didn't know it then, a tune of his own composition.

Evenings I might see him darting into a night club, sometimes with a guitar slung across his back. His hat would be pulled down low over his eyes as if he didn't want anybody to know he'd been there. He'd wait until the set ended, talk in hushed tones to a couple of musicians, and then they'd quietly leave, often through a back door.

But I'd also see him at the most unusual times, carrying a bouquet of sunflowers while skipping in the rain, working under the hood of a Pontiac in the dark of night, or playing an imaginary game of hoops in the Panhandle without a ball. He'd catch the invisible basketball, cradling it in his hands as he brought it into his body and pivoted, rose up and flicked it off his fingertips. The cement courts were a couple hundred feet away and in the opposite direction of his shots. If he'd had a basketball it would have bounced into a grouping of nearby bushes that separated the park from traffic.

The day when I talked to him for the first time, he sat stooped over on a bench not far from the merry-go-round in Golden Gate Park. It was the weekend and there were children everywhere. In the middle of them all, The Prophet, oblivious in concentration, rubbed his fingertips across the palms of either hand. His motions, strangely elegant with purpose, reminded me of tai-chi, or a ritualized dance between partners.

A butterfly, burnt orange with black stripes drifted past his forehead, fluttered up and up into a high blue sky. It was followed by another, blue and black with zig-zag patterns. The next was olive brown with yellow spots.

Butterflies flew one after another in a loose column above him. They flew out the palm of his hands every three or four seconds, or so it seemed, a variety of colors, patterns, and sizes, no two the same. When I looked up again, the butterflies spread out and then regrouped into long snaking columns that twisted and curved. They formed into letters that changed my life forever.

FLORENCE

My name written in a cascade of shimmering colors above my head.

"Hey," I said, laughing as I stepped forward. "How did you do that?"

He smiled, tipped his cap. A butterfly four of five times larger than the others flew out from beneath it. The words LIFE and DEATH were written across its wings. It flew behind a copse of trees and disappeared.

The Prophet spread his arms out wide as he stood up from the bench. As he did so there was a sound like the breaking of a tree limb and the butterflies above my head scattered in all directions.

"Kenny," he said and stuck out his hand.

He was younger than I'd thought, perhaps eighteen. I was twenty.

"That was beautiful," I said. "How . . .?"

He looked down at the ground.

"It's just a magic trick, nothing special."

He looked amazingly vulnerable, this young man who'd filled the sky with teeming imagination. He didn't seem to be flirting, but there was something he wanted.

"I needed to talk to you," he said. Or maybe he was flirting. I wasn't used to feeling this out of my element. I was out for a stroll in the middle of the day in Golden Gate Park, surrounded by shouting children who had all but disappeared.

"Yes."

"I need a favor."

He pulled a manila folder out from underneath the bench where it had rested on warm concrete. Very carefully he pulled out a sheaf of papers and handed them to me.

I took the papers from him. They were hard to read–some sort of advertisement for a band named The Pathfinders, led by someone named "The Prophet." The text had been hand drawn in pencil on plastic stencils and then cut with some kind of blade.

"That you? The Prophet?"

"Yes," he said. He shrugged. "A stage name. My brother started calling me that—as a joke. It stuck."

"What do you want me to do with these?" I asked.

"I thought since you worked in an office . . ."

I did then, for a time, as a glorified coffee bringer. But how did he know?

"You want me to make copies?"

He nodded.

"I can't make them myself," I told him, "but I can ask somebody at my office who can use the Gestetner." The magical copy machine in those hallowed days before the internet and photocopiers in every drugstore.

A week later I joined the band as a backup singer. I joined up, or was drafted, when I came by the abandoned warehouse in the Mission where the band practiced, dropping off a second batch of flyers. Something had gone wrong and people were arguing, there must have been a dozen of them but at least four were quitting to form their own band. The Prophet's brother Lamond was yelling from the stage at the deserters.

"You don't deserve to be paid," he yelled, gesturing at them, then putting his hands in his pockets, then taking them out to curse at them and gesture again. The deserters were scurrying to pack their instruments and get out. Others were trying to engage those leaving in conversation, to make some of them stay; it seemed like most of the people with the real instruments were leaving. Some of the people leaving were trying to convince some of the others to come with them. I heard more than one of those staying say, "The Prophet's here, stay here. The money is bullshit."

The Prophet himself stood aloof from it all, at the back of the stage, half in darkness, talking to a large silhouette over his shoulder that I couldn't quite make out for a moment. It seemed distorted, its proportions stretched like a cartoon character's. I tried to keep to the side of the stage along the far wall, away from the people moving, stopping, clumping, arguing, fleeing for the doors, coming back in to yell a point or going to the door to beg a friend to stay.

The Prophet, Kenny, I finally saw, spoke to a black bear standing erect on two hind feet. It didn't appear to be someone in a costume; it was a bear, talking, gesturing in normal conversation as the two conferred. The bear caught my eye and nodded solemnly, then it winked, turned and seemed to slip through a space in the back wall I hadn't noticed before, through a crack in the warped wood somewhere.

Lamond had come down from the stage, yelling, and picked up a metal pole, hefting it, sending the remaining band, "deserters" and "remainder" alike, running out the door.

The Prophet turned to me and nodded once.

"What was that?"

"It was nothing. The music was dying. We'll find other musicians."

"No, the bear."

"You saw it?" He broke into a huge grin. He took my hand, removing his dark glasses. From distraction, his attention focused on me, something electric arcing behind his eyes.

"Lamond," The Prophet shouted, "Lamond!"

Lamond stood in the doorway of the warehouse, waving his metal pipe, shouting something unintelligible and angry.

"Put that down. We have work to do. Music to make."

Like that, everything had changed again. Lamond turned, and seeing his brother suddenly so animated, Lamond's angry face drained of emotion, then he smiled wearily, hopefully.

"Music," he said. He looked doubtfully at the metal bar.

"Let's go round up our band from the bars and hideouts you sent them to." The Prophet clapped Lamond on the shoulder and laughed. "Meet Florence," he said; still holding my hand in his other hand, he gestured his arm out in a half turn, displaying me to Lamond. I had seen him, but never been introduced. "She's in the band, a backup singer."

"I can't sing," I said. Lamond's small smile seemed to fade, replaced by an "oh-no-here-we-go-again" look of resignation.

"We need real musicians this time," Lamond said in a flat tone, voicing an argument he had evidently made and lost too many times. "She said she can't sing."

"It doesn't matter," The Prophet said. "You have style," he told me. "I can see it. You have to sing with us! Say yes!" His eyes burned into me. Lamond appeared displeased but resigned.

"Get something to wear, something with more colors, or shorter, and with baubles, beads, something freaky, and meet us back here. Let's go!" he said to Lamond. Lamond nodded.

"Let's go," Lamond echoed, and the brothers walked quickly into sunlight.

I looked back one more time at the spot where the bear had been, then I left the warehouse, closing the door on emptiness. Maybe in the darkness at the back, animal eyes glittered.

*

"The music doesn't matter," The Prophet said the night of my first show. "It's the places you can go. Let me take you somewhere you've never been."

The reconstituted band, now called Sun Dreamers, played two amazing weekend shows at a small movie theater with couches instead of seats that sold carob cookies and spiced cider. The stage was only fifteen feet deep. We packed it like a commuter train. We were to be the warm up before a Russ Meyers titty flick, but we never gave up the stage. The bear was there, too, both nights, at the back, unnoticed, sitting up splay-legged before a drum he brought himself from somewhere behind the wall, beating a rhythm with the pads of his front paws.

"Did you ever feel there was a veil over the world," The Prophet said, "hanging over something else, some presence— some heartbeat waiting for you to hear it?"

I had dressed in a blue skirt adorned by silver crescent moons with smiling faces and a tight-fitting tie-dye blouse, but I was not outrageous on that stage. Two of the men, burly ex-bikers with long beards who played in the horn section showed up in drag and The Prophet loved it and made it a theme. The second night everyone came in drag, and the buzz from the first night had the theater packed with more crowd outside wanting in.

Both nights The Prophet chanted long hallucinatory stories and we danced until we were naked. The crowd joined us dancing onstage or in the aisles. Before morning came we would burst out onto the street for sunrise and an ecstatic "washing clean" in a pond in Golden Gate Park, all of us, the band, the crowd, people who just joined our naked parade to the pond.

Before the police and fire marshals could shut us down, Lamond set up our show in a bigger venue for the next weekend, a real performance hall. We ran around before the third show buying clothes at second-hand shops, flapper dresses, colored beads and leather skirts, preening in the Haight and on Polk, the Sun Dreamers, famous for being outrageous, the crazy of the crazed. We loved it. But The Prophet didn't show up and no one could find him for ten days, not until I did. By then, the promoter Lamond had hooked up with was gone, despite Lamond's threats if he pulled out, and the band had disbanded again.

*

I found The Prophet sitting crossed-legged on Hippie Hill in Golden Gate Park. The more distant sounds of a carousel mixed with the steady beat of a circle of bongo players at the bottom of the hill surrounded by a large semi-moon of dancers who swayed, or jumped wildly, often sitting for a respite or falling back onto the grass only to rise again and take part in the ragged dance to the sun. The Prophet lay on his back, his face impassive, eyes covered by dark glasses, looking upwards into the sky.

"Do you see them, those clouds, the light yellow then silver-hazy around the edges? Do you see them?" His voice was flat. I put my hands in my pockets, suddenly awkward. I looked up.

"Yes," I said.

"I don't feel them. I don't feel anything. The life in them, the shaping."

I licked my lips, then sat down, folding my flowing skirt under me like a blanket.

"Do you feel them?" he repeated. His voice dropped to a whisper, "I used to . . ."

"I—I don't know. I suppose—"

He reached out towards the clouds, I expected a butterfly, or maybe that he'd pluck the cloud out of the sky and give it to me, or we'd eat it like cotton candy, licking it from our fingers. But he began to cry instead. I touched his cheek. I removed the glasses to look into bloodshot eyes. When had he last slept?

We kissed. We kissed for hours until the clouds gathered into a storm and dropped a rain that brought us sitting up. The bongo players were gone, everyone was gone, the sun was setting.

We ran home, laughing, kissing, to my bed. We stayed until he had to go, finally, to write a song. I became, he told me, some new part of him . . . a place to run to. I knew, even then, that it was a bad idea. But I grounded him. I could talk to him and bring him back to us better than anyone . . . even, after a while, his brother. I knew it would have to break someday, but he took me up into those clouds sometimes, when he felt good. When he felt it, I'd never known anything better. Tomorrow simply seemed far away.

The end came sooner than I expected. How many shows had we played? A dozen maybe. We were rising again, the music flowing again, when it ended as it began, abruptly.

"I'm sorry," he whispered to me one morning. "I have to go."

It was two more years before I saw The Prophet again. I went back to work at the office, became a full time secretary, and eased back into everyday life.

I checked with Lamond a few times in the first couple of months, but nobody knew The Prophet's whereabouts and without The Prophet there was no band, no community.

Lamond seemed concerned, but he said his brother would come back when he was ready. I wrote my name and phone number on a piece of paper and went back to work.

My life was like the fairy tale of the boys who wander into a cave only to discover that while they've been away an entire generation has passed. I'd only been with the band a short time, two or three weeks before the Prophet had disappeared the first time, then we had become lovers and that had lasted a couple of months, that's it—but I found it very hard to readjust to living under corporate rules. But in time I managed.

I went to the reopening of the Palace of Fine Arts in Summer 1966 with Roy, my boyfriend from accounting. The Palace of Fine Arts was all that remained of the 1915 Panama Pacific Exposition, a spectacular World's Fair that had returned San Francisco to international prominence after the desolation of the great earthquake of 1906. Not concerned with longevity, the original Palace of Fine Arts was built with plaster and burlap. The decayed landmark had recently been rebuilt with funding from a group of San Francisco boosters.

Through the large crowd, I spotted The Prophet sitting on a bench by a nearby lake, lobbing bits of bread to ducks. The Prophet tossed the wadded up bread over the heads of a picnicking family that seemed oblivious to his presence.

We'd planned to meet Roy's friends, a couple who volunteered for a local children's charity and were interested in recruiting me to help out. They waited for us beside an ice cream vendor whose cart was nestled in the shade of a large, flowering tree.

I wanted The Prophet to wave me over but he didn't seem to notice I was there. I shook hands with Roy's friends quickly. A well-groomed but rather plain couple, they seemed flattered that anybody might care about anything they had to say. In truth, I'd have cut my arm with a knife right then just to feel something, anything. But The Prophet? I hesitated a moment—the knife was probably safer. But what choice did I really have?

I managed to disentangle myself, promising to return as quickly as I could, and made my way back along the path toward The Prophet, ducking children and bicycle riders, nearly sending a roller-skating child dressed in a frilly pink tutu into the drink. Her heels caught just in time and she managed to stop her momentum and fall less than gracefully onto her backside.

I was relieved when I found The Prophet still sitting on his bench. He was no longer throwing the bits of waded up bread to the ducks. The ducks had made their way up the grass and were standing in a row before the bench while he fed them by hand.

One of the ducks hopped up onto the bench beside him.

"Don't be greedy," he scolded.

To my amazement the duck hopped down and took its place back in line.

"Florence," he said, turning my way. "I'm glad you came back."

I must have stood there dumbfounded, worried that if I said the wrong thing he might vanish in a puff of smoke, or turn into a butterfly or a duck and fly away.

"I need to get another band together."

I nodded.

"My approach was all wrong," he told me. He stood up from the bench and took both my hands in his. He hugged me gently, turned me around so that we both faced the path.

"I have so much to tell you," he said. "I've been doing everything all wrong. I see that now."

If I didn't know him, I would have thought him crazed. But the light was back in his eyes and he was excited by the prospect of playing music again, with a band, with me. Nothing else mattered.

I walked with The Prophet and caught the bus back to his brother's house, leaving Roy and his friends waiting for me. When I saw Roy the next day at the office, he wouldn't talk to me, wouldn't even look me in the eye. None of it mattered, though, because I quit the job two days later and never saw Roy again and didn't go back to work this time forever—not anything most people would call work, anyway.

"Each musician," The Prophet told us, "is a separate voice." Where before we'd worked on harmonies and chords, blending the voices of the singers into the melodies of the musicians until it was hard to tell where one stopped and another started, now The Prophet instructed us in "controlled dissonance."

Every note we played or sung was meant to run counter to every other note. "Like the Tower of Babel," The Prophet said when we questioned him. "Imagine the entire world praying to God all at the same time. What God hears isn't English or French, it's an amalgamation of all the languages everywhere as one." He was trying to recreate through music, the original language lost after the fall of Babel.

Try as we might, though, none of us were very good at giving him what he wanted. It ran counter to everything we'd ever learned, ever played. He told us to be patient, that we'd get it eventually, himself included, but that it would take time.

The band started playing afternoons at an outdoor bar down by the piers called Munich Gardens with long, peeling wooden benches and fake-German barmaids carrying large steins of fake-German beer—it was a nothing gig, a place where no one listens to the band and everyone shouts "beer" at the top of their lungs during songs and laughs stupidly from drunkenness and heat exhaustion. Anyone reputable who remembered The Prophet wouldn't book us, and told everyone else to stay away, too. The Prophet had burned a lot of bridges on the way out, and even Lamond couldn't bully us into anything better. But the music had something again, something even more than before, and we moved up quickly into nightclubs, first opening, then headlining. Man, it all came together fast then—just as fast as it all fell apart fast later. The music just lit up and burned though us. I don't remember doing much except playing music, as if I just curled up when I left the stage and slept until it was time to get out there again, into the real, when the world seemed to offer up its secrets to us in pulsing sound, light, sweat, shimmering dreams and endless jams that made the animals howl and dance in the forests of the night.

Once, standing offstage waiting for an encore, drinking water spiked in I-don't-know-what in long gulps, I finally asked, "Where did you go, those two years?"

The Prophet had never told me, though sometimes he acted like I already knew where he had learned about the lost chord, "controlled dissonance," all that stuff he told us about when he tried to tell us how to take it higher.

"Egypt."

When I stared back uncomprehending, he added, "Not now, then." As if that would clear everything up.

The Prophet's eyes shone like the sweat on his face; he turned a beatific smile on me and I almost forgot what we were talking about in the mix of feelings he could raise in me, in anyone, just like that when he looked at them: trust, lust, joy, and more, a longing I could not define. But what he had said confused me, and pissed me off. That smile began to seem, for the first time, more moronic than beatific.

"I'd rather be there, back there dancing and dreaming. If not for you and Lamond, I would have stayed."

He smiled again, his eyes holding my gaze tight. My cheeks flushed at the compliment. I paused and realized what he had said before about "then" and "now."

"When were you?" I asked

He shrugged. He had his shirt off, and the sweat defined the muscles on his skinny frame. He looked like a boy and an old man, his skin smooth but mottled, darkness marred by light patches. He looked strong but attenuated, somehow faded, like the old or the strung out start to look. His muscles were taut, but his frame seemed so thin like he hadn't eaten enough in a long time. He had about him something innocent and something cynical and sharp-eyed that could make his expression unreadable, swirling with thoughts and memories in his eyes until I felt I might drown.

"I was in the time when the stars came down from their places and became gods."

I could see it on his face. It might have been true, but it wasn't. It was a line, a lie, but there was something to it.

He smiled at me again, but that trick was starting to get old—like the flash of cheap strobe lights hiding a washed out bump-and-grind down at the Condor.

"Tell me about it" I said.

"I lived with a music healer," he said. "He used sound—pure notes, the mesmerism of the beat—to bring people back to life, out of themselves, out of suffering into harmony, into ecstasy. I met musicians in the City of the Dead. It's hidden, but I know where to find it. It's here."

He reached out with one large hand and started thumping quietly on my chest, over my heart. It startled me out of all proportion, like an acid flashback, like an insight, a glimpse of truth unrealizable, a perfect line of poetry, an orgasm, a simple 12-bar blues line made somehow indefinably great when you hear it sung right. The crowd out beyond the stage had started to yell louder as some of our guys started to walk back on stage, take up their instruments, wait for The Prophet. But he gazed at me with an intensity that made me want to run away. I felt flushed, hot, burning.

"There's a beat to open pathways between worlds—to bring us closer."

The room shimmered with heat. I felt fevered, like I might fall over. Like it would be best to just fall over and sleep. He reached out with his other hand and held me steady. He never lost the beat over my heart.

"Like the bear," I said.

"No," he said, "the bear didn't think big enough. I've headed somewhere new, toward something more."

A thing moved inside the heat shimmers, just out of focus, large, upright but an animal, a tail, a snout. It seemed to bend away like a shadow then flicker back into sight, but still too dark to make out clearly.

If not the bear, then what?

It danced, keeping time to The Prophet's beat—or was it the other way around? The drumming grew louder as my heart picked up the beat. I felt my nostrils flare, smelling incense, wine, a musky animal smell, my ears hurt with the sound of a high whining, and my eyes watered in the heat.

The dancer fell into focus and I screamed.

"Stop," I cried, "Stop."

It was a wolf. A great wolf standing upright like a man.

The heat popped, vanishing, like a bubble, leaving me in a sudden cold sweat. My head felt light.

"I'm sorry," I started to say, but The Prophet pulled me out on stage with him, up to the mike.

"Tell it like it is!" he cried, half to me, half to the crowd shouting his name.

I looked out dazed at the audience hidden behind the lights in my eyes, then back offstage at nothing, at a darkness and emptiness that danced. Turning back I brought up something from deep inside.

"Well, all right," I said, as loudly as I could, finding energy from somewhere.

"What do you want to hear?" The Prophet shouted to the audience.

"Music," a couple of voices said.

"Give the people what they need," The Prophet shouted and the band slid into a music like no music I had ever known before I met The Prophet, music that clanged and humped, that moved backwards, that made the stars come down from the sky. I believed it all at that moment.

I laughed a long time until I cried and danced until sweat washed my tears away. Until we climbed inside the sun, and it exploded in heat and light and sweet regret.

I awoke to a loud banging at my door. I was in bed at the flat I shared with three other band members, two college students, and a flight attendant.

The banging on the door wouldn't stop. Where was everybody? Cops, I thought. I dragged myself up and put on a dark green robe with little paisleys. I shuffled my way down the corridor of the narrow San Francisco Victorian toward the door.

"Who is it?"

"It's me, baby, open up, hurry."

I opened up on The Prophet who hurried in and shut the door behind.

"I need your help."

Oh no.

He wore his torn T-shirt inside out, had on dark glasses and jeans, grimy along one side like he'd been rolling in grease. His face excreted sweat that dripped from his ragged beard.

"You need to come down, honey." I told him. "I'll get you some coffee."

"No," he said. "It's not like that." He held something under his shirt, cradling it against his body. "I need you to keep something for me."

"The cops? I don't want the cops in here." Like a lot of people, I used whatever came my way, which in the band was everything, a lot of everything the more time passed; but I didn't carry and somehow thought that made me clean, like it wouldn't get me that way.

"Not the cops, baby. This isn't drugs, it's a book."

I looked at him. He was haggard and hung-over, used up. Maybe it really was a notebook he was trying to give me, but the drugs, whatever it was that he was on, were clearly coursing through his system.

I wasn't in a mood for games, for parlor tricks, for madness. I suspected he had other women he was fooling with sometimes. I loved the band, and him, and the things we shared, but this seemed like too much. He kept some secrets and I let him. But right then I didn't think I was up for any of it.

He showed me the book. It looked dirty and cheap. Wrapped in a faux-leather binding and torn around the edges. It looked like crap, as if someone had taken a new book and rubbed dirt on it, not like anything anyone would come looking for. Nothing ancient or interesting or expensive. Trash.

"Get out." I crossed my arms and set my face against him.

"I never asked you for anything like this before." That much was true; he just took off and didn't come back for two years. Two years.

"I'll never ask again, baby, you're the best."

He peered at me over the top of his sunglasses as they slid down his nose from the sweat pouring off his body. His whole body shook now, like he was cold. His eyes were like a puppy's eyes, helpless, pleading, and, on a grown man, pathetic beyond belief.

"All right, I'll keep the book for you. But don't ask me again."

"You're the best, baby," he said. "You know you're the one."

"Give it to me and get out."

Every extra minute I looked at him right now was just another minute of me knowing I was a fool. I didn't like the feeling.

The Prophet put the book in my hands, looked at it like he didn't want to leave it behind after all, which pissed me off because he should be looking at me that way, though it made me wonder. He turned to go, stopped as if to tell me something, and then abruptly trundled off. I looked at the book, but didn't open it. I shoved it in the back of my closet.

About a half hour later, someone banged on the door again. It was Lamond. He was dressed nice, sharp like someone going out on the town to somewhere expensive, a green V-neck light sweater with a white border at the neck and sharply creased black pants. But they were night clothes, meaning he hadn't slept either, like The Prophet. He looked angry, as he usually did.

"Where is it?" he said as he pushed in. He clenched his hands into fists, unclenched, clenched. His mouth moved constantly, even when he wasn't talking—like he was having a running argument with himself. He radiated intensity, like his brother did, but angrier, even more self-involved, if that was possible, for he never seemed to be thinking about anyone but his brother and himself.

"Hello yourself," I said.

"The book, where is it?"

"You know about the book?"

"Give it to me."

So I did. I didn't care about the book. I didn't care to tangle with Lamond about it. He looked at it like I'd handed him a severed head.

"What is it?" I asked as he turned to leave.

"Didn't he tell you?" He laughed in a mean way. When I closed the door I thought that would be the last of the book. But it wasn't. Not at all.

Two hours later, the bear showed up at my door. Filling the frame and more, towering above me. He had soft brown eyes that seemed about to cry and his short snout had crumbs and twigs in the fur. He had knocked politely. I had opened up the door and we stared at one another wordlessly for a long moment. Finally I said, "Lamond took it."

The bear turned and waddled away.

I knew not to follow him down the rabbit hole. I knew it, but . . . what choice did I have, really?

"Wait," I called out, hopping out the door, bent over, putting on my slippers. I was still in my robe.

"What's going on?"

The ground swayed beneath my feet as I lost my balance. I fell but never landed.

I must have slept for I only found myself when I awoke. Or, I don't know how to put it . . . I awoke and saw something from the corner of my eye, out of focus, and when I turned to it to make it resolve itself and go away, there it still was, the impossible, the unexpected.

The Prophet.

"I'm glad you came," The Prophet said. He was holding my hand as I lay flat on my back on green grass beneath a copse of tall trees, some kind of stiff cloth beneath me. He wore what he called his "raiment," his work clothes, metallic gold cape and glittering bead skull cap, a faded Superman T-shirt, a short tight dress over tight black stretch pants and dark glasses. When was this? How much time had passed? Where was I just a moment before?

The trees shaded my view of where I was, but there was something not quite right about this place. The grass was too green, the sky not blue enough, and the air shimmered as if it were full of magic, or radiation—as if a glittering ash from a terrible explosion were raining gently upon us.

In my present condition, all the shimmering did was to give me a headache.

"Where . . . ?"

"Egypt," he said. "This is it. You came through."

I looked around. No pyramids. No desert. But a figure just out of the reach of my vision, where things blurred away, seemed to be half man and half bird. Or else the nose on his face was impossibly long. But that faded, or withdrew.

"When?" I asked.

"It's the Egypt from the world behind the sun, hiding in its shadow."

I looked blank.

"Of my imagination, if you like," he said. "The way I thought it would be at the very beginning of civilization."

"Back in time?"

"No. There's no such thing as time. It's an illusion. Like this city, these trees, this sky. San Francisco, too, is an illusion. I've peeled reality away, stripped it, and replaced a small pocket of it with this sanctuary."

I nodded as if I understood.

"Or," he added, "it reached out to find me, maybe."

I ignored that.

"This is where you were those two years?"

"Something like."

"On this hill?"

He shook his head no.

"I've got something to show you," he said. "Can you walk now?"

Surprisingly, I could. He helped me to my feet and we walked up the path through the copse of trees to the top of the small hill. I found I now wore my Sun Dreamer's outfit—a loud neon green short skirt, pantyhose with a faint paisley print, and a tie-dye T-shirt hung with a pink boa. When had we changed? I still wore my slippers, though, as if to prove my memory had some value; over-furry and overlong to be outside, they immediately began to collect dirt in their long pink fur.

I remembered the bear—I followed the bear—where was he?

I was not prepared for what I saw when we reached the summit. Row upon makeshift row of houses, yellow stone buildings mazed with empty streets, unpaved and dusty.

This was the place he'd called the City of the Dead. It was a city. It went on, mazing streets buildings piled haphazardly, as far as I could see before vision blurred . . . from heat or magic, I couldn't say.

Suddenly, people milled about everywhere, jamming the tiny streets with their day to day tasks. They didn't emerge from the buildings, they just filled it up like water poured into a glass. Dark robed figures were gathering in front of what looked like a large public building. Everyone was robed, sandaled, many wearing skull caps to protect from the sun. Voices mingled in the late afternoon air, spirited, jesting, in a language I'd never before heard.

I shrank back.

"Don't worry," he said. "I won't let anything happen to you." He took my arm and led me out of the park and down a side street.

The ground was solid. The smells of food and dust and waste were all unmistakable. The air was warm, hotter than it almost ever gets in San Francisco.

The Prophet led me down a street that ran alongside a short canal.

"It's all wrong," he told me. "The Egyptians built their homes from mud and brick, not stone like this. They were mostly farmers and craftsmen, scribes. This," he gestured in a circle above his head, "is something else entirely."

"Do you mean to say that you created all of this," I asked incredulously.

"No. I think I was drawn to it. I think it's as real as the other Egypt, as San Francisco or New York. We get so wrapped up in the details of our everyday lives that we lose the ability to see the greater truths."

I had no idea what he meant by that.

"Here we are." He pulled a curtain aside that hung from the balcony of a two-story building and ushered me inside into a small room. It contained a couple pillows, a mat filled with straw and covered with a crude fabric, several earthen plates, a few sheets of thick paper that might have been papyrus, a Fender Stratocaster guitar with a rosewood fingerboard and three-tone sunburst finish, and a saxophone.

"My teacher lived here, but he's left. I can still use it, though."

"What greater truth?" I asked. "I still see what you see, don't I?"

"Do you know what color blindness is, Florence?"

"Like when someone sees the world in black and white? Like a television set?

"No. That can happen, but it's rare. It's the inability that many people have to distinguish between the colors of a particular hue. Red, blue, or yellow. My father is color blind. He can't tell the difference between blue, violet, lavender, or purple.

"There are also people who can see subtler variations in color than the rest of us, just as there are also people whose taste is more precise than the rest of us. They can tell you whether a pickle came out of a jar or barrel. I can do something like that. But with sound. If I can make the right sound or melody, I can interact with it, become involved in the act of creation."

"I'm not sure I understand."

He motioned me to sit. I knelt on my thigh at the edge of the makeshift bed.

With great deliberation, he clasped his hands together in front of his chest, squeezing hard. He tapped his foot in a slow rhythm on the floor. Then very slowly he pulled his fingers apart. The space between his hands was dark, like the space I'd fallen through when I'd tried to follow the bear. In that dark space, I suddenly remembered what I saw—or realized what it was I dreamed—when I came from the hallway outside my apartment here to this Egypt. How had I possibly forgotten? I stepped out my door and fell into stars, winking and burning, an expanse of space that seemed to go on for millions of miles, all of it now between The Prophet's fingertips. Then the cloud of darkness and stars, galaxies spinning like jewels, closed in on itself and disappeared. His hand made a fist.

"I'm so close," he said. "So close. But I don't know what to do. I need the book back."

He glanced distractedly at me, knowing he had imposed, unwilling to keep my gaze. He scratched his beard with those fingers that had opened on galaxies. I stared at them as they moved, but now they were only fingers, thin and delicate.

"It's all right," I said, looking up at him and the first time truly seeing the immense power coursing through him. How did he survive it, day after day?

"I need the book back, Florence. I should not have burdened you. You have it safe?"

How long ago had he left it with me?

"I think I have to leave you," I said. "I think I have to go."

"The book?"

"Let it be so," said a voice from behind me. Turning my head, I made out the soft brown folds of skin hanging under the bear's arm, swaying like a curtain as he gestured out in earnest entreaty.

"It's too late," The Prophet said to the bear.

"I have to go," I said. I even made to rise. I nodded politely at the bear, like to an acquaintance at a party, someone you had shared dope with and talked to about everything that mattered— but someone you wouldn't remember in the morning and you knew it and were sorry about it. I wanted to forget what I knew, what I'd seen, to be myself forgotten.

"I have to go," I repeated. I was thinking of getting my old job back—maybe getting myself into school, and never thinking about this or The Prophet again. Suddenly I had hit a conceptual wall, the opposite of a conceptual breakthrough. I could understand no more, could fit nothing new in my head. This had to stop. But first I had to find my way out of Egypt.

"You didn't bring it?" The Prophet said. I looked at him as I had never seen him: he looked scared, confused.

"You don't have it?" The Prophet said, angry. He moved forward.

"Lamond took it," I croaked.

"What?" The Prophet shouted and tried to grab me by the shoulders. I leapt backed and the bear, walking forward on all fours, stepped between us, blocking his path.

"Lamond," he said, something fierce sparking in his eyes. I thought, Cain and Abel.

"Lamond," The Prophet shouted, and the stone walls themselves seemed to warp as he shouted it, or billow in a wind as if they were but curtains, suddenly without supports, loose.

Through the warping, another presence slipped out of the edges of my vision into the room, a long, lean, powerful shape— the wolf, tall, adorned with silver and gold armlets, wearing a short skirt-like wrap and sandals; it had a man's body, if the man were ten feet tall, and a wolf's face, cruel, sneering.

"What's this?" he hissed. "Have you failed me?"

I almost laughed—it would have been a madwoman's laugh— at the absurd danger. I was near hysteria. I was Little Red and we had taken the wrong road to Grandma's house. There wasn't a woodsman in sight—not The Prophet, certainly.

The bear bristled, fur rising on its back and shoulders, but it stood only slowly, turning itself, awkwardly shambling forward a step, shaking as it rose up, looking dimly toward the wolf as if not quite able to see him and sniffing, swaying his head from side to side. Already a heat shimmer and smoke filled the room, and my brain, until I could hardly see myself—I felt sick. There was no way out.

"You're leading him too far," said the bear to the wolf.

The wolf looked much more powerful but kept his distance, seeming to hide behind heat mirages, smoke and unaccountable distances even here inside the house. I was close enough to whisper and blocks away as the room warped and shimmered.

"What you think is irrelevant," the wolf said.

"Enough," The Prophet said. He waved his arms as if clearing cobwebs from a dusty corner.

"Lamond," he shouted.

The world lurched.

My vision contracted and everything went dark. I could hear the faint rhythmic tapping of a nearby foot. The curtain rose on the stage. From there, we could see a multitude clapping in anticipation.

The Prophet strode up stage.

"Give the people what they want," he shouted. He whirled, his gold lame cape billowing, and the band, ready and waiting, started up, loud, clanging, wild. Turning, chanting something now, his eyes closed, The Prophet's voice was lost in the din—the shouting and clapping of the concert-goers. We stood on stage at the Ice Flower, a firetrap with a large stage peeling black paint and an open warehouse for standing-room only. At the back, a makeshift bar had been set up behind planks of wood on concrete blocks. It wasn't for alcohol—LSD was handed out, tabs with the wolf's heads printed on them passed out in little paper cups. The smell of marijuana wafted and mixed with the patchouli oil.

San Francisco. Not Egypt. Late November. 1966.

What had happened?

"Are you ready?" shouted a voice. I turned—it was Harold, an ex-Hell's Angel, a huge bear of a man who played in our horn section. He wore a pink tutu with black fishnet tights, a white tank top and a felt top hat. He had one hand on a sax strapped around his body. On him it looked ridiculously small.

The Prophet had already wandered away from me on the stage. He talked to the crowd, then started a call-and-response to get them fired up for our second set.

I remembered everything now—we had played a first set before writhing hippies who adored us, freaks with long hair and magnificent, ragged, glittering clothes. They were dirty and sweaty—they were dancing, whirling in clouds of smoke and strobe lights. I had taken the LSD with the wolf's head.

Where had I been? I had been here. Danced through a set. But I'd been somewhere else at the same time, too. Hadn't I?

"I'm ready," I said to Harold, who grinned; he had gold glinting in place of one of his top teeth. The drugs, the heat, the bear—it was all so neat, so easy to explain.

Except it was horseshit and I knew it. I think it was the stars I had seen in his hands that were just too too much. If that wasn't real, nothing was. I had been to Egypt, or something like Egypt, the City of the Dead, and seen things I hadn't wanted to see. And I knew I had failed The Prophet in ways I could never guess by giving the book to Lamond.

Harold and I walked up stage, joining the others; everyone was smiling and it was infectious; though I didn't want to, I had to smile until my cheeks hurt. I had to dance in the clouds in the sky until sunlight came streaming though the doorways and I stumbled off to bed, grateful for sleep that opened on stars floating, bobbing, rolling down a broad river. I watched, laying on the bank, waiting for one of the lights to drift ashore to me.

The Prophet had sung like nothing else—like something new that made the people respond, twitch and sway and dance. The band had been great and strange, honking, harmonizing, breaking down, pulling together, waves of the ocean sound buoying us up through another great night for the Sun Dreamers—the best band that ever burned up and rose as smoke into night as if it never existed.

Everything about the gig was perfect. Except Lamond, playing mean and hard at his bass, had a wicked shit-eating grin on his face the whole night like he knew he'd made it happen and no one could stop him.

The Prophet had clearly wanted to talk with him afterwards, but he vanished, leaving word through Harold that we had another show next Friday. The next day we all had envelopes with our names scrawled on them and money inside left in our mailboxes.

But Lamond, the money man, was nowhere to be found until the end of the week.

The Prophet took it with a strange calm.

For the first few days of that week, everything seemed normal. So great. Perfect. We had The Prophet back, smiling, laughing, moving though the crowds on Haight Street like he was JFK risen from the grave, people wanting to touch him and get some of the magic. I had him back. He held my hand and we walked in Golden Gate Park and rode the merry-go-round with the painted horses and stood in museums laughing at what other people thought was art.

Everyone in the band had money and time to shop for new outrageous clothes, neon paint, drugs. For a while we had The Prophet, and we were the Absurd and Majestic Royalty of Haight-Ashbury, hangers on giving us free tokes or bringing us to all night parties as the guests of honor, the tourists pointing, shocked to their delight to see such weirdoes as we were then. We loved it.

I had to ruin it by asking a question.

About five of us were shopping in Uncle Shady's Used Clothing Store, trying things on, trading huge-brimmed purple hats, opening the changing room doors to flash everyone—laughing, singing, playing. Buying cheap baubles and new boas, beaded skirts and belly dancer scarves.

The Prophet looked like a proud parent as he leaned on a rack of leather jackets watching the tomfoolery. He was dressed casually in his jeans and pink ruffled shirt, dark glasses hanging in the neck. And without even thinking, I said: "Why are you doing this?"

And he knew exactly what I meant. Why is he doing everything? Everything . . . how does it add up? What does it mean?

He looked at me for a long time. "For love," he finally said.

He leaned in to me, seeming suddenly gaunt and drawn thin. And me suddenly remembering I should have left him. That I meant to leave him. That this was no good for me.

"What else is there but love? Death? The Big Bang—all the stars hurtling away from one another forever? It's a reality too big to comprehend."

He looked at me intensely. I shivered. He could melt stone. What wouldn't I do for him?

"Or there's love. Desire. Sex. Generation, life. Sunlight. The roots of trees and plants intertwined and integrated with the work of bees and ladybugs and all that. Chewing, eating, integrating. Gravity. We began as one dot, one thing, all together, undifferentiated, one harmony. That is the thing we lost.

"Music and cacophony, silence and choirs, everything at once—you and I can finally be together then, really together, understanding each other for the first time, can't you see? Not just us, the entire world can be healed, made right. Eden. No more pain. No more loss. No desire. Knowing each other's thoughts. Don't you see?"

I was terrified because I did see, a little. Because of all that I had seen, that Egypt, those animal spirits, the book, I understood he might be right. We would be destroyed as we became the thing he dreamed. One.

He put his arm around my shoulder. He was trying to comfort me, as if the look on my face was because the dream was too happy for me to suffer any longer without its fulfillment.

"It will be all right," he said, squeezing my shoulder. "Don't worry."

Mostly, I wanted to go home, sleep for a week, and pretend my life had taken a different turn. Maybe in one of the other worlds, some alternative reality, I'd become a painter or a carpenter and was happy.

Lamond said he didn't have the book and The Prophet believed him.

"But I gave it to him," I protested.

"It wasn't him, baby."

"I was there, remember. If I didn't give the book to Lamond who did I give it to?" I was challenging him to call me a liar.

"Maybe the man I stole it from."

I laughed.

"That soiled, moldy book with the hand drawn scribbles? You stole that?"

"From an Egyptian priest . . . a Sorcerer. I'm not actually sure what he was. He wasn't human. His eyes were round and lidless, like a chicken's, and the sides of his head were smooth with little tiny openings, slits really, where his ears should have been.

"I'd seen him in the street the day before. A crowd had gathered and his soft, soothing voice brought a pleasant chill to the stifling desert heat. I had no doubt I'd found a powerful shaman in this strange, non-existent place.

"I followed him and his entourage after they left the square. I couldn't talk to him then. He was surrounded by too many people and I couldn't speak the language. Not a single word. Couldn't even say hello or ask for a bite to eat without resorting to pantomime.

"But I went back to where he lived the next day. I could hear music when I got there, a barely detectable murmuring that was barely audible from the street.

"I wasn't sure I should interrupt. He sounded so hard at work. I opened the door a crack to peer inside. The room was empty, a doorway in the back separated by large tan curtains led to rooms more important than this antechamber. But in the middle of the front room was a pedestal, with the book on top, laying open. I wanted to go in and read it. I could see the words on it, squiggling as they tried to make themselves legible to me. If I only would come closer.

"I'd looked so forward to talking to the shaman, but now I knew I'd never get the chance. Not if I was lucky. I could feel the power pouring out of him as he chanted in a back room. His voice, though, was mechanical, emotionless, uncaring. There was a sinister quality to it that made me imagine a scientist pulling the wings off of a fly to see if he could figure out how they worked.

"I backed out of that room, not daring to close the door behind me in case it made a sound. Somehow, when I came out, I was holding the book. I must have gone to it, unknowing and begun to look at it before that voice had penetrated and I'd realized how controlling and different it was from what I wanted.

"The book, though, was a treasure. It was filled with strange symbols. When I went went to my friend, the music healer, he had abandoned me. I have never seen him after what I'd done. I went to the library here to help decode the book. It was then that I discovered that this Egypt that I'd stumbled on to, it wasn't our Egypt in any tangible way. There was nothing like these oddly shaped triangles and squiggles, always stacked in piles of three or four, that didn't remotely resemble anything that our archeologists had dug out of the pyramids. Nor the strange faces that rimmed each page."

"Black magic," I said.

"What?"

"Your book was filled with black magic." I laughed thinking of all those old movies on late night television. Everything he had to say was so insane. "Arcane arts, not meant to be known by mortal man."

"I suppose," he said calmly, unnerving me. "The closest analog I could find was the *I-Ching*. It was like having a list of all the hexagrams, but in some strange unknown language. I began using the *I-Ching*. Singing and throwing the coins. I could feel something happening, but it was subtle. It wasn't until I began combining the symbols that strange things started to happen.

"I had to add an extra coin for it to work. There were three times as many symbols as there were in our book, three sets of sixty-four.

"Strange things often happened when my last coin would turn up tails, changing the hexagram into a septagram from the third set. Once an empty goldfish bowl turned into a large vase with a carp. Another time it hailed ice cubes. Sometimes nothing happened at all. And that was scarier still. I'd walk outside and wonder what may have changed. I'd imagine odd spectrums in the light. Or hear feral sounds and wonder if they were caused by cats or something else I'd created. I worried about all the things I may have done.

"That's why I gave you the book. I realized I had no control. I didn't dare use it. Not here, anyway. And I was too scared to use it there. But I would use it if left with it. I had to get it away from me fast—but keep it safe."

He looked shaken. He held his head in his hands and I could see the sweat pooling about his neck, soaking into the collar of his shirt.

I squeezed his shoulders. There wasn't much I could do for him, but remind him that he was human.

Still, I was glad I'd given the book back to the Shaman or Lamond or whomever it had been. I didn't want it around tempting him into who knows what.

Of course, it wasn't going to be that easy. The dreams, the nightmares, started soon after.

The wolf came rifling through our dreams, looking, I knew, for the book, stealing our memories, or putting them back in the wrong order. Everyone in the band felt it, even The Prophet. Everyone began to act like The Prophet. No one showed up on time anymore. We began to disappear into realms we created and come back different, confused, crying, wonder-struck. And the wolf was seeking us there in those worlds we wandered in. We huddled together in the back room of Green's, a bar in the Tenderloin, and confessed our secrets to one another, dour, distressed, not making eye contact.

I think the wolf even killed one of us, but I no longer remembered who it could be. Our memories of him, I suspected, had been taken along with his life.

Lamond was furious. He yelled at everyone for being late, even The Prophet. He got beaten up by a pair of Hell's Angels on Market Street over a parking spot before a gig. They split his lip and bruised his shoulder so badly he couldn't lift his arm for nearly a week. He got into a shoving match with the police when they hassled us about an illegal event, a happening we put on in the Park where we passed a hat as we played. Live performance was illegal in those days without a permit. But we couldn't get many real gigs with half the band not showing up and we needed the money.

Lamond was as embarrassed as he was mad; he was always professional, always on time. I'm sure the nightmares were getting him, too, not that he'd admit it to anyone. He looked as bad as the rest of us. So when he showed up at my door at five in the morning, I winced and waited for him to start yelling because I'd missed our last practice to get some sleep.

Instead, he scuffed his shoes on the doormat and looked uncomfortable. His face seemed drawn back at the sides, like he wore a mask. His eyes unfocused, his mouth made a long grimace. He was dressed impeccably in a well-pressed black tuxedo with a flaming red cummerbund, with a battered green top hat listing precariously, white gloves and a black cane with a silver handle. He had something to say, but didn't know how to start. I leaned against the door jamb in my faded blue robe, loosely tied, a pair of men's boxers, a man's undershirt, and a new set of pink fuzzy slippers that replaced the pair I had ruined in the fake Egypt. I yawned. I had no intention of helping him. He could hang for all I cared.

"I'm not the bad guy here," he finally said. He took The Prophet's well-worn book from behind his back. It looked like it had been dunked in water. Handling the ragged thing with his gloved hands like it was a holy relic, he carefully leafed through it. It still looked like a cheap notebook to me. I wouldn't have picked it up from the gutter if I'd seen it fallen in the street. "Can you return it? I don't want him to think I took it."

I looked at him.

"So you did take it, after all."

"No," he barked fiercely. There was the Lamond I knew. "I got it back. You lost it. I found it."

I straightened and tightened my belt. Like the book I was bit ragged. From the nightmares, I guess. From the whole thing. But Lamond had come to my door to mess with me one too many times.

"No. Take it to him yourself."

I moved back to close the door.

Lamond put his hands up to plead with me to wait. He looked both ways down the hallway and glanced behind me into the apartment as if he was about to reveal state secrets. I wasn't sure if I should laugh at him or be impressed that he would tell me anything, even a good lie.

"He's drifting away from me," he said. "He'll drift away from you, too. You've been good for him, Flo. You're a good one. But he'll leave us. Please. Give him the book. Don't tell him I was involved."

I took a deep breath and let it out. Lamond was hard to pin down, like his brother, but there was something there that wasn't completely false.

"Us?" I said. "I saw you, Lamond. I was there. You took the book from me, remember?"

"You saw me," Lamond conceded, shrugging, "but it wasn't me. It was and it wasn't."

"I'm not sure I understand," I said.

"I'm not sure I understand, either." I could tell that whatever had happened to Lamond, it tore him up to admit to it.

"I've some lost time. Kenny told you, right?"

I nodded warily. He hadn't told me anything about that, but I didn't want Lamond to know that. And I honestly couldn't say what I knew—was there a difference between what I experienced firsthand, what I had been told, what I dreamed, what I hallucinated in a drugged out stupor, and what was just a lie I told myself to cover up knowing something much stranger, much worse? I could no longer say. Lamond looked like he'd said something he wished he hadn't, his mouth puckered as if he'd eaten something sour.

"Look, the story . . . here it gets weird. Won't you just take the book back to him? You don't need to know this."

"*Here* it gets weird? *Here* it gets weird?" My hands balled up into fists at my sides.

"You don't want to know," Lamond said, holding the book out to me.

I really did close the door that time. He pounded it twice, stopped. He knocked softly. He really wanted to talk to me. I opened the door. I crossed my arms.

"You wouldn't understand," he pleaded.

"Oh, you'd be surprised. I might not believe it, though."

"I killed a man to get the book," he said quietly.

Considering, I believed Lamond could do that, if he thought he had to. I pushed my lips into a line.

"When?"

"Last night."

"No, I mean when . . . in time, where in time?

He looked surprised.

"Egypt," he acknowledged. "Or a pathway that led there. I found the thing hiding."

"And it wasn't a man."

"No. It was more shadow than human. It was lost, trying to find its way home with the book, back to the Sorcerer. It looked like me, the way it dressed, its build, probably had once looked *just* like me, but it had begun to dissipate."

Lamond's eyes always rolled, his body always twitched. It

wasn't often he just looked at someone without also glancing behind them, seeking exits, watching for traps, searching ahead for
something better. But he just looked at me now.

"Go on," I said.

"You have been hanging out with Kenny too long," he finally
said in a quiet voice I'd never heard him use.

He held out the book to me and I took it.

"How much do you believe?" I asked.

"Everything. I've seen it all. Too much."

"What is it?" I hefted the book. It's tattered binding hung in
threads—dabs of hard glue showing through.

Lamond looked down the hall, at the ceiling, behind me,
twitching again.

"No matter what anybody tells you, there ain't no revolution
going on. The whole 60s thing. It's fashion. People will forget why
they dressed how they did, why they thought what they did. These
kids ain't going to change the world. Not now. Not later. They'll
grow up to be tomorrow's bankers and diplomats, all the things
they despise now."

He actually turned around in a circle, so nervous with energy
now.

"Kenny. This book. Maybe he can change the world. He's going to need to learn how to control it and he's going to need our
help. I can't do it alone. You've got to help me."

I thought about my conversation with The Prophet in Uncle
Shady's Used Clothing store.

"He wants to thread the worlds together," I said. "One."

Lamond put his gloved hands in his pockets.

"Yes, but we can help him . . . not do it wrong. He might bring
us somewhere dangerous. Believe me, I've seen his heaven. I don't
want it. It scares me. I'd stop him, if I could. But there are terrible
things out there. And he's the only one who can stop them."

"That's why you took the book?"

"I didn't take the book." The words exploded out of him. He
took his hands out of his pockets and jabbed a finger at me. "That
thing fucked with me and I fucked with it. It took the book and I
took it back. It wasn't me."

He stalked away, stopped, half-turned.

"There are things coming through, worse things than shadows shaped like me. Even if we just get him to close the door, we have to get him to do something about it. He needs the book."

I thought of the wolf.

"He's got to continue his work, for now. Fix some of the things he's done, if he can. Give him the book. I don't know what else to do."

I promised I would.

Instead, I went inside and laid the book out carefully on the kitchen table, moving dirty plates, silverware and empty cartons of takeout Chinese off the table to the sink. I retrieved Chinese coins from a jar in one of my roommate's rooms. I shook them and threw them on the table beside the book with two hands—divining. The coins heaped and spilled with a dull metallic clinking. I flipped through the book, turning its limp, water-damaged pages with two fingers. Somehow the squiggles, the symbols, the writing—I understood enough, somehow, to find the symbols I needed to see, the ones waiting for me to find them. Some of them seemed to move, to transform as I looked at them—perhaps no matter what page I looked at I would find the right symbol, the next one in the sequence, my fate.

When I finished my reading, I looked up.

I sighed.

Nothing had changed.

I placed the book on the top shelf of my closet, high enough so that I'd have to get a step stool to take it down. I tried not to think about the book. I didn't know when I'd see The Prophet again. I didn't know if I wanted to give the book back to him. Mostly, I was torn between forgetting about the whole thing and taking the book down and using my coins to try again to see if I could finally make something happen.

I watched the news on television, but had to turn the tv off when the Indian came on, before the test patterns and the static. Wind swept through the old house, making it creak and groan like the bowels of a ship. With nobody home that night, it wasn't hard to imagine I was on a ship. Outside could be anywhere, any-when. I felt directionless, cast adrift.

Still dressed, I wrapped myself in a blanket to stay warm. Suddenly I was frightened. I'd played with the book. The Prophet had told me about strange things that happened when he attempted much the same. "There are things coming through, worse things," Lamond had said.

I wanted to shrink into a little ball, become as small as possible, so small that the nasty, predatory things that I knew were searching for me would fail to notice me and pass on by. But they knew where I lived. If The Prophet and Lamond could be believed, the pseudo-Egyptian Sorcerer had sent Lamond's doppelganger right to my front door. What would happen when the Sorcerer realized that his minion hadn't returned?

I gave the book back to The Prophet the next day. He accepted it wordlessly, without even saying thanks, like he was receiving a sandwich on lunch break, like he knew it was coming back.

We got a review in the *Berkeley Barb*, the same newspaper that had made bananas famous a month before. They'd run a satirical article claiming that dried banana skins contained a psychoactive substance known as "bananadine." The article was taken seriously by the mainstream media, included in William Powell's *The Anarchist Cookbook*, eventually leading to an FDA investigation into the psychedelic properties of bananas. Their review had a similar effect on our flagging careers. Suddenly we were booked into a half-dozen venues and The Prophet was interviewed by all the major newspapers about the burgeoning San Francisco scene. Most of the column space from those interviews went to Janis Joplin and Jefferson Airplane, but suddenly we were part of it all.

We had never played the kind of venues we now played, never opened for the kinds of acts we now did, and never made as much money, either. But The Prophet was wearing down quickly. Lamond drove him to all our gigs and led him by the hand to the stage. The Prophet's back was stooped, his skin blotched with acne. He seemed like he might collapse at a moment's notice.

He wasn't sleeping, of course. He was working with the book late at night and into the morning, rehearsing during the day, and playing in the evening. I worried for him, but I worried just as much for myself and the other band members. For what might be stalking us, in the audience, backstage, or on the street after a performance. I didn't even know if he was trying to fix things or delving further into the unknown.

As bad off as The Prophet was, the band never played better. With our new found success, we all felt freshly invigorated. Each one of us stepped up our performances, even as The Prophet seemed to lose interest. His life was spent working with the book and, to a lesser degree, experimentation in rehearsal. Some nights he hardly sung at all. A couple of times, when he seemed incapable of performing, we hustled him backstage, and Star Baby, who'd recently joined the group, took over and fronted the band. Star Baby had a beautiful voice that carried us into waking dreams and forgave us all our nightmares.

"Flo, look, I took it," Lamond said. "I'm sorry I lied."

Lamond stood before me bristling; his shirt off, I could see his muscles taut across his torso, sweat drying rapidly, glistening to a dull film as the stage lights went dark following our show. He didn't look sorry. He looked, as usual, mad.

Lamond had led the exhausted Prophet off stage and away into a back room to lie down. The rest of us returned with Star Baby for the encores. The night had been another huge hit, guys in suits sitting in shadowed back stalls behind the hippies and groovies. We were something to see now for the agents, the power brokers. I thought I saw a long canine snout stick out of the shadows, a pair of paws coming out of a smart black suit to lean on the table as the figure leaned forward. I was high, and so thought, the Big Bad Wolf, and laughed. Now, though, as I left the stage, I had slowed to glance back again but could find no wolf among the fold filing out. Lamond surprised me when he stepped up and stopped me. I took a moment to process what he had said.

"You took it?"

"I'm sorry." Not easy, not often from Lamond. "I had to stop Kenny. I took the book. That's the whole story."

"You're a liar." I didn't say it angrily.

"I know. I lied. I just needed the book, and I'm sorry." I looked out at the people in the club lighting cigarettes, laughing as they exited, still jacked up on the music. I knew what Lamond now told me was the easy answer—Occam's razor and all that. But it was a load of crap.

"No. You're lying now. You killed the double. It fucked with you, you fucked with it."

Lamond shook his head. What was his game? He leaned in, warming to the argument.

"No—that's all bullshit—magic, unicorn crap."

"Shut up," I said quietly, annoyed.

Lamond looked truly distressed.

"You could just back out now," he said, "forget this shit—just play music. No more wolves."

"You're giving me an out?"

"Hey, what I say makes a whole lot more sense, sounds a lot more like the truth than anything else."

"But it's not the truth."

"All right, then, you're in."

He turned and stalked off, the muscles on his back hunched up, twitching as he walked away, disappearing behind a curtain to the back.

In too deep, I thought.

"Too late anyway," I said to no one.

It's funny how you can seem to meet famous people twice the first time you meet them. You feel like you already know them but then the things you know about them get mixed with the real thing and you can never quite remember if you learned it first hand or heard about it or if it was some performance, some part played for you and everybody else up on a stage. Our lives had been like that, the real and unreal mixed up like a salad for some time, so maybe it was destiny we would start to meet the famous, the bigger than, the never really there at all. Man, that was us. We knew more people than ever and could trust no one but each other.

Other musicians came to hear our shows. We met Garcia and some of the others from the Dead. We even partied at their house. Some of the Airplane came to hear us and stopped by backstage to shake hands. There were others, more all the time.

The Prophet, he was like everyone's secret right then. People started coming to every show—deep fans, you know: were you there that night when the set list was in this order and The Prophet never stopped speaking but just seemed to chant until he faded into smoke at the back of the stage sometime after four am? Were you there when the stage caught fire? Were you there when that one song came out like a wail and flying pigs floated by way up above in the rafters?

Finally, one night The Prophet collapsed. It had been coming for some time, the way Lamond worked him, the way he worked himself. It made me mad but he had stopped listening to me so I didn't know how bad off he was, although if I'd been paying even the slightest bit of attention I would have known.

He went into convulsions. He'd slumped down to his knees, cradling the microphone, but his eyes were closed and he wasn't singing. He slumped a little to one side.

Everyone in the band just froze, waiting to take his lead, wondering what he was up to this time. The audience thought it was part of the show, too. Some of them even imitated him, dropping to the ground. I started toward him and saw a short figure taking the stage. The wolf, I thought at first. Then, perhaps some other creature? But it was a woman dressed in leather pants that sagged like she'd worn them for a week, a ruffled shirt open over a white men's cotton jersey undershirt, beads and feathers and purple granny glasses. I'd seen her before, recognized her instantly. She hobbled up on stage. She could seem drunk even when she wasn't drinking, but she knew what she was about. She had a crooked, sweet smile on even as she came to help. The audience started clapping like she was coming on to sing until she silenced them with a hand wave.

I knelt down next to Janis Joplin as she propped up The Prophet's head. The Prophet had vomited. She turned his head and he coughed everything out. She cleared his tongue out of the way as she let him lie back, still shaking.

"It's cool, baby," she said to him and to me. "You're going to be fine. I been there before."

Still on her knees, she motioned for the mike. Lamond handed it to her.

"You know," she said to the audience, "every once in a while you've got to think about when the party's over. It's time to go home. The man needs a rest—so let's all go quiet and with love." And she laughed.

The crowd filed out, shuffling and respectful, while Janis took The Prophet's pulse and asked for a cold cloth. The band started to gather round, wide-eyed, in a circle until Lamond said, "you, too, time to go," and everyone began to pack up their instruments.

Someone turned on the house lights and, at Janis's directions, turned off the hot stage lights.

After a while, The Prophet sat up groggily. Janis introduced herself and sat down on the floor, her legs out before her like a little girl in a sandbox. She chatted with him easily. She had some kind of goofy grace about her, some way of making herself at home. She was keeping The Prophet from standing up too soon, ministering to him as well as Lamond or I ever had.

I sat with my feet over the edge of the stage and cried. The club had long since gone dark and chill. But I wasn't ready to face anything more. Finally, I went home, walking through streets interpenetrated with a deep, obscuring San Francisco fog.

A couple of nights later Janis came back with a long, sallow-faced guitar wizard, Jimmy James. His band Jimmy James and the Blue Flames had been playing mostly in clubs and cafes in Greenwich Village and, like us, making a name among music people. Unlike us, he really was on his way to the big life right then. It's hard to remember how young everyone was then. How young the world was. Janis had recently returned from Texas and was about to hook up with Big Brother and the Holding Company. Both, already doing well separately, would break big together at the Monterey International Pop Festival in the summer of that year. Janis's transcendent blues vocals were sung with a voice that seemed torn out of her, intense, exhausting and exhilarating all at once. She made other singers sound like they were afraid to really let go and *sing*. Jimmy James would break big at the Festival, too.

First he would have to lose the Blue Flames and move to London at the request of his new manager who would put him together with guitarist-turned-bassist Noel Redding and drummer Mitch Mitchell. Jimmy James would return to the States as Jimi Hendrix with the just released *Are You Experienced*. He would burn his guitar on stage at the Festival and on D.A. Pennebaker's film and people would really notice what he could do with a guitar, even without the cutting-edge phasing and other sound effects he would employ on his records. The rest is history. In six months' time Joplin and Hendrix would be the rock gods we remember. But not that night. It was just three up-and-coming musicians with some respect in the business and not much more.

Janis and Jimmy came back stage and sat with The Prophet in a small dark room at the back crowded with large wooden blocks for the stage and frayed curtains stored in plastic wrapping. Kenny had seemed too comatose to speak at first. I had gone to change clothes for something semi-clean and to talk myself down from the performance high with the others. I thought when I came back to check on Kenny the visitors would have gone and I'd find him alone. Instead, he seemed revitalized. Jimmy, wearing a long fringed leather coat and black mod boots, was explaining a trick with a wah wah peddle to Kenny, gesturing with ringed, slender, expressive fingers.

I sat just outside the circle of the three young musicians, listening. Later when I read of the teenaged Mary Shelley (then Godwin), as described in the introduction to *Frankenstein*, listening silently as the young Romantic poets, her lover Percy Shelley and the infamous Lord Byron, talked of the secret electric wellsprings of life, I felt I knew exactly how she felt, and how she couldn't explain what it was like, really. Because the conversation took place between minds that understood each other and so much could be communicated without having to be spelled out. Jimmy James launched into a long discussion of what he called "earth" in music, the beat underneath the music, and "space," the turning, whirling improvisations Hendrix would master on his guitar. He searched, he said, for the balance that would make for a "healing chord," the lost chord to bring a broken world back together, at least partway.

Kenny leaned in close and whispered "yes yes yes yes" throughout. Janis smiled her crooked smile and leaned back with closed eyes.

And Kenny, to my surprise, told them everything, laid out our strange story, the book, that Egypt, the wolf in the shadows and in our dreams. When he finished Janis took a long swig of whiskey but didn't look surprised.

"You've got to listen to the bear," Jimmy James said.

Kenny looked like he'd been hit in the stomach. He actually recoiled.

"I can't do that. I need to see, I need the power to complete these visions—you, of everyone, you should know. Man, I see the shadows falling from other places, outside here. I need to light the darkness."

"It's too heavy," Jimmy James said, "too heavy for you to carry like that."

Janis came to more of our shows. She'd sway and dance backstage as we played. She sang with us once, took the stage as part of our encore, and brought the house down. The power of her howl and startling vocals ripped through the crowded auditorium. A neighbor, convinced that some poor woman was being assaulted onstage, called the cops, adding immensely to our legend.

Kenny and I visited Janis at her house and at her local hangout, drinking and playing pool, talking to all hours of the night.

One night, at her place, Kenny showed her the trick that had frightened me so much back in Egypt. He clasped his hands together and pulled them apart until he held part of a universe between them, before it collapsed in upon itself yet again.

"I can't do anything like that," Janis told him.

Kenny seemed surprised.

"Remember I didn't start singing until a few years ago. That doesn't mean I don't know what I'm doing." She moved a stack of 45s off the floor and fumbled for piece of chalk tucked into a small box of art supplies.

"I want you to think about Egypt," she said. "Your Egypt. And I want you to sing."

The Prophet closed his eyes and hummed, tapped a beat against his chest. The air in front of his face shimmered as if his face was a furnace.

Janis reached into the air in front of The Prophet's face. She slashed a hard horizontal line with the piece of chalk, a fierce cut, as if she wanted to remove his head.

"Keep singing," she told him. She made three more cuts, another horizontal slash above his head and two vertical ones.

"You can stop now."

The Prophet looked drained. I stared at Janis as if she'd just proven she was a mad woman, and perhaps she had.

"Now watch," she told us. She took the flat of her palm and thrust it inches from The Prophet's face. The room filled with light, a square of daylight bursting forth in front of The Prophet. I could hear the wind rustling and a bird calling.

The Prophet squinted.

"Is it?" The Prophet asked.

"I don't know," Janis said. "Probably."

"How?"

"I was a painter long before I began to sing."

The Prophet stuck his head through the hole.

I actually don't remember what happened next. It had been a long time and I had been drinking. I guess we left it there, a hole to nowhere.

Janis tried to teach The Prophet the trick with the chalk, but his talent seemed to be entirely musical and he was never able to get the hang of it.

We were all tired. Janis was on the road. Jimmy James was in Europe. People were coming and going in our lives faster than I could keep up with.

Record companies were calling every other day. The Merv Griffin people wanted The Prophet on their show, then they changed their minds.

And through it all, The Prophet worked harder than any of us. Rehearsing the band so that arrangements got tighter and tighter, our music more frenetic yet controlled. And he was still working on other things too.

"I saw him yesterday," The Prophet told me one night.

"Who?" I asked, but I knew.

"The Sorcerer. He was waiting in line to buy a ticket. He looked human. He had a knit cap pulled over his head to disguise himself, but his face, the way he was dressed, his posture, stooped over and bobbing slightly like an old Jewish man at prayer, I knew him instantly."

"He bought a ticket?"

"I didn't dare wait to find out. I ducked around the back entrance before he saw me."

"He wants the book back." I wished The Prophet had thought to just hand the book over to him there on the street. He could have gotten the book from the dressing room and come back, and there would have been witnesses.

"I hope that's all he wants."

Lamond gave us all a few days off and he and The Prophet disappeared. They went to St. Louis, hooked up with a band there, and cut a single for a local independent record company that ultimately sold the two tracks to CBS records.

The record didn't sound like our music at all. A slow, driving love ballad that mixed country and gospel stylings, nice as far as it went. The band played sappy strings behind him and hammed it up. The record broke into the top 100 on the pop chart, but just barely.

The Prophet never said why they went to St. Louis or whose idea it had been to make the recordings. Lamond said something about not being able to afford to send the whole band. But it was just another unexplained event in what was becoming a long string of unexplained events. This one seemed more eerie for its apparent normalcy.

The rehearsals we now went through became legendary, the sources of many stories told late at night among musicians after gigs.

It was hard to tell exactly how much of what we did was preparation for performance in public and how much of it was unorthodox musical therapy. The Prophet would demonstrate what he wanted us to play. If he couldn't describe what he wanted, he'd resort to pantomime. It wasn't unusual for him to physically move the musicians' arms or feet, to straighten their posture or make them slouch, until he got just the sound he wanted.

He made us all write poetry, at first sonnets and then, when that didn't seem to work, free verse. He had us beat on pipes or flooring. He made us act out scenes in which we were our own instruments.

We chanted nursery rhymes. We described scenes from our childhoods. We recanted our attachment to the natural world. We made costumes and props for non-existent shows.

We'd arrive not knowing what the day's activities might bring. We might go running around Golden Gate Park, play capture the flag or do somersaults, or we might practice meditation and hardly move a muscle all day.

"Translate your spirit into music," he told us. And we tried as best we could.

Star Baby, though, was smooth and seemed to handle all our exercises with an uncalculated grace. The Prophet tried to push him harder than the rest of us, but without, seemingly, much result.

Watching Janis rip apart the very air with a piece of chalk and open a door to The Prophet's Egypt had unnerved The Prophet in a very fundamental way. Up till then he'd always believed that only musicians wielded the power he sought to control. And now that he knew that there were other methods he wanted to try them all, with us as his guinea pigs. So we went to the beach and drew childish pictures in the sand; we painted murals; roasted a pig in the park; performed Shakespeare for a family of four; went fishing off a pier and caught a giant stingray.

Even if we found that one of us had a talent like The Prophet's or Janis', I don't think The Prophet would have been able to harness it, let alone recognize it.

He needed Janis, but Janis was on the road most of the time now and usually too busy to join us when she wasn't. She had burst forth like a comet from the local scene to national notoriety and then to superstardom. She was our envoy to the real world and we all loved her for it. But we missed her just the same, The Prophet more than any of us.

I had a beginning once. A place I came from before I stepped off that bus and saw The Prophet playing saxophone for change. Like anyone, I had parents, a younger brother whom I sometimes fought with and sometimes protected. I had a bed with an old quilt on it made by my grandmother and the whole thing was always covered with stuffed animals. I had swim trophies on the mantle and a glass cabinet full of china dolls. But I don't have a beginning now. Nobody had done anything so bad to me as all that. Nothing disturbing or dramatic, but it wasn't me, being there, where I grew up. I didn't belong in that life and never did. My whole generation felt that way once, I think, a lot of us anyway. No direction home.

I thought it all through one night when I couldn't sleep after a show and feared the return of the nightmare wolf. That beginning did not fit this life now so it is not my beginning. I just stepped into this life fully formed. There is only this story. There is no back story missing, no secret from my childhood to tell, nothing that happened to me before this that matters at all. I don't have much more to say about it all except I was encased behind glass like the china dolls but I'm the one who escaped. I have no beginning, only an empty space in a glass case where I used to be that I think about sometimes. I never saw anyone from that time again, not even my parents. Maybe sometimes somebody who knew me then dusts the empty spot and wonders. But I will not go back.

And if I have no beginning, you see, I have no end. I will only go on and on, expanding into everything; I will trail The Prophet like the tail behind a comet. I will have no end and the story will only exist now. That's what I believed in then.

That's what I believe in now.

I'd never seen The Prophet and Lamond really fight until one day The Prophet had us rehearsing on stage without our instruments. Lamond grumbled about how stupid it was and made little snorting noises until The Prophet said to us, "come on now, play louder."

Lamond pretended to smash his imaginary guitar.

"This is asinine," he said.

"Lamond, we don't have much time." The Prophet said it quietly, so quietly Lamond should have known better than to antagonize him further.

Instead Lamond pretended to urinate on his guitar. Slowly lowering an imaginary zipper, he made a show of reaching deep into his pants before he silently guided the stream onto his imaginary instrument, turning back and forth until, after a long moment, he shook himself dry. He grinned.

"Yeah, we don't have much time for real rehearsing, and none at all for bullshit."

The Prophet hit him hard across the jaw. Then followed with a left that smacked Lamond in the middle of his chest. Lamond retreated a step, stunned. I hadn't known The Prophet could move like that, with the fury of a caged animal, but also with a precision that clearly demonstrated he knew how to use his fists. I heard his Uncle had been a boxer, and maybe he had learned something from him.

The Prophet leapt on Lamond like a cat, grappling him by the shoulders. Lamond was bigger and built much stronger—wider and thicker—but it was clear as the two rolled across the stage that Lamond had a problem: he desperately didn't want to hurt The Prophet.

"No," Lamond said, "no, no."

Like with everything, the band was slow to react because we could never tell the difference between what was real and what was part of a lesson meant for our benefit.

Until the two really started to kick each other and The Prophet tried to bite Lamond's ear, we didn't even begin to drop our poses with our imaginary instruments. It's like we all lived in amber, locked inside our own heads, unable to tell the difference between reality and smoke and mirrors.

Lamond's dark glasses (which he wore all the time now to cover his bloodshot eyes) were broken on his face, leaving a large blood-stained scrape across his left cheek. He was crying, not from the pain but frustration. The Prophet looked furious, eyebrows and eyes scrunched up, teeth bared in a terrible grimace, nothing I had ever seen from him before. He tried to choke and scratch his way free from the embrace Lamond held him in now on the side of the stage. Kenny kicked his brother hard in the groin and Lamond curled up. I touched The Prophet's shoulder as he rose to his knees. Desperately, Lamond lurched up behind The Prophet and swung wildly at the back of his head before falling back to the floor. The Prophet somehow was able to feel Lamond's presence and ducked out of the way, but the blow hit me hard in the face, blood gushing out my nose. I sprawled back, nearly blacking out. Through the swarming darkness, I swam back hard, fighting against the current as it ran over a waterfall, an abyss behind me somewhere. The Prophet turned back to Lamond, to finish him. He was about to do something he would always regret. I tried to move forward, but I could grab only air as I fell back, my arms windmilling.

Someone caught me and propped me up, someone big, moving me back to standing and putting me aside easily.

I looked up into the face of the bear. He grumbled at me before ambling forward to The Prophet. The Prophet rose up and hit the bear, but the bear kept coming and grabbed him tight in his embrace. The Prophet was immobile, shaking with excess energy and fear and anger.

The Prophet began to cry now, gripping the bear to him.

"I'm sorry," The Prophet said.

I held my nose. It had stopped bleeding as quickly as it had begun, but I could feel it swelling. I was shaking.

"You've been protecting us, our dreams," I said suddenly, realizing something through the pain. How did I know all this? "You've moved our dreams somewhere else, somewhere where our dreams don't belong. Somewhere the wolf can't find us. But it's driving us insane, Kenny. It's making us all go crazy."

Kenny looked at me, noticing the blood on my face for the first time, his eyes uncomprehending for a long moment, loosening his hold on the bear without letting go.

Kenny pushed himself back from the bear.

The bear nodded imperceptibly as if in agreement, then he was gone. He didn't amble off stage. He half-turned into somewhere else and slipped away.

"I just thought—" Kenny said, "I thought I could keep our dreams free from the Sorcerer."

"There has to be another way," I said.

I moved forward and touched Kenny again, warily. He took hold of my hand urgently. He looked lost, disoriented.

"We're going mad," I said.

"There are places to hide dreams, places between where no one can stay long."

"You're over-reaching. You have to stop."

I held Kenny, too, like Lamond and the bear before me.

We stood there for a moment, me holding Kenny, Lamond and the band looking on as if this were, indeed, another instance of clever theater, more smoke and mirrors, and not the impossible come home to roost. And then, emotionless and drained, we filed out into the night. Rehearsal was done for the day.

"The bear came back," said The Prophet. We were in the back of a dark saloon with Janis.

"You should listen to him," said Janis. "He can protect you."

"But that's all he ever does," said The Prophet. "I need answers. The universe is such a simple place, but my time to find the answers is finite. I need to know everything. The wolf will help me."

"We don't get to pick our spirit guide."

"I have. I chose the wolf."

I wondered if I had a spirit guide, too. One I couldn't see, perhaps we all did.

"It's getting dangerous," I said instead. "Just being around you is dangerous. I don't know who to be more afraid of—the Sorcerer, the wolf, the bear, Lamond, or you.

"They're all dangerous," said Janis, but she didn't seem serious. "You don't want to return the book," she said to The Prophet. "That leaves you with only one option. You can't keep waiting for him to take it from you. You're going to have to go after him."

"What would you do?" he asked her.

"Me? I wouldn't do any of the damn fool things you're doing—I'd live a different life entirely."

She grinned but The Prophet didn't crack a smile, and looked frozen like a photograph on fire just before it folds up and burns to ash.

The winters in San Francisco aren't like the winters in other cities. Summer doesn't make its arrival until Fall and then stretches on for months until one day you wake up and cold grips the air around you. Then it rains and rains. Pours for the entire month of December. No snow, just wet, and almost as cold, as the perpetual damp soaks through to the bone.

Theaters in winter became a refuge for us. Cold but dry, holding the world at bay. Bundled up in coats and scarves and mittens, running through our paces, learning to hit our marks, learning to really play. Serious musicians call it woodshedding, keeping to oneself, playing music hour after hour, day after day, letting the world go by. That's what we did. But together.

The world outside, meanwhile, was flying by. We barely paid attention to the war that wasn't really a war. We cheered after the fact when the district attorney dropped all charges against a group called The Diggers, an anarchist guerilla street theater group, for performing a Halloween puppet show at Haight and Ashbury. We paid no attention when Ronald Reagan was sworn in as Governor of California, jokingly telling U.S. Senator George Murphy, a former song-and-dance man in a succession of Hollywood musicals, "Well George, here we are on the late show again."

We should have been paying attention, as the new year hit— 1967—the world was beginning to pop all around us and would soon explode.

One night just as rehearsal was starting the bear joined us again. His drum looked ancient, the wood body blackened with age, covered with worn leather drawn taut along the sides. It was a good-sized drum but looked small in his massive paws. He held it with respect, careful not to mark it with his claws.

Even sitting down with his drum between his splayed legs, he towered head and shoulders over us. But the band did little but nod hello. The bear pursed his lips thoughtfully and nodded back.

When I'd first seen the bear, that first day I joined the band, only Kenny and I could see him. Things had changed. The bear, we all seemed to know, was on our side—I mean, look how he'd broken up what had come to be called The Fight? Only a couple of guys too stoned to be only stoned—out beyond stoned—remained oblivious, staring into nothing.

When The Prophet finally noticed, he frowned at the bear.

"You. You don't belong here. Get out."

Lamond grinned, and for once it didn't seem edged with sarcasm, for once I had a good feeling about it, like our luck was changing.

"I've heard him," Lamond said. "He can play that thing. He stays." He laid his palm out flat.

"I don't need him here." Kenny turned back to point at Lamond.

"Imaginary bear with imaginary drum, he fits right in." Lamond laughed.

The Prophet seemed pained, then like a miracle he laughed, too. He reached out to touch Lamond's shoulder.

"You know I trust you, Lamond, with the money, with everything."

Lamond nodded.

"All right, little brother," he said, "then let's play. It's getting better, stronger."

The bear was good, too, playing like nothing mattered but the music. And then, when I started to sing, I knew the bear was right.

When my dreams returned from wherever The Prophet had sent them, they crashed through me like waves, pulling me deep.

I awoke one afternoon in Golden Gate Park sitting out on the grass with a bunch of wonderful hippie kids I had just met, a busload from Oregon wearing goofy grins, felt hats, leather vests over bare chests, getting stoned and curling the hair on their toes (for these were hobbits, you see, fresh from the Shire, wanting to know what the nightlife was like in Mordor). I made butterflies with my own hands. They rose up from nothing in my open palms and flew away.

I didn't mean to, but I was telling a story about The Prophet and, unthinking, I just did it. Maybe it had something to do with the book, something that came to me when I played with it in my apartment that night.

Anyway, I startled myself and laughed. The Oregon kids took it harder, first asking, then demanding I explain the trick. Then they just took their pipeweed and went home and probably never came back out again. I laughed long and hard, still laughing when I thought about it until late into the night.

Now that The Prophet had stopped hiding our dreams, he seemed more confident, more powerful, and more purposeful in everything he did. Sometimes his body radiated heat as if from an invisible furnace, and when he sang he was like the sun, warming all of us.

One band member, Joe, a skinny horn player from Memphis who had seemed skeptical of the whole hippie scene out west, rose back up like Lazarus when The Prophet touched him. You know, like most converts he had become the one most into expanding his mind with the drugs and the music, but then he died. At least that's how I remember it. So much of what I remember from that time seems like it couldn't possibly have happened. Certainly not in the order I remember it happening. And yet I believe it, almost all of it.

Joe had been becoming increasingly comatose for some time. These days, we'd say he was clinically depressed, but having his dreams hidden from him was sapping his vitality in a very fundamental way, shutting himself off emotionally. He hadn't spoken to any of us in a long time.

When everyone's dreams came back, most of us were lit up, talking non-stop to one another for days, except Joe who seemed to be staring inwardly at something startling inside. One day, during practice, he stopped playing. His horn was still pressed to his lips, his eyes wide open, but he'd stopped breathing. He just slowly slumped down and left us. He lay a moment inert. Dead. But The Prophet laid his hand on his forehead and shook him and he woke up.

He hadn't been sleeping. Lamond tried to tell me Joe had just fallen asleep, or had gone into a drug-induced coma. That only made it more certain he hadn't been sleeping, or in a coma. He had been dead.

Joe looked up at The Prophet with a smile.

"Well, here we are," he said.

"For now," The Prophet said, "we need to be here and play the music, O.K.?"

"Yeah. Oh yeah," Joe said, standing up like a boxer who'd been saved by a long count, shaking his head. "Yeah I'm ready."

And he really was fine.

The Prophet changed the band's name to the Solar Children after that, a new beginning. One of hundreds, of millions like new stars forming in the heart of the sky.

*

Now that our dreams had returned, I had all sorts, dozens that I remembered vividly each night. In one I stood beside Kenny under an orange-colored sky roiling with high clouds, lightening flashing soundlessly in their depths. I don't know if it was real or not, so I offer it to you as part of this story. It happened to me.

Kenny and I stood naked before a large, burning funeral pyre. We were high up and in the distance was another city, not in the Egypt of The Prophet's making, but perhaps another one much like it.

I must have just come up unnoticed on Kenny for he seemed surprised when I spoke.

"Who is it?" I asked, indicating an immolating body obscured in the shimmer of heat and the roar of flame.

Kenny looked at me and smiled. His cheeks had tear-stained tracks disappearing into his beard.

"I hoped you might come," he said. We hugged and kissed.

"It's the healer I studied with when I lost you." When he lost me? He left me. "His name is William Blake."

I paused.

"The poet?"

"He was an emanation of that Blake."

"A what?"

"The one gave rise to the other," he explained. "But this one isn't fully human."

I looked into the flame again. The shape seemed human.

"Their hearts don't burn," The Prophet told me. "We must wait and then, before the flames die down, you must reach in and pull it out. Your hands will burn. It will hurt. But there is no other way. I will heal you."

My heart began to race and I pushed away from The Prophet. Some primal reaction to suffering took over and I shook with the urge to run away fast into the cool of the desert.

"Why don't *you* do it?" I demanded.

"This is not my dream."

The heart felt cold as ice when I gripped it. The flames peeled my skin off in waves of intense pain. I screamed until the skies broke and it began to rain from that roiling, alien storm. With useless eyes, my body blackened and grotesquely thinned, skin cracked and bubbling, I could not even hear my screaming for the roar of my blood boiling in my ears.

I held the heart out to The Prophet. He took it, a sweet smile on his face that froze my heart despite everything.

I awoke in my bed, The Prophet beside me sleeping. My arms were whole though oily to the touch, and I think whatever fine scars I might have had were now gone, burned away in the flame and the rain from another sky.

If The Prophet had taken the heart, I couldn't find it. I checked everywhere.

"But you were taking drugs," you want to say to me. Those things couldn't possibly have happened.

Most of them did. Just the way I say they did. My experiences are clouded a great deal by time and, I admit, by a lack of understanding of the principals of magic. But the drugs were more innocent in those days, more powerful, but also more pure. They helped open us up so that we could see the reality beyond everyday life. And we needed them, because we'd left everyday life far behind.

When I arrived at the theater before one the final rehearsals we had before everything came crashing down, Lamond was unpacking rifles out of crates.

He turned to face me and I screamed. I thought he was going to shoot me.

"Relax," he said. "You want one?"

I shook my head no.

I found The Prophet at the back of the theater in a cold dressing room, the back wall hung with a decaying red curtain bordered by limp, tangled yellow fringe. Two dilapidated wooden chairs waited before the vanity, while a sagging couch practically blocked the door despite all the space. The floor had a layer of useless things no one bothered to clean or even look at too closely, wrappers from candy bars, old show flyers, broken guitar strings, old feathers from our boas, hair and dirt and a great pool of black oil or tar by the far wall. The Prophet sat cross-legged, meditating on the floor. He rose to greet me, smiling. And when he touched me, the warmth from his hands spread down my shoulders and into my back and hips.

"What is Lamond doing?" I asked. This was months before the Black Panthers marched on the state capital carrying loaded weapons.

"It doesn't matter," The Prophet said.

"You're not carrying, are you?" I asked.

He shook his head, smiling in that way of his.

"It won't help," he said. "But Lamond senses something's about to come down. I'm ready. We're ready."

After coming to grips with the situation, I confronted Lamond on my way out. I told him he was being stupid, bringing trouble down on us from the cops, endangering our shows. He shrugged.

"I want to be ready for the Sorcerer this time," Lamond said. "Kenny says he's not as powerful as the Sorcerer, not yet, and maybe he never will be. But our technology is 5000 years more advanced. We can blow the fucker away if he comes back." Lamond grinned. He hoisted the rifle onto his shoulder, sighted down the barrel, and pulled the trigger. I jumped when I heard the rifle's hammer strike. Not loaded.

Janis didn't like the idea of the guns any more than I did.

"I know it seems like a good idea," she told Lamond one day. "But I think you shouldn't rely on that advantage too heavily."

"Why the hell not?"

Lamond, Janis and I were riding in a multi-colored bus on our way out to a party on a commune slash farm in Sebastopol that would last all weekend and include long jams between lots of Bay Area musicians, and an impromptu orgy one night. The Prophet appeared to be unconcerned with whether Lamond had a gun or not.

"I'm just not sure things are as simple as you think they are," Janis said. She began to gesture, setting into an argument. "We agree that that world and our world are one and the same, ultimately?"

Lamond nodded. "I've been there. They're connected."

"Then reality must be mutable in a very fundamental way. We

can change that reality by altering our perception, through music, painting, dance, whatever, right?

Lamond nodded again. He knew he wasn't going to like what he heard.

"If the Sorcerer doesn't know what a rifle is, will it hurt him?"

"It's a rifle. It'll blow his head off if my aim is true."

"Yes," Janice agreed. "It'll blow his head off if reality behaves the way *you* think it will. But what if it behaves the way *he* thinks it should. Then all you've got is a big stick."

"It's a rifle," Lamond repeated. "We didn't need to teach the Indians what a gun was before we—or, you know, they, the white men—took their land and threw them out. And they did a lot of praying for protection—the ghost dance and all that."

"They lived in our world," Janice said, "even if they saw things another way. This guy doesn't, so things might be very different."

Janis leaned toward Lamond. Her granny glasses slipped down her nose revealing brown eyes in her roundish face that had a startling depth and attention.

They looked at each other closely for a long moment. Lamond waved her off, unwilling to speak, unnerved.

"Maybe it'll work," Janis said, leaning back, letting the argument go. "I just don't think you should count on it."

The argument with Lamond led Janis to have one with Kenny, too, in a last ditch effort to save us before things got worse, I guess. She was trying to get him away from all his experimenting with the book. They had the argument before our last show as the Solar Children, as it turned out. We still had several hours before things started when I walked in on them. I thought about turning around, but they didn't seem to even notice me. Kenny was leaning against the edge of a make-up table attached to the wall before a large mirror lined with mostly burned out lights. The ones still working were the only lights in the cavernous room. The glare of the lights burned intensely but weakly, cutting harsh shadows against their faces but barely sending any light out into the larger gloom.

I closed the door quietly and sat down in a battered, round-backed chair by the door. The bear eased out of the darkness and sat, still in shadow, across the room from me.

"You don't need the book," Janis told The Prophet, holding his hand tight, pulling it toward her to make her point, trying to physically move him to her side of the argument.

The book sat open on the table, *I-Ching* sticks fallen haphazardly beside it. How many fates had been changed, or revealed, or hidden, by The Prophet's experiments?

"The book holds the key to everything," The Prophet said, incensed.

"You never needed it. You're more than it is. It's merely a cipher."

"I need more time. A few more days." He looked about the room but didn't notice me. "They're everywhere," he said. "Foxes in the henhouse. Wolves at the door. You saw them. I know you did. That's why you're here, isn't it?"

"You're out of time, I'm afraid. I've been waiting for you to realize it. But now I think you never will. You're too much of a dumbass."

Janis rarely spoke in anger. She spoke loudly, laughed loudly, when she felt it. She sang in a tremendous wail. But she could be so humble, so vulnerable, for someone who wielded such power. She never raised her voice. But now her voice was rising as she couldn't even get Kenny to follow what she was saying. She stepped up to him, nose to chest. I knew this was it. She was giving it one last try. And I knew there wasn't a chance in hell Kenny would really listen.

"Kenny just give it back. Or, hell, destroy it. You don't need it."

"I'm almost there."

"It's in your way. It's stopping you. The kind of knowledge your looking for doesn't come with short cuts. It's a cheat. It's blinding you, stopping you from realizing your full potential."

With each exclamation, she hit lightly on his chest. But his eyes remained vacant. His face expressionless. She finally stopped and stared up at him for a long moment. Then she turned and left.

"Maybe you'll know what to say," she said to me as she left."

I shook my head.

"You get out, too," Kenny said to me. "And take the damn bear with you."

*

I passed Lamond in the corridors below the stage. He walked with a stiff gait, as if he were drunk or limped on a hurt foot. He'd stuffed a rifle down his baggy cargo pants. I wrinkled my nose like I'd encountered a bad smell.

"You some old-time gangster," I said, frustrated he would be out here playing around when The Prophet needed him.

He stopped as if had something to say, but his eyes were shifting. He wasn't looking at me.

"Or just a moron," I said. "I don't think these guns are going to do anything."

"I saw a pack of wolves—wolf people—wolfmen, something. They're at the back of the club smoking, huddled in a circle. They're wearing big coats. They think I can't see the tails coming out the back, but I can." He laughed nervously.

"It's all going down tonight," Lamond said flatly, frowning with worry. "But I'm ready."

"Janis is gone," I told him, "probably for good. She can't take this anymore. You've both lost it." I wanted to tell him that I was next, but the crestfallen look on his face stopped me.

"We need Janis here," he said. "She's the only other person besides Kenny who has any idea what's going on. You've got to get her back."

"Call in the National Guard," I said, flippantly.

Lamond exploded. "Don't you see we're all going to die!"

"You're yelling at the wrong person. Tell Kenny. Make him give the book back. Janis says he doesn't need it."

Lamond started to brush past me.

"I tried that," he said. "I've yelled at him my whole life and all he's ever done is whatever the hell he wanted."

I stopped him with my hand on his shoulder. He turned to look at me.

"Lamond, I don't know what's going to happen. And neither do you. You need to stop pretending you know what to do. It's just making you crazy. And we need you level headed tonight. Every night."

Lamond chewed on his inner lip a moment. Then he turned and began to limp off into darkness. He stopped.

"Don't *you* go anywhere," his voice came to me. "We need

you too." Then he was gone.

Looking after him, where he had been, I saw that the bear had followed me out of Kenny's dressing room.

"Come on," I said, motioning to the bear. "Let's go get ready. We've got a show to do."

I was beginning to think Lamond should always stuff a rifle down his pants. Whether it was because he liked the feel of a long pole down there, or because he was afraid he'd get his balls shot off if he messed up, whatever the reason, he was playing like a man possessed. His bass work was always top notch, but never, until tonight, inspired. When I told him so between songs, he said, "Yeah, I try to avoid that fancy shit. I told you before . . . I've seen Kenny's dream, and I don't want it. I know what can happen when you throw yourself into a dream and don't come back. I never wanted it. But it just doesn't matter anymore."

We had a large audience of stoners and hipsters and scene-makers, maybe two hundred or more, mostly burn outs decked out in spectacular tie dye, colorful bandanas and a haze of marijuana smoke. Our people. They were clapping and dancing in hypno-tized rhythms, either slow, like they were underwater in a dream, or whirling too fast like leaves on a breeze flying away. I envied them what they couldn't see. Here and there among them, standing at the edges of the dance floor, or below the speakers off stage right, Lamond—doppelgangers like the one who came to take the book from me. So he had been telling the truth about that. There were four or five that I could make out for certain; who knew how many more Lamonds might be milling about in that crowd?

Lamond had said, If I remembered right, that they were some sort of shadow thing shaped to look like him. They wore sim-ple white T-shirts and jeans, looking angry, fearsome, not at all one with the groove, waiting with hands thrust into their pock-ets. Waiting for some sign to burst upon us. Upon me. I could see more than one eyeing me, calculating how easy it would be to choke the life out of me, rip my throat with its teeth. When I looked over at the real Lamond, he just shrugged.

I also saw the wolves at the back that Lamond had told me about, moving in a slow circle now, beginning to growl and slaver, hungering for the wilding moon. They had been upright and wearing clothes, but as the concert continued, they began to shed their clothes and trench coats and drop down on all fours. No one in the audience noticed a thing. And where was the Sorcerer? Somewhere in the darkness, certainly, he sat watching. He would give a signal to the doppelgangers, and probably the wolves, too and that would be that.

I began to feel a coldness at the pit of my stomach. Dread. But there was something else, a counterforce behind us. The back of the stage was slowly expanding outward. A vastness manifesting itself. And in it, stars winking into being like when twilight falls, The Prophet's universe taking shape at last. I wish I'd understood what that all meant, then.

Our show itself was smoking. We were playing for our lives, one last gig before we died. And we all knew it.

I think Kenny had put himself into a deep trance before taking the stage. The book had become everything to him, a new drug, inspiration. I knew he had taken to keeping it about him always. He wore a purple strapless evening gown torn down the side on the bottom right so he could move his legs. He had pulled on baggy orange sweats underneath. He had layered beads, silver, red, gold, and strings of sparkling baubles around his neck. He wore a many-colored dreamcoat made of the remnants of an American flag stitched together incongruously, fabulously, hung loosely over his shoulders. He had on a tiara and a peacock feather stuck in his Afro. He led us through the songs with assurance, smoothly, but without saying a word to us, gesturing elegantly and expecting us to follow. And with a faraway look in his eyes that left me cold like the dark between stars.

The darkness deepened and two moons, one crescent and the other full, climbed in the alien sky behind us as the Theater filled with stars beyond measure and we played on and on, later and later into no time, holding the new world in our songs. Someone had given me something and I had taken it without asking questions. Like Lamond, I knew it didn't really matter anymore. So I wasn't surprised when I saw the river. The one I'd seen before only in my dreams. It flowed out of the night sky, winding out, like a tributary of the Milky Way, to flow behind us at the back of the stage. I heard the water lapping and looked back, one long look of acceptance. Far off in the empty sky, something was coming. And who would be sailing to us across the gulf of stars? What strange thing? I could hear the words intoned by a deep voice on a Saturday night Creature Feature movie—*what strange thing?*—and it made me laugh until I shivered.

I don't know how long we played. The Prophet had led us through all of our material. I no longer knew when or where we were. We had been doing longer and longer jams at the ends of songs, unwinding them until nothing remained. Most of our players were in drag, too, of course; we looked like a mockery of the Amazon Queens of Mars from some bad 50's sci-fi nightmare, flashing and glinting in our sequins, our tie-dye beehives, our torn but elegant gowns, our lacy, frilly frocks and silver space miniskirts. The beefy guys in the horn section had on matching hot pants—I have no idea how they found any in their sizes. But when they set up high kicks to fill our ragged sound out, the crowd went wild.

The bear sedately laying down a beat with his drums at the back was the most normal looking of us, which about sums it up.

At the end of one of the long jams, The Prophet let the music die and the silence linger as he leaned over the microphone like he'd given up and would never be back. Like he was just too damn tired to go on now that he'd brought the river and just couldn't keep the monsters at bay anymore. I looked out in the crowd for Janis, hoping against hope to catch her out there, somewhere away from the terrible Lamonds that still prowled the theater. But she wasn't there.

I saw the Sorcerer though, just off stage. I don't know how I recognized him—same as The Prophet had when he said he saw the Sorcerer waiting in line for tickets to one of our shows. He looked human. He looked like no one, a stagehand, wearing some workman-like overalls, stained and frayed, and black English shit-kicker boots, knit cap pulled down over his ears. But his alien eyes told me just who he was.

Kenny looked out at the crowd, at all those terrible imitations of his brother, glanced over at me and the stagehand beyond, the Sorcerer readying to make his move. Then The Prophet's face filled with a look of triumph and, what looked to me like malice.

I saw him mouth "fuck you" at the Sorcerer.

"I have a new song." He was telling all of us because whatever it was would be new to us, too. We'd played everything we had. The band all looked to him, fingers poised, waiting to find the new rhythm for the final jam.

"Oh yeah," someone in the crowd yelled.

The Prophet held his arms out, palms down, holding us off, letting the energy and anticipation build. The first verse he spoke with no instruments accompanying his voice. He growled out the lyrics, slurring his words darkly.

> *Counter clockwise*
> *Sideways down*
> *Turn around*
> *Fall down*
> *All away around*
> *Underground*

He released his hands and the band gave him a beat, and then we all followed Lamond as he led us into something that sounded like a dirge with a backbeat. A march straight to Hell.

"*4 AM in Wonderland*," The Prophet said. "*4 AM in Wonderland*," he said with more force.

He spoke over the music, words whispered about you by the wind that suddenly you understand. He sang:

> *The vampires are out*
> *no reflection in their eyes*
> *they can't see you pass through mirrors*
> *into Wonderland tonight*
>
> *Down, down*
> *smoke and stars*
> *caught inside your eyes*
> *deeply stranger*
> *than you know*
> *truth behind the lies*

Counter clockwise
sideways down
turn around
fall down
all away around
Underground

The Prophet took the mike off its stand, trailing the long cord, and began to dance, gathering us up with him in a circle, but the circle was ragged, broken from the start. I joined in, too, laughing with fear. I tried to fill the gaps but I could not. The song was *wrong*. Things were going wrong, terribly wrong. The crowd was restless, upset, visibly frightened as they began, against their will, to sway and raise their arms. It was a spell, I knew. He was casting a spell. He was taking us into some vast whirlpool of his own empty heart.

Something touches you like rain
or the spray of waves on the shore
something chills you to the bone
a raven calls nevermore

You're going to die tonight
Not knowing what for
Not knowing why you came here
Knocking at a door
Why did you come?
What do you want?
Who do you think you are?
What have you forgot?

Counter clockwise
Sideways down
Turn around
Fall down
All away around
Underground

I know who you are
I know why
I know the secret you forgot
why you're going to die

The Red King rouses in his sleep
And calls out a name
You no longer know is yours . . .

You're all just a pack of cards.
You're nothing but a pack of cards.
You're nothing but a pack of cards

The song didn't finish it just broke off.

Lamond, one of his many shadows, leapt on me and grabbed me by the throat. He was so strong. I couldn't do anything. And then he shot him, the other one. The real one shot the one who grabbed me. When had he taken the rifle out of his pants? Had he done it during the performance, when all eyes were on The Prophet?

The now headless body lost solidity, toppled, vanishing almost before it hit the stage. At least there was no blood. Our Lamond had a huge grin on his face as he reloaded. Even better, to me, was being able to breath.

Wolves came streaming through the crowd at us, leaping up on stage. We flailed at them with our instruments. The bear waded forward, swatting away wolves and doppelgangers like so much wheat before the scythe.

I heard more gunplay.

A carved wooden boat, long and skinny with eyes painted on the prow, appeared at a bend of the river, still too far away. But its path was blocked. Dark clad figures were pushing poles against the current to bring their progress to a halt, peering at us from the boat deck and frowning. Something was blocking their passage but I couldn't see what. The Prophet kept turning his head, first to look at the boat and then back to the smiling Sorcerer. The Prophet wasn't the only one who could manipulate reality. The cavalry was running late.

The Sorcerer's minions were pushing us to the back of the stage. Soon there would be no retreat.

*

But then The Prophet finished his spell, picking up his broken chant, tears in his eyes he gave up the boat, gave up everything.

As The Prophet repeated "you're nothing but a pack of cards," again and again, our minds and bodies unfolded. Each of us became insubstantial enough to see through.

Casually, he took the book out, still singing, and burned it up in his hands. He didn't light it with something, but it burned nonetheless, smoke rising into the night.

"I don't need it," he said to the stagehand behind me who tried to come forward then, but too late. "I never needed it."

Then the spell finished us.

We were become nothing.

The theater, the people dancing, the band. The wolves, the doppelgangers, the sorcerer. All faded away into nothingness, The Prophet's chant a whisper . . . and then gone.

The river, too, faded, dried up, rolled back. From the boat, the wolf god cried out to The Prophet, who ignored him.

"You called me," the wolf said, snarling.

"You're nothing but a pack of cards," The Prophet repeated, only turning his head to glance coldly into the open night, unconcerned.

"I will not forget."

We all. Everything. Were unmade.

Existence must build on something. Faith can be built in the world, in God, in ourselves, in anything you like. One thing to measure the rest against. I had been to Egypt and seen the river, how hard could it be to exist in mere reality?

After an eon, I sighed and, tired, tried.

Time came back to me; I came back; pain came back. I thought then about what The Prophet had done. I existed again, the I who loved him and had not really been loved in return. Desire and suffering, my two friends who emptied me and filled me, who told me who I was, settled in my heart like two escaped birds returning happily to their cages where they are so well fed and loved—so happy to be wanted again they burst into a song of torment and nostalgia. I broke into tears, then laughed because I cried over a flicker in the same grey nothingness of existence and nothing more.

I was in nothing. Fog and swirling shadow.

You can imagine how I felt when the flicker took on color as I approached something. I was walking, without knowing it. I approached a warming orange and yellow—a fire, large and unruly as hell, rebelling against the grey of heaven.

There was a figure at the fire.

Janis, sitting on, of all things, a rolled-up sleeping bag. She wore her old leather pants, so casually cool yet hanging off her in an ungainly, used up sort of way. She had a silverwork Indian belt hanging loosely around her waist, beads around her neck and silver bracelets. Her hair had been tucked under a large cowboy hat that looked as if it had been recently tossed on the highway to be run over by a caravan of freight trucks and she had on a pair of red fretted cowboy boots. She wore, I swear, rose-colored granny glasses and a goofy crooked smile wrinkled her baby-fat cheeks. She looked beautiful.

She reached over to her gear—it appeared to exist, I thought, only as she reached over to it—and threw me another sleeping bag.

"Sit down," she said. "Have a toke."

I caught the bag. She held out the fat joint she had in her pudgy fingers. When I didn't immediately take it, she brought it back to her lips and took in a long breath. When she finished, she held the smoke inside, motioning me with her head to sit down and holding out the joint again.

I sat down. I took a toke.

I know it sounds ironic now, but I thought: this woman knows how to stay alive. And despite what would happen, it was true. In the beautiful mess that was her life, she always knew the right thing to do. Sometimes that's not enough, that's all.

When we finally released the air from burning lungs (she had held hers almost twice as long as I could hold mine), the smoke rose up into a night sky full of stars. Steady stars, familiar and riverless.

I goggled at them through teary eyes.

Never take anything for granted. It may make your life a little more comfortable to do so, but I'm here to tell you it's not worth it. It's not the way things are. Things are wonderful beyond belief.

"Texas," she said. "A large Texas sky. I grew up here. I had to leave. I heard the siren call of San Francisco, of destiny. And things here were too hard for me. But you never forget where you grew up. And when things get bad, these kinds of places are the easiest to remember."

She reached beside her and picked up an open bottle of whiskey and took a swig. She handed the bottle over to me.

I took a swig, pulling my arm across my mouth to wipe up.

"Well, that was a hell of a show." She laughed.

We laughed together.

Then we spent some time just looking into the fire or up at the stars or out into the tumble-weed night of a West Texas prairie, lonely as anywhere you would have thought if you'd been anyone but me. I knew what loneliness really looked like.

Finally, perhaps sensing I was content and would never break the spell, Janice tried again:

"You need to stop him."

"Me?" That got me. I looked over at her.

"He doesn't listen to me anymore," I said. "He doesn't listen to Lamond, or anyone. Not even you."

I paused.

"And isn't it too late? Why didn't the damn bear stop him? He's his spirit guide."

"The bear's not his spirit guide," Janice said.

She looked at me, and I knew what she was going to say before she said it.

"The bear is your spirit guide."

We looked at each other without speaking.

"You didn't know that? That explains a lot. You've always had the power to effect things. I thought you were just choosing your moment."

The bear came then, shambling out of the darkness. Stopping just outside the firelight, he put his nose out and turned his whole head and shoulders back and forth, surveying us with his dim eyes and smelling us, as if uncertain. Had he been out in the nothing? Had he been nothing, too, until I brought him back?

"Why don't you stop him?" I asked her.

"I'm not really here, Florence. I'm . . ."

She groped for the word.

"An emanation," I finished.

She nodded. "That's right, an emanation. You've been pay-ing attention. I'm not here, but I left this behind to talk to you if things got bad."

She took another long hit of her joint and passed it over. I felt obliged.

"To talk to me," I repeated tonelessly before inhaling and holding. I was still getting used to the idea that she would want to talk about all this with me. That I had any role in this at all besides backup singer and washed up girlfriend.

The bear came up and sat next to me companionably with a grunt of greeting or relief.

She blew another lungful of smoke into the Texas sky which drew it up toward the stars.

"Go to him," she said, kicking my foot with a cowboy boot.

The bear stood up and hunched down for me. And though before my last hit I had had a bunch of questions about what this all meant, instead I just stood up and climbed up on the bear's back and we ambled, not without a twinge of regret, away from Janis's fire and her wide open west Texas night and back into nothingness. I hugged the bear. Its fur was soft, except for the bristles just at the hump between his shoulders, which scratched my face but I didn't mind. His skin hung loosely and bunched up in my fingers. The muscles beneath rolled with power, pulling me along easily through the grey twilight.

It was different though to be out there with someone else. Especially if that someone is called your guide. I mean, then I had to be in the right place, doing the right thing, going the right way. How often do you get to know that in life?

We found Kenny curled up asleep half-covered in the grey ash or sand of nothingness. He had his hands between his legs and he shivered coldly but there was a light sweat on his forehead.

"The Red King sleeps," I said, "what will happen if I wake him?"

I slipped off the bear's back and knelt next to Kenny. I shook his arm.

He opened his eyes. He smiled at me and gave an exaggerated sigh. "Man, I had such a dream," he said. "I thought I . . ."

He saw the bear behind me, then the nothingness.

His face crumpled in disbelief and sadness.

He reached out and held me. I wrapped my arms around his head, cradling him into me fiercely.

"I wanted to bring together everything," he said.

"I know," I said.

"I must have been insane. I brought us into nothing."

"Yes."

"I wanted the One. I brought us into nothing."

I thought about Janis's fire. Her Texas sky.

"We're in Golden Gate Park," I said. "A summer day. The drums are playing on Hippie Hill. They will be playing all day. We are laying on the grass. Sunlight on our faces."

He looked up into my eyes as I spoke. He nodded wordlessly.

We heard the ragged drums, their polyrhythms, playful and wild, so different from that deep, hypnotic beat The Prophet had tapped against my chest when I had first seen the wolf. Or that he had used to drive our songs relentlessly into madness.

The Prophet sat up, disentangling himself from me. He took a deep breath of air into his lungs like Janis taking a toke on her fat Texas joint.

The sunlight against my cheeks was like a benediction. The grass was pushing up against us, growing as we sat there. The world pulled us down in its gravity well, trying to bury us into the earth as we would one day be. Pulling, pulling, pulling. Every day we rose against it, every day until we failed. But not yet. Today we would walk in the sun. I welcomed the fight to stand up, to be, to exist.

"I can't tell you how happy I am to be here," I said.

The Prophet smiled ruefully at me. He shook his head, but I don't quite know what he meant by that—that he was foolish for almost destroying all this? Or that he wasn't happy to be here?

We were dressed in the remnants of our stage clothes. I had on a short silver dress and a limp pink boa. He had on a purple dress over orange leggings. The dress was pulled down to leave him bare-chested. He removed his dark sunglasses.

"I still have some things to learn," he said. He paused. "The wolf will be angry."

I looked at him, worried.

He shook his head again. "He won't be back for a long time after what we did. That passageway is closed for a while. A long while."

"Egypt?" I asked.

"I don't think I'll ever see that place again," he said flatly. "I don't think I'll ever be able to remake that. I might be able to find another way in, but there's no guarantee it'd be the same place."

We sat a long time, feeling the wind ruffling our hair and clothes, watching the clouds sometimes cover the sun then quickly pass away.

"Do you feel them?" I said. "Do you feel the life in them?"

"I don't know."

I closed my hands and opened them, releasing two butterflies who circled each other fluttering, rising up into the breeze.

The Prophet laughed. He looked self-conscious. Like he had no right to laugh. I stretched.

"I'm hungry," I said.

"Me, too."

We stood up, brushed the dirt from our bottoms and legs, held hands, and started downhill. The wonderful hippies around the drum circle—still young, still thinking that something would work out if they just believed hard enough in utopia—they flailed and hopped, their shirts off, their hair long and free. I glanced back to see the bear, his nose sticking out of the bushes behind the hill, turn then and walk away. We had triple-stack pancakes and (in honor of Janis) Texas-style omelets with salsa and hot peppers at 3 PM in the afternoon at a greasy spoon. And felt *here*. The cheap plastic stuffed seats of the booth squeaked when you adjusted yourself on them. The dirty floors made you not want to look too closely under the tables. *Here*, for a while. The hot peppers, each one, with each burning taste, made me think: thank you, thank you, thank you . . .

After that, there are only more stories. We kept playing music, for a while, under a new name, buoyed by all the energy released by The Prophet then, in that place, and all the answering echoes of all the fabulous artists who sensed a possibility, a miracle of rare device, a soap bubble of iridescent impossibility about to burst.

I don't know if you will understand me when I say we gave birth to and ended the Summer of Love that night (1967 not 1968 as the media, and some faulty memories, sometimes think).

The wake of all that we had seen would catch us all up into its embrace and carry us far out to sea like a Tsunami receding, but it was all already over. We would be washed up on the shore all too soon, alone.

Oh, I could tell you stories what happened next. But we'll leave that for now. Our music floated up and out, and everyone heard what we made, the clash and bang and beat and dream of it. After the summer, our band, by whatever name, would crash down again, breaking into a million pieces, burning up, scattering ashes into the wind, but sending out embers too that would ignite new dreams and bring the people to San Francisco, to the City of Love by the Bay, in droves. The tourists, as usual, would ruin the scenery. The flame would burn out spectacularly after a few years, and as Lamond said, most of the people there would forget it ever happened and fall back into tired ways and, years later, checking their thinning hair and stock portfolios, would say to themselves (to quiet those voices, insistent, still calling to them) "it was just the drugs—just a hoax." Nobody ever really thought they could change the world, did they? It was just fashion, just people wanting to get laid, right?

No. But let's leave that story lie.

Me, I would stick with The Prophet, part of the core, along with Lamond and Star Baby and a few others. The Prophet left us for a time, but we all hunkered down on a commune in Northern California and played music for ourselves alone, music to rock the stars to sleep, to raise the sun in the morning and bloom the flowers. A kind of healing, or penance, for those of us who had been too close to the rend in reality that The Prophet had made. The Prophet had gone to travel the world, to hear more stories about the Wolf, to understand what it meant and what he had to do when it came again. When he came back, he was unconcerned, carefree, easy to laugh, but distant. Beyond us all somehow. Stronger somehow, too, more substantial and deep like the stillness in the heart of the Northern California Redwoods. We were never lovers again. Something had changed. He loved me, I know, but we never reached each other again.

He gathered us up and moved us out to New York to hit it big as Egyptian Motherlode, the best funk band ever to land its starship on this pitiful little place. But that—what can I tell you?—

that is another story. Before the future came, before the loss, before the forgetting, before the call of new things, before lost love, before alien encounters beyond the rim of the solar system, we had that summer in San Francisco. It belonged to us alone and everyone. And if some have forgotten what it all meant to be there, all I can say is, I will never give it back. I keep it safe and when I feel it, I dance.

I dance the wolves away every time.

5
BALL AND CHAIN

San Francisco, 1965

I CHECKED MY NAME AT THE DOOR WHEN I JOINED the Sun Dreamers, useless baggage that had lost its appeal and become too much of a liability. I became Sunshine Sammy that first summer, then Diaper Dan, and finally Star Baby—reborn in the fiery cauldron of the 1960s.

I couldn't be Gregory McDaniel anymore, even though I hadn't answered to that name in years. I'd been Dan Gregory, Greg Daniels, Gregory Mac and so many other people, cardboard cutouts of human beings, that I'd lost track. That's the way life runs when you live it undercover, in the background, suddenly there, and then not. But The Prophet, maybe he just played me perfectly, though at first I would have sworn he hardly knew I was there.

He shaped me. I didn't believe in any of the crazy, harmless hippie bullshit of his—stuff you can hardly read about without laughing that we all treated like it would save the world but knew in our hearts was just so much nonsense.

I was sent out to California in 1965 after three East Coast members of a black power organization known as the Revolutionary Action Movement were charged with conspiring to blow up the Statue of Liberty, the Liberty Bell, and the Washington Monument. The students who made up the Oakland chapter of RAM were hardly interested in this extreme form of activism. That's what the report I sent back to Washington said. I hadn't given much credence to a pair of young recruits I'd helped to bring in who didn't see eye-to-eye with the rest of the organization, Huey Newton and Bobby Seale. They soon left to do their own thing. But I'd slipped away by then, too, so far underground that this time I never resurfaced.

I went with friends, members of RAM I was getting to know, to a concert in Golden Gate Park. My friends were harmless idealists who'd discovered Marxism while at Oakland City College. I was pushing them to make contact with RAM's founder, Robert F. Williams, a civil rights leader and former president of the Monroe, North Carolina NCAAP. Williams was currently living in exile in Cuba, where he was making regular radio addresses to Southern blacks on a station known as "Radio Free Dixie" at the behest of Fidel Castro.

We sat out on the grass, on old beach towels to protect our clothes, and watched what must have been a wonderful show. I couldn't tell you who played or even what they played. I was trying to figure out a way to bring Robert F. Williams to justice before he could take over the power vacuum left behind after the assassination of Malcolm X. Such were my thoughts, my concerns. I wasn't one of the good guys, even if the team I played for said so.

The Sun Dreamers came on last. They kind of stumbled out on stage, one after the other, each looking equally dazed, as if they were quite surprised to find themselves in front of an audience.

No two of them dressed alike. They stood in clumps and played what seemed to be two or three different songs at the same time. Half of their instruments were out of tune. The crowd was clearly distressed and many people had already gotten up to leave when The Prophet started to sing. He sang without words, his voice sharp and beautiful, lilting as it struck a primal nerve and sent a shiver up my spine.

Then The Prophet held up his hand just as the late summer sun snaked between the branches of a copse of nearby trees and he caught a jutting, long ray of sunshine in his big upraised palm. He made a fist and the light extinguished altogether, or else it fell once more behind the trees.

The band had stopped playing. Everyone was stunned, silent, looking at each other, wondering what we'd just witnessed, wanting to know if other people had seen it, too. And then the band started up again, in unison this time, suddenly tight, rocking at a breakneck pace, faster than seemed possible. The crowd roared its approval; we were ready for anything.

I couldn't get RAM to make contact with Williams in Cuba. They were more interested in local issues, mostly non-violent. As long as the Oakland chapter didn't lose interest and disband, I had a pretty cushy job. I attended classes at San Francisco Community College during the day, where I kept an eye on the curriculum of several college professors, drove an old, battered Volkswagen Bug, and maintained a modest North Beach apartment above a coffee shop run by an elderly Italian couple.

I was pushing RAM to do more outreach, most of which I had to do myself. I wanted to bring in more radical elements, more intellectuals. I needed to change the membership and its values in order to change the agenda of the group.

I saw the Sun Dreamers a couple more times, mostly as the opening act for a group that somebody else wanted to see. Their show was always untamed and unpredictable, highly entertaining if you liked watching chaos courting disaster. Somehow they'd managed to find a small following, despite the fact that no two sets ever repeated themselves in either sound or substance.

I was surprised then when Louis Armand, a fellow I'd recruited for RAM but hadn't joined, contacted me on their behalf.

"They want what?" I asked.

They wanted guns, lots of them. I couldn't get the story straight—something about a rival Egyptian band and apparitions or ghosts. It sounded like the plot of a bad monster movie. I didn't like the idea of supplying guns to crazy people but, at the very least, it sounded like a good opportunity to recruit some real black radicals to the cause.

The Prophet appeared aloof. His brother, Lamond, was the main force, not just in this deal but behind the band, always in motion, while The Prophet stood with his arms crossed barely even blinking his eyelids.

"Don't worry," Lamond assured me. I wasn't very worried. We'd go back and forth over the price, which wasn't important to me in the least; we'd argue over how many firearms I could deliver, the makes and models, and in the end I'd either sell them to him or I wouldn't. I was trying to figure out a way to use the situation to my benefit and right then I wasn't succeeding, and I couldn't sell them the guns unless I could figure out some way to justify the transaction.

"Can you sing?" The Prophet had been so quiet that I'd forgotten he was there.

"A little," I answered. I'd sung in the church choir when I was 14, but seldom since. I thought he was making some sort of desperate plea: *we're all black, we're musicians, sell us the guns.*

"I thought so," he said

"Not now," Lamond said, clearly agitated.

"You'll have to sing for us next time," said The Prophet.

"How do you know I'm coming back?"

"You will," he said. "You will."

I did, but I didn't sing then.

I came back to find out what they were doing with the guns. I was desperate. I needed something I could put in a report that would make it look like I was up to something very important. I needed to impress my superiors right away.

The night before I joined the band, I had to kill someone. It was a simple hit. I knew the man's address; I knew the layout of the house, where the bedroom was; and I knew what time he'd be asleep and that he routinely took sleeping pills. I was chosen for the job because there was nothing to connect me with the target and because I, and my various projects, were expendable. That's how I knew it was time to make some sort of impression.

The task itself was of little consequence to me, but there was always the possibility that I was being set up. Sometimes an attempted assassination, a botched one, could be as important as the real thing. I could be arrested or killed, all for the love of my country.

As it turned out, I was in and out in less than five minutes. The front door was unlocked. I padded quietly up to the third floor and left a small hole behind his left ear. No surprises. No wife, no mistress, no children—not even a dog—no complications of any sort.

The next day, I was back in Oaktown, catching the Sun Dreamers doing their thing with the intention of getting to know them better. I met some of my RAM friends at the show. I threw myself into the music, dancing wild, taking whatever was handed to me, alcohol, drugs, fruit punch, totally ignoring my intention to meet the Dreamers and open a dossier on its members. I wasn't sorry or guilty about the murder. It wasn't that. I just didn't want to die. And right then I wasn't sure about anything, except that if I kept moving I'd be a difficult target to shoot.

The audience surged up onstage to dance with the band, moving around and through the players, people taking turns singing into the mike while The Prophet went around blowing out these weird Bruce Lee-like "woo-oo's" at us. He had some sort of incense oil he would rub in his palms and then blow the sweet smell over each of us, some sort of blessing. I was flying when he stepped up to me and put his mouth up to my ear so I could hear him. I waited for the weird sound, but then he spoke.

"Looks like you've got company."

I said something that was meant to be "what?"

"Your shadow. He says it's all right. He understands. It wasn't your decision."

I was starting to freak out, but trying my best not to let it show. I was paranoid all by myself, and the whatever-I-was-on intensified everything. What did he *know*? Was he blackmailing me? I'd already given them what they wanted. Was there something more? Were the guns I'd given them the bait for a larger trap?

"He's not sure he can forgive you, but I think he will."

Then The Prophet moved on.

I kept dancing.

I woke up, slouched against the side of a building, somewhere outside, cold, to someone pushing my shoulder.

"Kenny says you're in the band." It was Lamond. He didn't look too happy about it.

It was near morning.

Lamond had a rifle I'd sold him stuffed down his pants. I giggled and avoided the obvious joke.

What the fuck did he think he was doing? These guys weren't revolutionaries. They were clowns. Dangerous clowns with guns down their pants, but still . . .

He seemed to be waiting for an answer. I needed a cup of coffee. "I'm not in the band," I said. "And I don't know Kenny."

"The Prophet," Lamond said harshly, like I was being an idiot. "He says you're in. Come on, the bus is leaving."

So I went. Dangerous clowns. They might even make a good report with some creative tweaking. And then I was Sunshine Sammy—The Prophet named me—and the next week I was singing. And I never knew I could sing like that. And I never wanted to stop.

I don't remember if we slept at all that summer. It was just practice and playing.

Before I knew it, without really planning it, I went underground.

I can't explain why, but I didn't ever tell my bosses about the Dreamers. At first, I just didn't get around to it—honestly didn't know what to say or how to make the band credible persons of interest. Then I just didn't want to. I kept a secret from them for a change, and felt like I'd found some little space for myself. I told them the guns I gave the Dreamers were for a RAM cell, one I invented. I told them I was on to something new and big. I got into it and wrote reports fueled by uppers and false promises.

I kept up my reports that Summer, but they became increasingly unreal, increasingly what my superiors wanted to hear. And I fell in deeper with the Sun Dreamers, unknown to anyone, least of all myself. When Pete Stalls left the band in the fall and immigrated to Liberia, I took on his persona of Star Baby. I grew a big bushy beard and donned the giant diaper, bonnet, and oversized glasses that had been Stalls' trademarks. To make the transformation complete, I gained 40 pounds on a steady diet of cheeseburgers and milkshakes. Through connections I had obtained a copy of Stalls birth certificate (a fake) and his driver's license (the real thing). Nobody in the band ever called me Pete; I was Star Baby from that point on. The Prophet called me Baby.

Deeply under cover, hidden in plain sight, I performed in my outlandish getup on stage nearly every night. I enjoyed the funky costumes, the bizarre stage antics. I didn't buy into the mysticism, even though strange things happened all around me all the time, or seemed to. There were drugs everywhere in San Francisco. Many people even suspected there were hallucinogenics in the drinking water, all part of some covert CIA experiment, and maybe there were. It would've explained a lot. But it wasn't my doing.

I knew enough about The Prophet now to know he was sincere, that he really believed in all his mumbo-jumbo. And I guess I saw enough, playing gigs with him in sudden sandstorms of my imagination pock-mocked by vast pyramids with mazes leading far below them, or drifting through psychedelic black holes deep in outer space, to know something really was going down; I did believe in something in a back-handed sort of way because I knew it firsthand. I knew something weird was true, something you could never put in a report. But I didn't want to know more. The Prophet wanted to know everything, which I thought was just foolish. Never know where the bodies are buried if you don't want to be buried next to them yourself.

My troubles worsened when a couple of the guys I'd made up in my reports, members of the imaginary ultra-radical breakout cell from RAM, showed up to get me in on a job. Their names, improbably, were Jo-Jo and Hieronymus. Jo-Jo was short, stuttered, was angry about everything, and never stopped talking; Hieronymus was long, lean and mean—and never said a word. They both wore knit caps—easy to pull down and hide their faces—black canvas jackets, and clean new jeans.

"We're going to blow up the Golden Gate Bridge," Jo-Jo said. "Make a statement. Those m-m-motherfuckers will know who we are and what we're about." Just like I'd written him in my report: he was from central casting. But at first I didn't notice what I should have—that they didn't exist. I just thought: this is big! Finally something big! So, I thought, dimly and stupidly, that I had to go along and do it. I dressed quickly in black, and shoved a small handgun in my pants at the back, hiding it under my long coat.

I tried to get Lamond to join us, to even the odds if I had to take on the guys I'd invented. Lamond was always the most radical and hard-assed of the Dreamers, yet I had no doubt he would stand by me in a pinch.

It was early morning when Jo-Jo and Hieronymus burst into my room. I told them to wait downstairs and woke Lamond, who slept by himself in the back of what was really a large walk-in closet. He snapped awake and looked at me like I'd slipped a dead fish in bed with him; the whites of his eyes seemed to glow with intensity, the red veins in them popping. He didn't say anything and waited for me to tell him what was up. When I finished he said, quietly:

"You're a god-damn fool."

I knew that. I didn't know he knew it.

Lamond had his rifle lying in bed next to him, under the sheets. It was not the time to tell him it was dangerous to do that.

"The Prophet is dealing with more important things than the U.S. government," Lamond said. "Go back to bed."

I nodded. What was I doing? I tried to concentrate and when that didn't work I shook my head, but my thoughts wouldn't clear. I knew I should take Lamond's advice and go back to bed.

Instead I headed downstairs and went walking with Jo-Jo and Hieronymus though a sleepy, damp San Francisco morning. We walked through empty streets, smelling salty breezes, cold whipping about our ankles and blowing under our dark caps.

Jo-Jo never stopped talking in a low whine about all the things he knew for sure had gone down that shouldn't have, all the people who'd get theirs in return, how his family would know he existed soon enough (the last made me laugh, although I couldn't quite remember why); Hieronymus just kept nodding, hands deep in his pockets, face hard as granite with high cheekbones and a prominent cleft over his upper lip.

I followed them all the way to nowhere.

We never found the bridge. We missed it in the swirling fog.

We came out by the water near the Cliff House, an old restaurant overlooking Seal Rock in the distance out in the ocean. Jo-Jo flashed his plastic explosives and detonator with a serious look that meant "let's get to work"—but there was nothing to blow up. The Cliff House was decrepit. The camera obscura out on a nearby promontory wasn't oppressing anybody. Hieronymus said his first words all day:

"Laughing Sal," he said, pointing.

Laughing Sal was the scary animatronic figure guarding the entrance to the local amusement park, Playland by the Sea, located just down the road a ways from where we stood. To get in the park, you had to pass under her lunatic gaze as she shook with peals of scornful laughter. I hated her, as did every kid in the Bay Area, I'm sure; but blowing it up wasn't exactly going to bring the

U.S. government to its knees. Was Hieronymus kidding? It had to be a joke, and as a deadpan statement of our futility. Maybe he really thought we should do it.

Without speaking, we descended below the Cliff House, down broken concrete steps to the ruins of the old Sutro Baths where sixty years ago white people in funny old-time swimwear used to cavort in droves. No need to blow it up—it had fallen apart a long time ago. I thought we went down there to have a dark, quiet place to confer but no one seemed to feel like speaking. We left the explosives there, buried in the sands behind an old ruined outbuilding of indeterminate use. I don't know why we buried them, why we didn't just go home to try again another day.

I wondered, *how do you put this in a report?*

Then I remembered Jo-Jo and Hieronymus didn't exist, that I'd invented them. My two figments wandered away, behind some old graffitied walls, or back up the cliff, or into the waves. I walked into some old caves people used to swim through, drinking champagne and twirling their handlebar mustaches. It was very dark and I stumbled into the water. I walked with the cold seawater seeping into my shoes and wetting the cuffs of my pants thinking at any moment the foot or so of water below me would open into deep water and I would fall all the way in and drown. When I made it outside again, I climbed the cliff face, clutching the tough plants that grew there, back up to Highway 1, crossed it, and lost myself in the endless blocks of city streets leading nowhere.

As I walked home the world woke up and went to work. Many of them off to drive unmolested across the Golden Gate Bridge.

I stopped sending in reports after that. Hieronymus and Jo-Jo may have sprung fully formed from my imagination like Athena had from Zeus' head, but unlike Zeus I didn't trust my creations. They were dangerous, unpredictable fools. Just like me. Instead, I faded completely into my new persona. I worked hard to improve my singing and guitar playing, even began writing some of my own song lyrics. I was Star Baby, "the newest citizen of the intergalactic universe" with "a passport from the Groovatron Nebula." At least that was the way I was announced every night.

I'd plug in my electric guitar and bend the strings. It wasn't

Jimi Hendrix, although we gigged with him a couple of times, more like Albert King, gut bucket soul. My guitar had a gripe with the world and everybody was going to hear how sad it felt. Me, I just smiled. The guitar had its own voice and I let it speak. There were nights I swore it told me what it wanted to say.

We had a quiet rehearsal space in an old, crumbling theater that would be condemned a few years later. After practice we'd walk out onto the steps out front and watch the people coming home from work. We'd get stares, sometimes curious and sometimes hostile. At the moment, we weren't getting much reaction at all.

The Prophet, Lamond, and I sat out front, sweaters bundled as wisps of fog rolled in off the Bay. The men in their hats and suits coming home from downtown office buildings now moved furtively around the clusters of teenagers gathered on the corners. The teenagers were pouring in day by day. Soon they would take over the entire city. Lamond had a beer. I had a Coke. The Prophet was trying to explain something to us about the mechanics of music. We weren't getting it and he was gesturing broadly with his hands.

The Prophet stopped gesturing. A lanky redheaded kid, face speckled with freckles, no more than sixteen, was standing two feet away from us. Two other teenagers, a boy and a girl, both white, stood several feet behind him.

We turned to look at the kid. He smiled slightly, but didn't say a word, just stood there, gathering his courage. The couple behind him averted their eyes. The Prophet waited for him to speak. Lamond shrugged his shoulders.

I said, "boo," without force.

"I need a place to crash," he finally said. "My friends do, too."

"Sorry, kid," Lamond said.

"Why here?" The Prophet asked. Lamond stood up and walked inside. He knew where this was going.

"The town's full. I need a place to stay and a chance to work."

"What about them?" The Prophet asked. "Will they work too?"

The couple stared at their shoes. They were thin and their

faces and clothes were smudged with dirt. They could have been chimney sweeps from Victorian London; something pathetic from a Dickens novel, maybe. But there was reality, too: taking in a couple of white boys would be bad enough, but the girl would be trouble. If she had a figure under the poncho that she wore we'd all be in for more than just a bit of trouble with the police. But it was The Prophet's move.

"Do you play an instrument?"

The freckled redhead shook his head.

"I don't suppose they do, either." The Prophet frowned. "Card tricks?" he asked.

"Yes," said the girl.

"Ah," said The Prophet. "Show me." He pulled a deck of playing cards out of the air, wrapped in cellophane, in a box marked with the ace of spades, and handed it to her. She fumbled with the cellophane, her hands awkwardly searching for enough purchase to start a tear.

"Pssst."

I turned my head but didn't see anybody.

"Pssst," louder. Who was doing that to me?

Somehow The Prophet was standing in the doorway behind me; he was sitting there with the teens; somehow he was in both places simultaneously. He—the one behind me—watched over my shoulder as the girl attempted the worst card trick ever—she tried to palm a card but it flipped up and hit The Prophet—the one sitting on the sidewalk—in the face.

I gazed in wonder at The Prophet behind me as if he would deflate at any moment. What was going on? Except for a pair of high top sneakers, he wore no clothes. Completely naked. The Prophet outside winked at me.

He gestured and I stood and walked back inside.

"This is our chance to talk," The Prophet said.

I wondered if The Prophet was naked in case I was wearing a wire. Then I realized that didn't make any sense and giggled.

The second Prophet—the naked one—put his arm on my shoulder and I turned inward, like him. The next step I took felt like I shed my skin. I turned back to see myself, like an image in a mirror, still standing in the hallway, watching the girl shuffling, getting ready for another card trick.

I felt like we were in a cave, as if I was under the Sutro Baths again. The Prophet turned and walked into darkness. I followed him. I was naked, too. Soon we were moving upwards, then climbing a staircase seemingly hewn into the side of a cliff, like Machu Picchu or some old Anasazi dwelling in the Southwest. The path grew so narrow that we needed to hug the mountainside. I could feel a breeze as if we were outside, but the sky was dark or there was no sky at all. There was a bit of light around us. But looking over the cliff, I could see no ground, no ocean.

Eventually, The Prophet led me to a little outcropping of the cliff with enough room for us to sit and rest. The Prophet sat dangling his legs over the abyss. I sat cross-legged off to one side.

"This is a good place to clear your head," he said.

"What is all this?" I asked.

"The cliffs? Sure you want to know?"

"No," I said. "I don't."

"Astral projection," he said. He touched his own chest, "astral body."

"Come on," I said. "I don't believe in that bullshit."

"O.K.," he said. He held up his hand and showed me two green gel caps—sleight of hand, elegantly done in stark contrast to the card tricks outside. "Then we must be high on something. Take these," he said grinning, "or the illusion will fade and you might fall into the water far below."

I took the pills from his outstretched hand, downed them without water.

I nodded as a strange vibration rattled up my spine and bent the world like Hendrix bending a note that reverberated and distorted.

"Wow," I said. There were no words; there was no such thing as time; there was no reason that the universe had to be anything at all. What was going on? No drugs I knew worked that quick.

"I brought you here, Baby, because it's time you cleared the air—told some secrets."

I tensed up. Tried to clear my head, but everything was rushing at me in waves.

What did he know?

"Lamond told me you tried to recruit him to blow up the Golden Gate Bridge."

"Is that what this is about—it was nothing, just some crazy guys I know who wanted to take a field trip, but nothing happened."

"I know," The Prophet said, "the fog came up. It wrapped itself around you, found your ears, your nose, your throat, entered your brain."

Had he been following me? Had Lamond?

"I want to make this clear," he said. "I can't tell you what to do. You want to play with your imaginary friends, play, but it isn't a game. None of what any of us do here is a game. The next time you set off to destroy the Golden Gate Bridge or the Washington Monument, the next time you go to the store to buy Corn Flakes, the next time you brush your teeth, whatever it is that you feel you need to do, you need to take it seriously. You need to do it. Just make sure that you're the one in control."

I nodded, even though I had very little idea of what he was talking about. The Sun Dreamers were starting to sound more and more like the secret service, only the rules, unspoken in both cases, made less sense than ever.

"What's happening to me?" I said. "What is all this?"

"Mind control," The Prophet said, frowning at me.

"How? Tell me!" The Soviets were rumored to be way ahead in researching psychic phenomena for warfare. Big money funded research here and no one would care how long I'd been gone off the ranch if I came back with the secret to mind control. That's how he made me see all this stuff. Maybe I finally had something for my report. On the other hand, maybe I'd been compromised and they'd need to get rid of me anyway.

"You want to know the secret?"

"How are you controlling my mind?"

"Uh, no—I'm not. No mind can control another."

"Right," I said, deflated. Of course.

"I used you to do it. You're controlling yourself. Simple, see? That's the secret."

I nodded, even more bewildered. So he *was* controlling my mind? How was he having me do it?

"Look, Baby, you've got some stuff to work out. We've got music to play. You've got to be the one in control—not me, not them, not your imaginary friends. You."

He looked at me with sad brown eyes.

"Next time, no fog—and you do what you want," he said.

I tried to protest, didn't know what to say but sneezed instead. I laughed, delighted, my imaginary body, my astral body, had sneezed.

"Gesundheit, Baby," The Prophet said.

And I was back outside, in daylight, sitting beside The Prophet. I must have dozed off—no big surprise as the girl was still performing card tricks. "Your tricks need work," The Prophet said, "but let's find you a place to crash."

The Prophet stood up, his knees cracking.

"What did you give me?" I said.

"The pills?" The Prophet said, motioning the kid and his friends into the theater, our rehearsal space. "Vitamin E—nothing harmful."

We would have to practice outdoors after that, as rotations of unwashed youth piled into our space on their spiritual journeys to "Baghdad by the Bay." The Prophet didn't like to say no to anything, especially any inner journey, no matter how ridiculous. Even mine.

Jo-Jo and Hieronymus showed up later that week with a new plan.

"You won't believe this," Jo-Jo said bursting into my room. "The m-m-mint—San Francisco has the m-m-mint. The m-m-money, that's the key to it all." He started gesturing, seeing the unbelieving look on my face. "Chaos and order, it's all in the f-flow of the cash."

I reached for my coat, caught myself. What had The Prophet said? The next time I set off, I had to do it? Make sure I was the one in control? No. Not exactly. I didn't really want to do this, not really. I wanted to go back to bed, slip underneath my blankets and dispel the chill that was growing around my life.

I looked out the window. Tendrils of fog where drifting in from the ocean, as if they were searching for a way into the house. I thought about The Prophet.

"Why?" I asked.

"We can disrupt the flow of capital," said Jo-Jo. "The whole system will f-fall apart."

"There are other mints," I said. "Philadelphia, Denver. The production won't stop." Jo-Jo frowned, started to argue. Hieronymus shook his head and glowered.

"Besides," I said, "the mint will be well guarded. You can't just walk in and ask to see the money."

"They give tours."

"That's the Old Mint. It's been decommissioned since 1937."

"Then let's blow that one up. It'll be sym-sym—" He stopped, motioned down with one hand flat: "symbolic," he said.

Maybe. Maybe it would, but the Old Mint was near Union Square, blocks from movie theaters and major department stores. Police would be nearby and available, one way streets could be cordoned off quickly, grinding already congested traffic to a standstill—too many witnesses if we tried to walk away. It would be a suicide mission, at best. Unless we used The Prophet's trick, shed our skins and headed for the surreality of the cliffs. But I didn't know if I could do that trick again, if it would fool anybody beyond a bunch of kids. And me.

What did we hope to accomplish? What did *I* hope to accomplish?

I certainly didn't need to be a hero. I possessed no desire to turn these two goofballs over to the authorities, but I didn't want to be responsible for them either.

"Sit down." I told them. "What would you like on your toast?"

The spare cabinets yielded half a loaf of bread, some jam, pancake mix, and packets of oatmeal and cream of wheat.

"Let's talk this over," I said.

When I turned around, though, the kitchen table was deserted, the chairs empty.

I experienced other hallucinations, strange things moving about in the fog, edging their way closer to my reality.

I stopped taking drugs, but that only seemed to sharpen my perception, my foreboding that something I couldn't quite comprehend was searching for me. I eliminated coffee from my diet and, when that didn't work, even chocolate and soft drinks.

"There's something out there," I said one day to The Prophet, "watching."

"There always is," he told me, "just don't look back."

I didn't feel reassured.

Jo-Jo and Hieronymus returned the next week.

They stood in my kitchen, heads bowed, exchanging glances. I knew by the way they shuffled their feet that they had something to tell me that I wasn't going to like.

"It's time you surfaced," Jo-Jo said, nodding at me.

I nodded, as if what he said made sense.

"You stopped giving reports a long time ago," he said. "The Man is getting suspicious."

I nodded again. The Man? Really?

"If you're not working for them, they're going to want to know who you are working for. You're going to blow our cover."

Were they reporting on me? Didn't I make them up?

I ignored them. I turned on the baseball game, then started switching between it and the Miss America pageant. Before long we were all settled in watching both. But I was beginning to feel as if I was a figment of their imagination, not the other way around.

When the game was over and one of the girls was crowned, the two of them at last got up to leave.

"You'll need something big," Jo-Jo said. "You've been away from the game too long to give them anything less. Think it over."

I didn't like the new tack. They were laying it on me. I didn't know anything at all. I just reported the news—or made it up—that's all.

I started catching glimpses of Hieronymus and Jo-Jo at the clubs we played, on the street, at Macy's or the Emporium. Wherever I went I'd see them, heads bobbing, flailing to fit into their surroundings. They'd bump into each other, look at themselves in surprise; they'd start talking to the people around them whenever I met their eyes. I felt sure they were following me, marking my "progress."

The shame was that I knew I didn't want to play revolutionary anymore. That was my old job and I hadn't enjoyed it then. Now

I simply wanted to disappear into the band. Whether it was an internal or external manifestation, something was clearly holding me back.

When the knock, loud, frantic, came at my door, I was sure it was my two ridiculous shadows. I grabbed my gun as I rolled up out of bed—suddenly wide awake.

I peeked out. It was The Prophet. I stuck the gun behind my back, in the waistband of my shorts. He rushed in, closed the door and leaned in to me.

I could hear voices raised outside, shouting, moving away through the night.

"Look," he said, as if finishing the point in a conversation I'd been participating in for some time. "If you could postpone the end of the world, would you do it?"

The Russians, I thought and reflexively looked up as if I'd be able to see bombs dropping somewhere beyond the ceiling.

"Is this it?" I asked. I'd played the spy vs. spy game seriously at times and cynically at other times. But wasn't this what it was all about? What I'd been trying to help head off all along?

"Calm down," The Prophet said. I must have been wide-eyed, on the brink of panic.

"We should get a car," I said, "head North. It probably won't do us much good, but it'll improve our odds."

"But would you do it, though?" The Prophet asked. His eyes were bloodshot. His hands shook. He looked pale, hollow eyed. "I mean, what's the use?"

"Would I do what?" Somewhere in the distance I heard an air raid siren.

"Stop the end of the world, man. The End Times. Apocalypse. Last Judgment. Do you think we deserve another chance?"

I'd turned my back to The Prophet, fumbled with the knob of the television. I had to know what was going on.

The Prophet grabbed my shoulder. His hands, hard like iron, turned me part way back towards him.

I wasn't thinking. I just knew The Prophet was strong and dangerous and that there might not be time enough for whatever I decided to do.

"Yes," I shouted. "Yes, of course. Stop. Postpone. Sure." Just let go of my shoulder.

"OK," he said.

And just like that everything was quiet. No air raid siren. I could hear the drip of water falling through a hole in the rain gutter.

"Right," he said, leaving, not bothering to say goodbye.

What the hell had that been about?

I locked my door and rolled back into bed, but couldn't sleep for hours. In the morning, I woke to find myself clutching my gun to my chest like a teddy bear.

It startled me that what I feared most when I'd thought we'd all be annihilated in a blinding flash was the end of the band, no more music. I tried to figure out if that was an appropriate response as I caffeinated (I was back on) and headed out the door toward rehearsal, hoping that the world would still be there, that the quiet wasn't the illusion.

After that night everything kicked into high gear, into the stratosphere, and the band entered one of its most productive periods. I was happier than I could remember.

I knew I had decisions to make that I was postponing, but I couldn't figure out what anybody wanted from me and, somehow, that mattered to me more than I thought it should.

My two clowns, my superego and my id, wanted me to do something stupid, anything as long as it created a spectacle and stirred up trouble.

Washington wanted me to find a patsy, somebody to take a fall.

I couldn't begin to fathom what The Prophet wanted. Somewhere, lost in all the mysticism and all the mind games, I was sure The Prophet wanted something from me—even if it was merely to be a witness to his folly.

The rest of the band ignored me. They were friendly for the most part but kept their distance. They had their own problems. I came to practice and to gigs and hit my marks, sang, and played. I needed more interaction, more feedback. The next time The Prophet decided to end the world, I wanted there to still be something to live for.

*

Our ranks swelled as several of the kids that had moved into our rehearsal space joined the band. One of them, a young woman with vacant brown eyes, looked at me throughout rehearsals as if she knew me. I'd never noticed her before, but now she wore a long purple dress, ripped out at the sides so it draped over her arms, beads like she'd just been to Mardi Gras, and a headdress with Day-Glo feathers. She held a scepter with a glowing red crystal at the end and her face was made up as if she were Egyptian royalty.

"Who's that?" I asked Lamond afterwards.

"High Priestess," Lamond said with disgust, putting his axe away quickly so he could exit first, "Our Lady of Chaos and the Dance of All Things Great and Small." He spat on the floor. "All I know is, if she stands in my way during a show again, I'm going to plant my foot in her ass and kick her off the stage."

Her part of the act was an invocation to Chaos, a theatrical bit with smoke bombs, weird kenning (naturally), neon make-up applied to her arms and lit by a blacklight, wild gesticulations, and partial disrobing—the last part, or parts, ensuring the success of the whole. I thought it was crap. I'd met the real Lords of Chaos, and they worked from behind anonymous desks in nondescript offices, sowing teeth and raising Cain.

During her number, The Prophet would fade to the back of the stage, facing away from the audience, mumbling and rocking up and down on his heels. He never bothered to place his microphone back on its stand. He still held it down at his side while she worked through her routine.

One night I saw the Priestess, during a show, at the side of the stage talking to Hieronymus and Jo-Jo. They nodded, serious, and moved away from her into the smoke and the sweating crowd. She walked over to me.

"The Harrowing of Hell has begun," she said, cupping her hand to my ear.

I nodded, smiled, waited for a moment of clarity that didn't come.

"What?" I asked

"Janis is dead." I felt my knees begin to buckle

"What?" I repeated, even though I knew.

I remembered running through the hallway of a narrow apartment, inside a rundown Victorian. Bookcases lined with battered paperbacks made the hall difficult to negotiate at full speed.

A large man in jeans and a leather vest loomed in front of me.

I shot him with the pistol in my hand.

He grabbed his shoulder and I shot him again.

The side of his head blew away, spraying blood and brains across the ceiling.

Janis Joplin sat calmly in the kitchen, waiting for me, a bowl of Corn Flakes on the table, an artist's sketchbook beside it. Her hair was a tangle of curls. She took a swig from a ceramic mug and winked at me. My heart raced. It was only a matter of time until somebody responded to the gunshots. I had to get moving, dump the weapon, fade into a bolt hole, clean up the loose ends.

But first I had to finish what I came here to do.

My hand shook.

I emptied the revolver.

I looked for the back door, found it. Janis' head lay crumpled in corn flakes. I didn't wait to see the color of the milk.

I fled, hopped a fence outside and found an alleyway that led to the street.

There is no way of escaping who you are or what you've been. All strategies end in suffering and pain. Pleasure is fleeting. All we want is illusion. We are never free, never alone. We seldom make the right choices. And even then, it seldom matters. All smiles are grinning skulls; all tears are crocodile's. I know because I smiled when Janis gave me the word that unlocked the bound suggestion inside my brain.

"Look," she'd said, holding up the sketchbook. A detailed pencil sketch of my face starred back at me. I took the sketchbook with me. After I'd jumped the fence, disposed of gun and gloves, a couple of bricks of heroin and a syringe, I sat at a local coffee shop and looked more carefully through the book. It was filled with pages and pages of drawings of me, sometimes as many as three to a page. There were illustrations of me singing with the band, some were from shows, others must have from been drawn during rehearsals. In one The Prophet held my guitar by the neck and pointed at the strings, attempting to illustrate some point. When had she drawn that? Had it even happened? I couldn't remember.

"Blackberries," she had said, and my mind clicked open. "Blackberries, blackberries, blackberries."

I heard a scream and the lights in the cafe blinked several times before going out.

"Hold him," I heard Lamond shout as if from a great distance.

Everything was impossibly black; I felt pinned in place by a massive weight.

The blackness subsided.

A crowd had gathered around me. Lamond looked down at me, concerned. The Prophet turned me over onto my back. The Priestess smiled.

I smiled back, happy, ecstatic. I still remembered pulling the trigger, the sketchbook, the coffee shop. But I also knew, despite the clarity of those memories, that they hadn't happened.

"You've had a seizure," said Lamond.

"A vision," said The Prophet.

The Priestess starred down at me with vacant eyes. It was only then that I recognized her as the card player who'd auditioned for The Prophet when he'd taken me to the cliffs all those months ago.

"He's all right," said The Prophet. "Help me get him back to his room."

Lamond shrugged, a small gesture, absolving himself of responsibility. He mumbled something. A tall lanky kid with long blond hair and mutton chops helped The Prophet lift me to my feet. Together they bore my weight, although physically I felt fine.

Something inside my head, something dear to me, something at the core of who I was, felt like it had barely escaped annihilation and now hung by a strand as insubstantial as a cobweb.

"Janis?" I asked. The Prophet and the Priestess, and the kid sat at my table where Hieronymus and Jo-Jo had plotted with me to blow up the mint. I sat on my bed on the other side of the room.

"She's dead," said The Prophet

"I shot her," I said. I felt terrible, responsible, although I hadn't been in control; I'd been directed by some unseen force. *Hadn't I?*

Someone had planted the orders in my brain, right? Or, no, Janis had said something, and then I had . . . what?

"I don't think so," said The Prophet. "Florence and Johnny said that she overdosed on heroin, but at this point anything is possible." I remembered throwing the sandwich bag filled with heroin over the fence onto a neighbor's backyard lawn. I'd stumbled into the man in the hall and had to take him out, made too much noise, otherwise I'd have . . . have what? . . . done things differently?

The Prophet dragged the story out of me, like I was a psychiatric patient describing a recent nightmare. "You had a vision," he said. "Nothing more. A lucid one from another world, a world in which, perhaps, you've done exactly what you say you've done. We all have them."

It sounded almost reasonable. But we all *who*?

"I've tried to take all of you under my protection," he continued. "I've been wrong, though. Wrong about so many things." His voice faltered, less certain, now that the subject was somehow swinging back to himself. "I've taken all of you out of your various realities, given you lives that you were never meant to live. There is a price to pay for such things. I understand that now."

I'd fainted, had a vision, lost control. Wasn't I the one who should be flipping out, mumbling incoherently? What the hell was wrong with these people?

"I want you to read this book." He handed me a battered paperback, worn from many readings. Where had he been hiding that? Under his robes? Up a sleeve? It was some sort of pulp novel called *The Sinful Ones* by Fritz Leiber. "I have a lot to consider," he said. "I want you to think about the notebook you took from Janis' apartment, visualize it as best you can. I want to know everything about it: the drawings, the color and thickness of the paper, everything you can remember. I'll be back when you've had some rest." Prophet and Priestess stood up together and walked out the door.

"Hey man, you sure you're all right," asked the kid. I assured him that I was. I slept soundly for several hours but did not dream.

The kid was still there when I awoke in the middle of the night. He sat at my kitchen table reading the slim volume The

Prophet had given me. He looked up when he felt me staring at him.

"Oh," he said. "This is a good book."

I gurgled something intended to be a response and he brought me a glass of water.

"Thanks," I said.

The kid had taken my shoes off after I'd gone to sleep, but I still wore yesterday's jeans and T-shirt. My forehead felt like I'd been hit with a two-by-four.

"There's food in the fridge," I said. I slipped into the shower. The warm water made me feel more human. It was nice to have a door between me and the kid, a chance to take stock, but the truth was that I knew neither the rules nor the stakes of the game.

I toweled off and took a handful of aspirin. Why didn't I keep anything stronger?

I opened the door to the smell of fried eggs.

"I didn't catch your name," I said, extending my right hand while holding my towel around my waist with the other.

"Oliver," he said.

I must have cocked my head quizzically.

"My friends call me Vee."

"Okay, Vee. Tell me about the book." Some of the books The Prophet had given me were abstract to the point of incomprehensibility.

"It's a novel," said Vee. "There's this guy. He works nine-to-five in an office downtown. There's nothing special about him. He meets an upset girl. After that he discovers other people who are behaving oddly that nobody else seems to notice. The premise is that the universe is a giant machine in which the people are the gears that keep everything in motion. When the hero stops doing his part in the machine it keeps moving without him. When he deviates from the pattern, only the others who have also broken their own patterns can see him. Everybody else acts as if he's still performing his job."

I stood with my back to the kid while I dressed. I took my gun from the dresser, took the bullets out, reloaded, and placed it back beneath the pile of clean socks. It was the same gun I'd used to kill Joplin, but all the bullets where still there and it hadn't been fired in months.

"There's a bunch of racy stuff thrown in, but the author seems to be making the point that most of the people who achieve freedom of awareness are content to live off the work of the others who are little more than puppets, automatons really."

"Except the hero?" I ventured.

"Except the hero."

Well that seemed clear enough, but it still didn't answer any of my questions.

"Do you remember where you were when you had the sketchbook," asked The Prophet. We stood outside the coffee shop, looking inside through the large plate windows. The sun was out, but shone only dimly against the windows.

"I was in a booth," I said, pointing. The last one, by the counter."

How had he found this place? I didn't think it really existed.

"Tell me everything you can. What color is the sketchbook?"

"Brown. The cover is thick, like cardboard. Denser, but not as heavy. The white paper is flecked with tiny strands of colored materials."

"When the lights went out, where was the book?

"On the table."

"Were the pages open? Were you still holding it?"

"Yes."

"What happened to the book?"

"What do you mean?"

"Did you put the book back on the table? Did it fall out of your hands? Fall off the table?"

"I don't know."

"This is important. I want you to think about this, carefully. Close your eyes and visualize yourself holding the book."

I closed my eyes. "I don't remember."

"That's unfortunate, but right now I want you to visualize the events, not as they occurred, but from outside your body as if you'd watched everything as it happened to you. There are no wrong answers, just tell me the first thing that occurs to you."

"Okay."

"You're holding the book?"

"Yes."

"How?"

"The back of the sketchbook is flat across the table. I'm flipping through the pictures with my thumb. I've got a cup of coffee in my other hand."

"That's when the lights go out?"

"They flicker."

"The lights? Or your perception?"

"I'm not sure."

"That's the last thing you remember?"

"Yes."

"I want you to put the cup of coffee down."

"Excuse me?"

"What kind of cup is it? A mug?"

"Cup and saucer."

"I want you to visualize yourself putting the cup back on the saucer. Then I want you to carefully close the cover of the sketchbook and place it on the table, so that the pages run parallel with the wall. Now open your eyes."

Nothing had changed. I half expected to see the notebook on the table, but a pair of teenagers hunched over schoolbooks sat there now.

"Were any of the waitresses present."

There were only two. Both wore yellow dresses with black aprons and had their hair pulled back.

"The blond."

"Close your eyes."

I did.

I could hear him tapping his heel to the ground in rhythm.

"I need you to stand up from the table and walk away. Walk out the door, but leave your point of vision inside the shop. The blond waitress sees your sketchbook, picks it up. She looks at the door, but you are already gone. She carries it behind the counter and places it in an orange milk crate on a shelf beneath the cash register. Keep your eyes closed."

"Now run through it again in your mind, the series of events, and then do it again until I tell you to stop." I did. Saucer. Notebook. Stand up. Walk out. Blond waitress. Orange milk crate. Saucer. Notebook. Stand up. Walk out. Blond waitress. Orange milk crate.

The Prophet began to hum and then started tapping me on the chest.

"Now let's go inside. You can open your eyes now."

I followed The Prophet inside to the counter. He asked the cashier about the notebook. She paused for a moment and then reached beneath the register, pulling out a milk crate.

"Is this it?" she asked.

It was. Everything was just as The Prophet had had me imagine it, except that the milk crate was blue.

Jo-Jo came up to me before a show, hemming me in before I had an opportunity to walk away. I sat beside the stage, my guitar held awkwardly in my lap as I absently prepared to tune it. Hieronymus, draped in a big faux fur coat and yellow hat, hung back, hands in furry pockets. Jo-Jo smiled and put his hand out. I put my pick in my mouth. We clasped hands. Jo-Jo wore a neat green turtleneck and brown knit, stovepiped-leg pants.

"Looking good," he said.

What was this?

"You think you've got it all figured out?" he said, nodding as he pulled me close enough to whisper in my ear. "That it's going to be this easy?"

"I don't know what you're talking about."

"Right," he said, saluting Hieronymus, "just as we thought."

He faded back like we'd decided something, smiling and nodding at me. I wiped my hand on my pants but I couldn't get the cold clam of his hand off mine.

"When do the living walk the paths of the dead?" The Prophet asked. Had we been rehearsing? Playing? I couldn't remember. We were walking down a street I'd never seen. Bright red trees overhung the road, their leaves filling up the gutters like paint. Odd, delicately thin cars that couldn't have held more than a single passenger lined the streets. We paused, waiting for a street light for what seemed like an eternity.

"When they're dead, too?" I asked, wearily. He insisted on asking me questions as if I were a philosophy major or a student of divinity. No matter how much I read, it was seldom enough.

The Prophet shook his head, the teacher reproving.

"You're a little overwhelmed, aren't you?" he said. "No—look, when the worlds are out of balance. When the worlds need to find equilibrium, that's when. Things must be taken and placed in and out of worlds—like shifting weights on scales that measure everything. Except it's not as simple as two sides to this scale—it's got dimensions, dimensions few of us have ever imagined. And somehow I've got to find a stillpoint where it all balances."

"Like algebra?" I ventured. "Like very complicated algebra."

The Prophet paused, considering, looking up over his left shoulder at nothing.

"Perhaps," he said, clearly humoring my simple assertion. "When it's time to let all hell break loose," he continued, "when everything is upside down. Topsy-turvy. When dreams are torn asunder. When the battle is lost or won. Perhaps then we walk with the dead."

The light finally flashed green and we found ourselves at the back of a stage as we walked around the corner. A show was going on in front of us. The Sun Dreamers played a wheeling kaleidoscope of sound, and The Prophet and I stood back and above, looking on as the galaxy spun, turning straw into gold.

"Which do you think it should be?"

Now you can think me a fool—now I probably think I am—but this was real with everything up for grabs on my say so. I did not want my "dreams torn asunder," again. I knew he had the power to do that.

"The world needs to live," I said. I had no argument to back that up and just hoped he'd take my word.

"I could leave you behind out here," he said, "as a counterweight. A living man in the barrows of the dead forever."

I looked down. That's where we'd been, I understood, now. We were still there, in between, liminal.

I felt tears, unbidden, beginning to well up behind my eyes. Where were we? What had happened to the stage, to the Dreamers? I tore my gaze from him and looked *back*. We were outside of everything on tracks of sand. Under bright stars spinning. There was a river flowing out of the sky.

"I want to live," I choked.

The Prophet leaned in closer to me, taking off his sunglasses.

"Then why have you been acting like an asshole all this time? The world could have used your help long before now."

Beside us, looming out of the sand, was a pyramid. It lay snug by the river where its waters came rushing to ground and flowed away. I could see inside the pyramid, somehow. There were rooms and rooms of darkness, full of the dead, milling about, blankly staring, pointlessly shuffling, no longer thinking, passing each other without touching. Dead and lost.

Over his shoulder, I could see the man I'd shot so recently. He was talking with Janis. They seemed to be waiting for something to come down the river. Maybe a ferryman like Charon. The two of them shared a joint. The man with the bullet in his brain blew smoke out the hole in the side of his head, making Janis laugh.

"I don't know," I said, desperately.

"Maybe it's a matter of perspective," The Prophet said.

Yes, it is, I thought. Could The Prophet keep plucking magic from this place forever, shaping it to his whim, without putting anything back?

I sat down where I was, in the sand. The corridors of the dead seemed to stretch forever in every direction, spiraling out of the pyramid, shooting through and around the stars.

"I'll stay," I said, resigned, tired beyond belief. I wanted nothing more than to curl up on the banks of the river and sleep among the reeds, on the off chance that I'd wake up in my own bed, but if not . . .

"Naw, you don't have to—I was just fucking with you. Sometimes I'm an asshole, too, you know?"

I looked at him and he was smiling.

"But maybe things will be different now, because you would have stayed."

"Yeah?"

"Sure. Could be. What do I know? I'm just a conduit. Like a spigot that's left on and flooded the garden. I don't know anything. Except that I'm tired of being used." He frowned. "I'm going to make it stop."

"The world?"

"No—the manipulation of the world by something I don't yet understand."

"OK," I said.

"OK," he said, and he began to sing.

He helped me up to my feet and we moved upstage, passed the necropolis of the pyramid, back into the world. From his robes, he pulled out the notebook, Janis's sketches and doodles of me.

As we moved from sand to wood, I was startled to confront Lamond's headless body. He stood, holding a rifle facing downstage and I knew things weren't what they seemed. There seemed to be a lot of people in action everywhere, some running away, some grooving to the music still, the beat of which never stopped, and some fighting. There were wolves out there, some wearing clothing as if they'd stepped out of the pages of a Saturday morning cartoon. And somewhere just in front of the stage, a great bear stood up on its hind legs and roared a warning. I remembered it playing with us, in my dreams. I decided it was on our side, if that even mattered.

When The Prophet hit the mike his voice filled the theater. He sang the world together, smoothing its edges, like an artist working a potter's wheel, wetting the clay malleable, making something whole and beautiful and right. I have no idea what he said but everyone slowed and stopped whatever they had been doing and watched him. And he took the notebook up and burned it in his hands. When he lifted it up, I saw Jo-Jo and Hieronymus stand up, comically pantomiming "that's it" to each other, one pointing, the other holding his hat. The Prophet didn't light a match or anything like that; he just seemed to rub his fingers together and the notebook went up in flames, curling, blackening, and then gone. Hieronymus and Jo-Jo did the same: curling, blackening, then gone.

I didn't have to look back to know there was no pyramid, no river. I groped like a blind man for my instrument and when I found it, I played the sun up in the sky. I hadn't known I could do that.

I slept for too many hours, woken up at last by the sound of knocking on my front door. I half-expected to see my bumbling evil twins, but found Lamond, The Prophet, and the Priestess camped outside.

"Great set," Lamond said to me and walked in as if the three of them came by my apartment all the time. Prophet and Priestess followed behind. I went to the kitchen sink and ran cold water over my hands and face.

The Prophet placed a canvas duffel bag on the kitchen table and proceeded to take out several incense burners, loose pages in plastic sleeves with diagrams of what looked like eyes and pyramids, and two 45 recordings of "Piece of My Heart," one recorded by Janis Joplin in 1968 and the other, the original recording, by Erma Franklin, Aretha's sister, recorded the year before.

"Séance," said Lamond when I asked.

"Of course," I replied. The Prophet didn't bother to look up. Chalk, charcoal pencils, pens, paints and, at last, the notebook emerged from The Prophet's bag, placed on the table, and the incense burners lit.

I sat on one side of The Prophet with Lamond on the other. The Priestess remained standing.

"Shouldn't we hold hands?" I asked. Nobody said a word. Lamond glared at me with enough menace that I decided to shut up.

"Put this on." The Prophet handed me the two recordings.

I looked at Lamond.

"Play the other one first." I grabbed my plastic, orange and yellow record player from the top shelf of my closet and plugged it in. It was a cheap child's toy with a built-in speaker. I lifted the lid, placed the Erma Franklin recording on the turn table, lifted the arm and placed it in the groove.

The crinkly sound of static filled the room, followed by a simple piano melody. The Priestess sang along with Franklin's voice. The first few notes were simple, too, but once the backup singers slid in behind the two of them, the intensity rose. Franklin's version was noticeably different than Janis Joplin's . . . and The Priestess' different still, too tinny, too white.

The record rolled for just over two minutes. The needle played to the end, popped the speakers when it reached the very end, and the arm retracted.

Where Franklin's version was a powerful performance, an emotional testament that no matter what her man did to her she would not be diminished, Joplin's, by contrast was Christ-like. She seemed angry at times, occasionally wistful, but the piece-by-piece destruction of her heart seemed like it would ultimately lead to some sort of redemption, a Eucharist. But for whom?

The Priestess dropped to a deeper register as Joplin started up, but then she began dancing with her eyes closed. Her voice tightened and she began to hit the right notes.

The record ended and she was still swaying.

She opened her eyes and looked me directly in the face.

"I knew you'd be back," she said and she laughed, a wild cackle. She turned to face The Prophet. "Hi, Ken. I see you got my message."

The Priestess—no, Janis, she moved like Janis, her wrist loose and casual, her back stooped but not bent, as if always mid-shrug, the way her legs bowed a bit, suddenly she was Janis, spooky and uncanny her; Janis stood up and moved over to my broken down couch and began explaining the rules of the dead to us. Telling us we didn't have much time. The Prophet and I sat before her on the floor on cushions stained with food and drink, burned by joints and incense sticks, discolored by I don't know what—blood or vomit cleaned up by bleach, it seemed. Everything smelled like deep down wet—a mold at the soul that never dried or a tincture of skunk smell you can't ever quite cover over; everything smelled fecund and overripe and bursting with life and death.

I took a huge hit of it all, breathing deep, shaking my head, trying to understand. But the talk—the talk buzzed in my head—I can't explain to you all they said. Everything. Nothing. Lamond didn't even try to listen but sat against a wall near the window playing his guitar, bent over each chord like he would learn it more deeply with some kind of sheer super-concentration; maybe he was on lookout in case the wolves or the bears came. I felt insane that night; I felt moved to tears, bored, startled, asleep, dead. They seemed to say one word over and over. They talked all night. They explored all the details of their lives—of other lives they had each lived in other times, other worlds, where they had been lovers, friends, enemies. I gathered at last that they were translating something—and about dawn, with a faint light rising like an impossible act of grace—why should the darkness ever lift? why did we deserve such mercy?—I understood at last that they translated something written on the inside of a coffin.

"Sarcophagus," The Prophet said.

"You saw words?" I asked, throaty with fatigue.

"Not me—not me me, you know," Janis said (which is ironic, I knew, even though I had long ceased to even see her "conduit," my bandmate, the Priestess—she was Janis, but not, and dead besides, and . . . my mind reeled and refused to think).

I made a face, trying to feel like—I don't know—myself. I looked at her. Janis wore a sheer scarf of many colors, ripped jeans, granny glasses that threatened to drop off always, a wry, detached smile, a lost look in her eyes but a knowing way about it all, jumbled together as she was; she knew everything, was cooler, somehow, then I could imagine—she was Janis—but could not be; she was impossible. She turned her head in puzzlement.

"Why would I be buried in a sarcophagus anyway," she said. "I was cremated and my ashes spread across Stinson Beach."

I laughed nervously.

"Was I there?"

"You will be."

"Well, I . . ."

"Earlier incarnations, see?"

"Emanations?"

"No, not this time."

I nodded like this all made sense. The student taking notes for the test: incarnations, not emanations. Check.

"See. On the inside walls, Baby," The Prophet said, leaning over from his pillow, suddenly close as if he would fall in to me. I put my hands up and caught his hand as he gestured out to me. It was rough and hot. He was sweating but I was cold. "The ancient Egyptians knew all this shit and they wrote instructions, warnings to avoid the traps and snares of the underworld, the journey into the afterlife—the otherlife. We need to know that now if I'm going to finish doing what *you* said I should."

"What I . . ." I trailed off. I guess I'd told him to save the thing, if he could. I thought he had—or was that still to come? The music never stopped—the beat—I heard it now—at heart's core, below the earth. Did my brain always feel so thick, desert sand packed behind my eyes, piling up to my forehead, a sharp pyramid wedged point ways in between my eyes? I thought I might scream if they kept talking to me.

"You said I should try to stop it all from ending. So I am, by giving up."

"You're going to kill yourself?"

Janis laughed at me, incredulous.

"Of course not."

"He doesn't understand," The Prophet said, pulling his hand from mine.

"I thought you said he got me through?"

"Yes, but . . . look." The Prophet turned to me. He peered at me over the sunglasses he had worn all night. "OK, Baby, what's the truth . . . of the world, you know?"

My throat constricted. This was it. I was going under the sand—or it felt like my neck constricted with bulging things— tumors like mushrooms sprouted suddenly cold and thick and choked me off. I couldn't speak while I thought of all I'd seen since I met The Prophet. The truth?

"The world," I croaked, a headache splitting my forehead, the weight of sand, all the time in the world jammed into the top of the hourglass impossibly, unbearably. I couldn't stand them and their talk or anything at all. I felt insubstantial, as if to touch something would make me cry and tear my skin—be crushed and broken, "its illusion. Its—"

Janis burst out laughing. "After all you've seen?" she said.

The Prophet shook his head. He scratched his neck.

"He did get you here. He's key, but he doesn't get it."

I started to cry then, dizzy with confusion. What did they know? What did they believe?

Suddenly things started to flow out—tumors deflating. Did I cry grains of sand? I lightened, and time ran down the hourglass again and I was left—nothing?

"What do you care about Ancient Egyptians?" I shouted, lost. The headache was broken and I wanted it back; I wanted the weight of things back. I was hysterical, I know. "Man, they're all dead. You're alive!" I paused, bewildered. "At least, you are," I said lamely to The Prophet.

Lamond, studiously trying to ignore this, snorted at me. I had the feeling he'd been in my spot before. It made me feel a wave of sympathy for him—maybe he was bravest of all behind his anger and bravado, because he just tried to hold on, to survive, like

I was, but all the time, for years, seeing things that his brother could do, knowing the places he could go. Why wasn't he insane?

I raved on, but don't know what I said, exactly. I was sick of The Prophet. Now I wanted them to stop desecrating the dead—disturbing the dead—with all their play-acting and occultism. I tried to lay the dead back in their graves.

"Gone," I spat out as I ran out of breath, "Dead. Past."

I keeled over, drool stringing from my mouth to pool on the floor below my face. When I straightened back to sitting on my pillow, wiping my chin, everyone looked at me impassively. The Prophet shrugged. He readjusted how he sat on his pillow—shook one leg as if it had fallen asleep.

"The past. The future. They're not . . ." he said. He sighed.

The morning light had reached the window and shone through now, visible through a marijuana haze of smoke—but who had been partaking?—we'd finished our last joint hours ago. Who were we then? How many days had passed? Which days? From when? Many different days from different ages, rolled into one?

"They're still around—present," Janis said. "There is only—"

She marked something out with one hand, awkwardly, as if she might topple down on the couch and fall asleep mid-sentence. Had I ever had a weirder conversation?

"Yes, but—"

I thought I was going to say something like, "exactly my point. Only now *now!*" like I'd proved something, when suddenly I saw it. Only present. Time a smear, a word connecting things. Nothing gone, only changed.

"The dead," Janis said, wearily, "the living—these might not be the most helpful distinctions, you see what I mean?"

She gestured down at herself—at the Priestess—at something of her before me.

I did see, actually. I'm not sure how I ended up sitting on the hardwood of the floor, splay-legged like a child with a ball, in front of me a piece of paper on which I was drawing hiero-glyphs—from memory. The floor lay littered with other pieces of paper. Janis leaned forward from the couch, her head resting on her hands, intent on my work.

"Don't stop," The Prophet said, "but we don't have time . . . for poetry." He waved his hand at what I was doing now. "Write some more about the sarcophagus, the warnings."

"Let him work," Janis said, without emotion.

I looked dazedly at the scatterings of scraps of paper spread along the floor, tacked to the wall. All by me?

"It looks like my turn again, anyway," Janis said. "I've read those inscriptions, waiting for the boat to come, and I haven't even told you about the alligators yet."

"Crocodiles," I said.

"Oh, yeah," she said, "right."

"The Nile. Crocodiles"

"I've seen some mean alligators in Texas," she said, "dated some, too."

The Prophet chuckled.

"Crocodiles," he said.

We drew a map of hell that ended at the gates of oblivion; a river to the edge of time that passed whirlpools of starry depths; a journey into a forest on a narrow path, overgrown and dark—into a mountainside, into darkness, through heat and pain, to gardens dark with sinuous rills. A way through peril to otherways—The Prophet's path.

In the waning light of evening, we rolled up our plans—our scattered chicken scratchings on tattered tears of paper—rolled it and tightened it with a yellow rubber band. The Prophet put it under his arm as he prepared to take off.

"Someone's got to die," I said, apropos of nothing.

"You do learn fast," The Prophet said.

"I think I've got that covered," Janis said.

I laughed nervously. Was that a joke?

After both The Prophet and Lamond, leading the listless Priestess by the hand, left me, I crawled into bed and slept—for nights on end—not consecutive nights, mind—but the forgotten ones, the leftovers, swept aside by history. I used about a hundred up. No one else was using them anyways.

The next morning, I couldn't hold it in my head anymore, whatever I thought I'd understood the night before. The Prophet was gone.

"He's not coming back for a while," Lamond said. "He's got

a journey to make. He said you'd take us where we needed to go next."

I didn't know anything about that.

"I need something to eat," I said. "I could eat a crocodile."

We made our way down to the Haight and ate at a little hippie hole-in-the wall with thick, wheaty pancakes covered in honey and butter with a mound of peppered potatoes high beside it. We didn't speak. I liked that about Lamond, after all his brother had to say. Back out on the street afterwards, with dirty cars with God's Eyes hanging from mirrors, tour buses of gawking Midwesterners, music rising from cross-legged longhairs, I shrugged at Lamond.

"I need awhile to think about it," I said.

"Sure," he said. "Take all the time in the hourglass."

I winced.

"Someone's got to die," Jo-Jo said to me. I already knew that.

Most of the band had drifted away as soon as The Prophet left on his journey. The Priestess was among the first to go, to my surprise. We never talked about the night she was Janis—I don't know what she knew. A core stayed around, waiting—Lamond, of course, some backup singers, Florence, most of the horn section. These people, like me, would wait forever. Our theater playing space emptied of stragglers. I don't think any more new space opened up in San Francisco for the tossed-up waves of flower children still cresting, but they couldn't seem to find us anymore, somehow. We'd lost our sun and so wandered into night. And all the satellites moved along on their lonely way in space without his gravity to hold us together. I sat, as I did most days, in the theater, trying to make the music sound right—but it didn't.

"I know," I said, "someone has to . . ."

Hieronymus grunted. We huddled together in a tight circle in the cavernous gloom at the back of the old stage, a council deciding fate. Old men going thumbs up, thumbs down—who lives and who doesn't. Empty boxes, loose cords, empty food containers lay about. There was a big box of cast off costumes that looked especially pathetic and abandoned now, as if the people in them had deflated instead of taken them off. Jo-Jo had on a loose faux-Indian print shirt, jeans and sandals. He had a colorful bead headband that hourglassed his new afro and a cheesy mustache. Hieronymus had on a trench coat, dark cowboy hat and glasses, like he was about to shake me down for money owed. He sort of was.

"Look, I'll do it," Jo-Jo said. "I've been sending the reports in anyway. I've been carrying you for some time with . . . HQ."

I looked away. I pretended I didn't hear him say anything that stupid. HQ? What junior spy manual from the back of the comic book did he get that from?

"I'll go," he said. "M-m-me."

"Really," I said. "You'd do that for me?"

"Not that. It just—feels right."

I looked back at him and he was me. He still wore the lame outfit but he was me, as I had been. It was like looking in a mirror—to the past, distorted. I was someone else now. He was the me who could return to . . . all the things I left, things I couldn't even think of or understand anymore. Did I really shoot someone in his sleep just because someone told me to? What kind of asshole does that? I looked away from myself then, the me standing before me, eager to go back—to be the sacrifice called for.

"They'll never notice you were gone," he said, "at HQ," he added, like he was really getting the spy lingo down.

I didn't crack a smile out of respect for the dead, or the soon to be.

"Really, it's more like I was never really there," I said.

Jo-Jo shook hands with me (but I still couldn't look him in the eye again). Then he shook hands with Hieronymus. Then he walked out. Not through the door. Just out. Do I really need to explain? Still?

Hieronymus stood there for a while. I broke out of my musical doodlings and found a tune, something coming together in my mind. I followed it where it led, thinking about how it could be the foundation of a song. Hieronymus cleared his throat.

"Yeah?" I said.

"Well, you know." Hieronymus never did like to speak. This seemed like a prelude to something longer. I stopped playing. "Like at the end of The Tempest. Prospero let Ariel go, too. Can I—?"

"Go?"

He reddened.

"Go," I said. He nodded and turned—like a funny turning image of a mirror falling, suddenly righted—into a bird—a little black thing with a white breast and red flaked along its neck; he flew away, singing songs of easeful death. I realized he was singing my new tune. I raised a hand in wonder, and laughed.

When I walked outside, I noticed my shadow was back, wavy but there. I think I had misplaced it for some time. When had I last had the sun on my face?

"Hello," I said, "which way?"

I led the core of our band up into the Northern California wilds and got us lost. We founded a commune of our own to hunker down in and wait for the next chapter. I knew The Prophet, after he had harrowed hell, would be back. We would need to be sharp, on top of our game, when the time came. When I found the spot, Florence took over again and Lamond kept us working—kept us in food and sundries. We played music—played and played—finding something there that does not belong in stories: it was a great time and I was at peace. And The Prophet did return of course, but that story is not this one. I leave that song to be played by another player, closer to the beat of it; someone who can hum it in their sleep. I will only say: if Hieronymus was my Ariel, then Jo-Jo was my Caliban, right? My monster. And I could only think of what Prospero said at the end of Shakespeare's last play.

"This thing of darkness," I tell myself whenever I lose heart, "I acknowledge mine."

Our music jostled up and out, rising high as those Northern California redwoods that seem to scrape the sky. They live before us and after us and understand things they whisper to us in our quietest dreams. You would not believe how high those trees grew, even if you saw them yourself. But then, who could really believe anything these days? Or who could understand how carefully we must choose what we fill with our faith—for grace is something, I knew now, that is not just given to us but something we must ask for. See? Be careful not just what you believe, but how. And, most importantly, why.

6
THE MOTHERSHIP
CONNECTION

San Francisco, 1976

ﬡN OPEN DOORWAY, HANGING ABOVE ME IN THE
pale sky, gaped in the side of the disc-shaped spaceship,
framing the spaceman—a black man in mirrored thigh high
boots, silver sparkle shorts, and no shirt. He wore a 50's-style
bubble helmet, clear so you could see the silver headgear that ac-
centuated his massive afro. He had a great, wild beard, tufts sticking out below the helmet.

He removed the helmet from his head, and I could see now
that it was, in fact, a very large, upside down fishbowl with a piece
of corrugated tubing dangling from the open top, a cheap plastic
castle of some sort welded to the bottom. The spaceman shouted
from high above me, but I could understand what he said clearly.

"I come in peace," he said, showing me his hands. "Take me
to the funk."

No, that's not what he said first. First came the sound—
Aauurch!
—like a jet plane mixed with the horn of a clown car—
Aauurch!
What? I blinked from staring too long. I lay with my back on
grass, the expanse of sky—the silver disc—the man in the doorway—far above me. How had I gotten here? It was all, I thought,
a dream I had had many times.

"Aauurch," the sparkle-shorted spaceman shouted to me from
the sky as he fell.

He looked off-kilter somehow, one side of him larger than the other, as he spun down closer and closer, descending toward me. It was all part of the beautiful dream I had been having for years. I always awoke before he landed.

This time was not any different. Except in every possible way.

I woke, opening my eyes and finding myself sprawled on the sidewalk, my head precariously close to a curb, several feet from a rain gutter. Feeling came back to me slowly as I felt pins and needles all over my body. A few bruises, too. I crawled on to nearby grass and lay on my back. The dream of the spaceman clung to me, but other memories returned.

I remembered a party that had sped out of control. I'd drunk half a bottle of whiskey to wash down several tabs of acid I'd been given by a dark-bearded shaman named Wild Side. Although in my memory I'd been sure he was a shaman, his image in my mind's eye looked much more like a hippie who'd forgotten that the 60's had ended seven years earlier.

I couldn't remember a thing after drinking the whisky except the dream of the spaceman.

A worn down motel stood nearby, fronted by palms, oddly built sideways to the rolling waves, refusing the magnificent view of the Pacific Ocean near San Francisco's Land's End.

When I finally thought to look up, I saw the spaceship, hanging silently like a silver piñata in search of a party. But I was awake.

I sat up quickly and my head swirled and I thought I might pass out.

"Time like a bullet lodges in my heart," I thought. "The loneliness of an empty dream is memory." They were the words the shaman, Wild Side, had made me repeat the previous evening, saying that they were very important and that I mustn't forget them, but the sentences meant nothing to me now—they were an answer to which I no longer knew the question.

The words flowed through my mind as the spaceman, turning like a rag doll, fell into the ocean, beyond my vision. I gaped a moment as the silver disc began to slowly float away out over the water.

I struggled to my feet. My mouth was dry, coated with the peculiar flavors of cigarette smoke, whiskey, and vomit. I stumbled across the street toward the water. I looked over the concrete railing and saw people on the beach: Frisbee players, kite flyers, dogs walking their people, wanderers whose lonely footsteps led along the ocean's verge. None of them seemed to notice anything amiss.

The spaceman had plunged into the Ocean. No one had noticed. Except me.

"Hey!" I said "Hey! Hey!" throwing up my hands.

I could see something silver out in the distance, in the water, sparkling flotsam in the waves.

I ran down concrete steps, falling when I sank in soft sand at the bottom. I shouted and ran into the water, the ocean rising to meet me, sucking me in.

The body of the spaceman floated ominously face down, just beyond the surf. I plunged under the next wave and paddled out to him—he was much larger than I had realized. I turned him over and, hooking his arm under one shoulder, dragged him to shore.

I shouted for help but still no one seemed to notice.

I knelt beside the spaceman, who coughed, spilling water out of his mouth. I held him in my arms to keep him from falling back into the shallow surf, shielding him as the waves reached out to reclaim us both. The spaceman had a worn face with baby cheeks. Unexpectedly, he opened his eyes and grinned up at me. He reached out and touched my face.

I started as if from an electric shock.

"Have you lost it?" he said, sadness and forgiveness in his eyes.

Around me, the light became more intense, preternaturally clear. I could see where the mylar and cheap gem studs on his costume had begun to fray. His whole outfit, wet and clinging to his body, seemed cheaply put together from the racks of a thrift store, perhaps several; none of the pieces belonged together.

Doubled over, with my arms still around him, he gradually regained his footing. He looked at me, a beatific smile on his face.

"There's no time," the spaceman said.

"Time's like a bullet," I said.

"I need Saul. You can take me to him." It wasn't a question. "He can find what you lost."

I nodded.

He reached back behind himself and fished out a soggy spiral bound notebook he had stuffed into his waistband.

"We need this," he said, thoughtfully. It was ruined, ink

smeared, pages hopelessly meshed together and disintegrating. "I can find another. I left it somewhere in my dreams."

He handed the ruined notebook to me and I clutched it. He straightened up.

"Take me to Saul," he said.

I can do that, I thought. *Saul lives in me.*

"The loneliness of an empty dream is memory," I said.

"Then stand up, my righteous man, and show me into the empty dream," he said. He stared into me like he was rummaging inside my head, finding it broken, inside my heart, finding it flawed, inside my soul, finding it stained—but accepting me anyway. "We have places to be, people to see¼music to make."

We?

I knew Saul. I'd said so, or perhaps only thought so?

"Tell me about Saul," the spaceman said, "as we move¼tell me the story."

I told him everything, like he was my shrink, or just the last person I found beside me on my deathbed when I had only moments to confess.

Saul Beckman played left field the day he underwent his transformation. It was a bright March day in San Francisco, cold dew clinging to the grass as we shagged baseballs beneath a high blue sky sprinkled with white puffs of clouds. Our cleats kicked up large divots as we moved, preparing for what would be yet another season for the green and gold of Everett Junior High.

I didn't see him fall.

Coach was showing me how to pivot my hips, to turn quickly and track down a long flyball. John Hall yelled for Coach. That's when I looked over and saw Saul crumpled on the ground. He'd toppled forward, lying face down in the wet grass.

Johnny Kimmelman knelt beside Saul, talking to him. Coach ran over to them. The rest of us approached at a slower gait, not sure what had happened, but wanting to be ready in case there was something we could do.

Johnny and Coach turned him over on his back. He lay there for a few seconds with his eyes closed, before something spooked him and he bolted to his feet, backing away from us. He looked at the baseball glove he was still wearing, took it off with his right hand and dropped it on the ground.

"Aauurch," he said.

Then he turned and ran, flapping his arms.

Saul wasn't very fast, even with a head start. We corralled him and led him back to the team bus. Coach asked him simple questions, the kind you ask somebody who has had a concussion, but Saul was incoherent and unable to string more than a couple of words together.

Later, in the hallways, I asked him what happened.

"I was an eagle," he said "Not at the end, man. I knew I was just a stupid kid flapping his arms. But for a second there . . . an eagle."

"Right," I said.

We didn't see Saul after that. I don't think he wanted to talk to me after his strange confession. The baseball season came and went. I watched almost all of it from the bench. I never did get my hips to turn properly, not in the outfield and even less at the plate where shifting my weight might have allowed me to hit the ball past the drawn in infielders who crept ever closer when I came to bat.

I didn't see Saul again until the summer after I washed out at college. I was delivering bottles of Dr. Tima's Honey Root Beer and Cola to the Jewish Temple on Clement Street. Dr. Tima's Honey Root Beer was a sweet, all natural soda that foamed up into a frothy lather when poured. The soda was delicious, made from all natural ingredients, and would have been more successful except that thick head of foam refused to settle back into the glass. The soda had to be poured slowly, but at least it was Kosher.

I'd left the truck double parked outside and was maneuvering my cart slowly along the carpet in the main room so as not to topple any of the boxes. I recognized Saul at one of the tables, clean shaven among a room full of old bearded men in black hats.

He was taller and paler, a bit more spindly, but it was him. I nodded to Saul as one of the bearded men took my clipboard and signed for the delivery. Saul's stare was vacant. I might as well have made eye contact with the couch. It wasn't that he didn't recognize me as much as I wasn't there at all.

A large black man came out of the synagogue as I packed up the truck. The man walked up to the window as I entered the cab. He waved his arms, signaling me to roll down my window, which I did, and he handed me a note written on yellow paper and walked back inside.

> Saul Beckman would like to see you. Tonight
> at five o'clock at the Blue Front Deli.

The note had been torn off a yellow, legal notepad and then folded in half. The ballpoint hadn't worked right away. I could see where a false start had been made before a scribble at the bottom had freed up the ink of the pen.

I refolded the letter and placed it in my shirt pocket as I pulled away from the curb. The rest of my deliveries, no more than three or four stops, didn't take very long. There wasn't much demand that summer for a foamy drink sold mostly at small, independent health food stores.

I spotted the man who'd come out to the truck as soon as I entered the restaurant. He sat in a cramped wooden booth against the far wall, bundled up in loose fitting fatigues several sizes too large for him. Saul, sitting beside him with the same glassy stare I'd seen that afternoon, seemed diminished by comparison.

"Lamond," said the man, offering me a hand twice as large as my own.

I took his hand, feeling suddenly like a little boy. He grinned, waiting.

"Bob," I said. "Bobby."

"Okay, Bobby." I looked at Saul but he wasn't talking. "You live alone?"

I did.

"How much do you pay each month in rent?"

I named a figure that was almost twice what I paid. I wasn't sure what was happening, but I wasn't a complete rube.

The corner of Lamond's mouth twitched slightly. "Saul needs a roommate," he said. "He can't stay where he's been staying." I hesitated. "I'll pay his share of the rent."

"If it doesn't work out, it doesn't work out," he said. He took his wallet out of his pocket and counted out fifteen twenties and placed the pile on the table and pushed them toward me.

I placed my hand on the bills and began to pick up the money before I realized that that simple gesture went a long way towards committing me.

"That'll do for the first two months," he said and handed me a card.

The card didn't have his name.

"Egyptian Motherlode, band manager" was written beneath an embossed ankh. There was a telephone number with a local exchange.

"Keep calling," he said. "I don't have an answering service."

Lamond handed me another five dollars.

"I recommend the bagel dogs," he said and left. Saul still hadn't said a word.

Saul slept in the extra bed; he went to the bathroom; he showered. Occasionally he went back to the synagogue. But he seldom said much of anything and only rarely seemed to see me at all. Early on, I thought often of getting rid of Saul—handing him back somehow, like in he movies when someone would leave an unwanted baby on the church steps and ring the bell—but the packets of money, left in my mailbox in tattered envelopes without postmarks, kept me from making waves.

When he did talk he'd bring up odd subjects like reincarnation, astral projection, or alternate realities. Several times he told me that he'd been reborn in left field that day when he'd collapsed back in junior high school.

"This dude," he said once "was coming at me with a knife in the middle of the street. It was dark and the warm air smelled of diesel. I threw my hands up to ward him off and I fell on the curb. I coughed, felt blood in my mouth and on my chin, and a musical note, as if I was preparing to sing, caught in my throat. Then there was nothing but pain and darkness.

"I floated disembodied for a long time, concentrating on blocking out the pain, holding on to my thoughts, my identity, until I heard soft voices murmuring. I tried to follow them but didn't know how. And then the voices were louder and I could smell freshly cut grass and realized I was standing on my feet, outdoors, a long way from wherever I had been. New York, Los Angeles, Phoenix, Flagstaff? I no longer knew or cared.

"Everything seemed roughly the same, but everything was different; the world was somehow larger than it had been."

That was how he told stories. They stopped as surprisingly as they started. Sometimes he repeated the same story again later, in exactly the same way. Sometimes twice in a row. Every once in a while he'd describe a random detail, never sure if the image had just come into his mind or if it was a memory. It could be a black woman in an apron bending over a hot stove who he was sure was his real mother, or singing in a Baptist church full of the spirit–and he'd sing a few bars for me that sounded really good, even though his voice sounded raw, like he'd been drinking whiskey.

Once he told me that he had a memory of drinking and playing pool until the sun came up and that he'd been very happy in that pool hall. We caught a bus that evening and rode down to the wharf and found a table at a bar. Saul put a quarter on the table to reserve the next game. When it was our turn to play, he beat me soundly, not missing a single shot and drawing the attention of more than a few of the patrons. He won several hundred dollars that night. Although we never went back to the bar and never played pool again, I suspected that he occasionally slipped out to play. I certainly would have if I could shoot like that.

A young blond woman with dreadlocks showed up not long after that and said she was Saul's nurse, and she could help out. She came to the house at least a couple of times a week after that. Sometimes she stayed overnight in his room, but not often.

I lost my job and never found another. Saul's center of gravity pulled me firmly into his orbit before I quite realized what was happening. Late at night, when I couldn't sleep, I often feared I would become like him; that we would both sit in the apartment, in our separate rooms, staring at nothing all day while mysterious benefactors brought us supplies when they felt like it.

In fear of falling into the black hole of his marginal existence, I eventually stopped hanging around the apartment so much.

Sometimes I didn't return to the apartment for days. I began to drink, as if that would help.

Saul joined a band. Maybe it took me being gone to light a fire under Saul, or maybe it was just time for him to make a change. Saul joined a band that played old soul classics from the 1960s on the weekends, playing gigs wherever they could find them: weddings and bar mitzvahs at first, but later small clubs as the opening act to bands that would remain mostly forgotten. Saul was the group's lead singer, all five foot six inches of him. The band members were all younger than him and all white, but they poured everything they had into their performances, making up for a certain lack of originality with the brute force of their desire to perform.

Members of Egyptian Motherlode, the band that Lamond ran, would come to the sets and sometimes sit in on the sessions. They would huddle with Saul between sets, their hands and arms gesturing wildly, while Saul canted his head in contemplation and his eyes would light up like nothing I'd ever seen.

I don't know how to explain it, what began to happen. The band was not much, but Saul's singing was a revelation. His phrasing was distinctive, like a drum beat or a horn riff, racing ahead of the beat of the band. He sounded like a combination of James Brown and the great New Orleans R&B singer, Ernie K-Doe. Saul's vocals, like Saul himself, had no humor; they were passionate but didn't seem committed to any genuine emotion, except perhaps a yearning for the music.

I wondered how I'd missed his talent for all the years I knew him, how this tiny Jewish kid who barely seemed capable of speech could possess such a big voice overlaid with bold and original phrasing. And why there had been no sign of it in all of this time. No singing in the shower, humming a tune; I couldn't remember him even listening to the radio.

About a year or so into my tenure with Saul, Lamond showed up late one night at our door with a gun. An old .45, a large gun but small in his hand. He held it casually the whole time we talked on the stoop. He didn't point it at me or even seem to notice he carried it, but I couldn't keep my eyes off it. He explained, patiently, that I had to be sure to watch out for Saul and to take care, that bad things were coming, that everything was going to change. He said he had to go away, go north for a while, but he would still be sending money, and he would still be watching. Then he turned around and walked down the street with the gun still in hand, low at his side.

Always eccentric and a little crazy, Lamond seemed to be losing whatever grasp on reality he had left. If I were smart, I knew, I would use Lamond's behavior as a clear signal to leave the house and not look back. I considered it coldly, analytically. I didn't possess any trepidation or fear. I knew that I had little desire to start a new life. I didn't want to move back in with my parents, didn't want to find a job. I was comfortable enough where I was, with the rent paid–although God knew how long that would last. I wasn't going anywhere. My only worry was that as Saul loosened up and took control of his life that the two us would somehow trade places, that I would become the social pariah that nobody appeared to understand.

The Dalmatian Club where Saul's band played one night was just off Haight Street, near the panhandle. The inside of the club was painted white with small black spots placed at regular intervals. The lights splashed so brightly against the walls that there were hardly any shadows. It was a hard venue to play. Every fault—duct tape on the drum snare, the dandruff on the collar of a saxophonist, or the too dilated eyes of Saul Beckman—was exaggerated.

On this night Harold Lennox, the band's trumpet player, asked me to stick around after the set, through the next couple of acts, including a punk rock band whose lead singer kept a live parrot on his shoulder and a disco cover band that only knew about six songs, half of which sounded the same and two of which they played twice. When the disco band started to play, the club switched to black light. The theater went dark and the white walls and ceiling glowed as if the club itself hung suspended in stars—stars with a dirty floor, rickety chairs thrown against the walls, and angry drunks spinning and speaking incoherently.

Harold found me after the show and I waited with him, drink in hand, as everybody filed out. He motioned me to follow as he went looking for the manager.

"Just stand behind me," Harold said, "try to look tough."

This didn't sound promising for either Harold or myself. I was taller than most of the band members, particularly Saul, but I was also skinny. I doubted that my Chuck Taylor Converse, flared jeans, or my Farrah Fawcett T-shirt added much, if any, toughness. I pocketed my glasses, figuring that I didn't need to be able to see to look the part.

We walked past the bar and Harold peered into the kitchen, didn't see what he was looking for. The kitchen was dark and empty, with stools propped upside down on the counter. I looked questioning at Harold who shrugged.

We found the manager behind a desk covered in cassette tapes, hundreds if not thousands of them. A reel-to-reel machine took up part of a wall behind him, but it hadn't been used in a long time. A thin line of dust coated the present tape.

The man looked up at the two of us, surprised to see us, but unconcerned. I tried to look tough by straightening my chin and squinting my eyes, but his eyes and face were fixed on Harold, saving me from embarrassment.

"The answer is still no," he said.

"C'mon, man," said Harold. "We're ready. You know we are. You saw that audience." The audience had in fact been excited and grooving, but there'd only been about twelve people, half of which must have been there to see the other acts.

"If you want a better spot," the man said, "You've either got to bring in more people or you've got to pay a booking fee. There's no way around it. We're not a charity here."

"We can't pay the money," Harold said, "but people will come once they've seen us. You know they will." Harold's face had flushed and sweat beaded along his brow, for a brief instant I thought I was going to have to restrain him.

"When you've got the money," the man said calmly, "we can talk." He picked up the telephone receiver on his desk and pushed a button. "Right now, I've got a phone call I need to make."

Harold's chin sunk about an inch and he sputtered a couple of barely audible syllables.

"Tell you what," I said. The man looked up without moving his head. "Give us the second spot and we'll double the crowd."

"How will you manage that," he said. I could feel Harold's gaze on me, too, wondering the same thing.

"We'll manage," I said. "If we don't double the crowd, you can take all the money."

"Kid," he said, "I already take all the money." Then he laughed. "Sure, why not?"

I began managing the band.

We didn't get any more people to come see us when we played the second slot at the Dalmatian and we never played there again.

I changed the name of the group to The Solomon Blue Band and called what they played "Western Soul," a phrase I'd made up to capitalize on the popularity of "Northern" or "Blue Eyed" soul groups, designations that indicated that the performers, unlike the music they played, were white. I was able to get them better gigs, still nothing really special. But we started opening for Egyptian Motherlode when they played locally and sometimes when they went out on tour. They had a few hits to their credit, and drew fairly big crowds, although they were missing their lead singer, a man called The Prophet.

"He's on a vision quest," Lamond said. "He's going to want to meet Saul when he comes back, so keep him safe."

He didn't offer any other explanation.

Solomon Blue was a good warm up band. We played standard soul classics that everyone knew and we could be counted on to get the crowd moving, into it, ready for the main event. With Motherlode, you never knew what you were going to get. Their songs, often written by The Prophet, sometimes entirely improvised, tended toward themes of spirituality or a strange, surreal sort of gospel. Their deep, funky sets could be either brooding or rocking depending on the mood of the band.

Saul became Solomon, although we never legally changed his name.

Solomon was at his best singing hard driving funk. He learned how from Egyptian Motherlode. They groomed him, and talked to him about phrasing and the beat, but also about ghosts and emanations from the stars—the music of the spheres.

Nights after a show, I would lead him home. He would be catatonic. I would drop him in bed, and he'd sleep all the next day. That's where I expected to find him now, in his bed, awake but glassy-eyed, so that's where I took the spaceman who fell from the sky. But we didn't find him there. Instead we found two men in black suits, black ties over white shirts. They packed heat—pistol-like weapons with strange markings. We had entered the apartment without noticing them; I had fumbled the keys in the lock, then thrown them on a nearby table. We had walked along the narrow, Victorian hallway toward Saul's room at the back. The two men stepped into the hallway.

They raised their guns. The spaceman raised a hand.

"Stop," he said. He coughed, bending over. But the men did not shoot.

I heard a weird keening; it was coming from the spaceman.

"Drop," he said, "the guns." The words were spoken in a lilting accent, almost sung.

Two guns landed on the floor. The two men turned to face each other. They seemed surprised, unsure what to do next.

The spaceman, his hair still bristling with saltwater, shook his beard and wriggled his fingers. He spoke rapidly, and the sound was like scales played up and down on an instrument I had never heard before. He moved forward and touched their foreheads. Their faces looked to be made of twine, papier mâché and odds bits of metal. The two men crumpled to the floor, flattened and disappeared as if they'd been pushed out of existence, like paper slipped under a door.

The spaceman's strength left him suddenly and his legs collapsed. He leaned on my shoulder for support as I struggled to keep us both upright as I led him down the hallway, into Saul's empty room.

"They'll be back," the man said, gasping.

I remembered something Lamond had said—something I had taken for incoherent ramblings.

"Are you The Prophet?" I said. "You're The Prophet."

The spaceman stopped and, as if remembering over a long distance of years, said, "I've been called that."

"I heard you were coming," I said.

"I've arrived." He looked hard at me. "We need Saul. I need my notebook."

"Did the . . . black suits take Saul?"

"No, they wouldn't have been here waiting. They would have been long gone, through cracks in the cosmic egg."

On the table beside my keys we found a note from Saul—he was playing a gig with Motherlode that evening at an old warehouse south of Market. The Prophet was delighted, and the world around us brightened. I felt dizzy as if I had drunk two cocktails faster than I should.

"Where the fuck were you?" Lamond said, before taking The Prophet in a bear hug. The Prophet had taken an old sheet from Saul's room and tied it around himself, including around the top of his head like a kind of turban. His sparkling shorts peeked out on one side. Lamond wore jeans and nothing else, not even any shoes. Everyone else in the band had on colorful clothes, loose-fitting, bright, sparkling with glued-on glitter; they were wrapped in scarves, shaded in dark glasses, kicking up paint-splattered boots.

The Prophet returned the hug, but seemed to struggle before saying, "Lamond?"

"Yes, damn it, Lamond. Your brother."

"It's been so long."

"OK," Lamond said.

The music had begun, a deep funk groove with nowhere to go yet. The drummer, a guitarist in a diaper and a raincoat splattered with paint, and Lamond's bass had laid down the beat. Lamond had broken off to come off stage when he had seen The Prophet. But the music continued, unbroken. Saul stood among a knot of singers on the far side of the stage. The group on stage hummed and wailed around the grove. They had their arms around one another, like children or ecstatics in a church.

"There was a chance to fix everything that was broken, but I blew it," The Prophet said to Lamond. There were tears in his eyes now.

"Kenny," Lamond shouted back. "Forget it. Come play."

Lamond looked at me, pain etched on his face. He spoke to his brother.

"It's all right," he said.

"He took our chance. Now—it's over. I'm just trying to keep us from losing everything."

The Prophet looked down at his empty hands.

"And to keep a channel open where a few might get through. The god wants to walk the earth again, to destroy us. His avatars will confront us, obliterate us if they can. I need time. I need Solomon."

"Saul? He's over there," Lamond said, pointing. I pointed, too. The Prophet stumbled on stage. He took the microphone. Members of the band began to shout, to sing greetings, to cry, more of them came on stage, a dozen, more. Lamond began to play again, wandering back on stage.

"When I broke, I had to go, to learn more," The Prophet announced to the crowd. The audience seemed to take this as part of a conversation they had been having all along. I saw heads nod. People crowded the stage. They began to sway. "The gods were interfering, dreaming me into their worlds—their dimensions—trying to rob me of humanity's inheritance. But they still have much to learn. I can open doors, too."

At a hand signal, the music rose up, enveloped me. The Prophet began to sing. I took a deep breath and didn't breathe again for what seemed like hours on end.

I don't know how long passed until The Prophet came up to me. He leaned over me.

"Beware the Jubjub Bird," he wailed. The crowd roared its approval. "The jaws that bite—the claws that catch!"

He touched me and an electric current went through me again and I began to dance. Everywhere I looked I saw stars.

The concert started strong, but The Prophet soon tired. Not long after he finished his fourth number, a rambling chant of the names of ordinary and famous people along with the names of the planets in the solar system and the various moons of Jupiter, Lamond helped his brother off the stage, wrapping him in a blanket and giving him a cup of coffee in a Styrofoam cup. I followed and stood nearby, afterimages of a starry sky still fading in my eyes. The music continued on stage unabated.

The Prophet closed his eyes as if in sleep. Lamond took the cup from his hands and placed it on a nearby table.

"I couldn't shut the gate," The Prophet said. I nodded forlornly, but he was talking to Lamond.

Several Motherlode band members stood on stage, forming a circle again in which they joined hands and sung rounds of harmonies. The words were all improvised clichés on the themes of peace, brotherhood, forgiveness, and redemption. It sounded beautiful, perhaps it would even have been transformative for the right person, but it all faded into the background as I watched the pained look of resignation on Lamond's face.

"What does he want?" Lamond asked.

"He wants our world and our discoveries."

"What have we discovered?"

"Not us, this world. His world is round like ours but it floats alone in space with only the moon visible in the night sky. He'd never seen the stars until I brought them there."

"Until you *brought* them?"

"Yes. I expected to see stars. Sure they were all jumbled and out of order, constellations unlike any I'd ever seen. I thought I'd gone back in time and the stars were simply in an older alignment, but it was the result of our two realities merging, altering our perceptions."

"He's been after us all these years because our stars are pretty?"

"No, he wants the planets circling the stars. He believes that they each possess countless other dimensions. He could devour them for eternity."

"Are they?"

"I tried to tell him, 'no.' But if I can bring the stars to an ancient, alien Egypt maybe he can bring life to Mars. He's only just beginning to realize how vast distances can be. He has no concept of how cold and unforgiving it can be out there."

The Prophet laughed. He looked up and saw me with half-closed eyes.

"My rescuer," he called to me. "Where is Saul?" Although I didn't expect to see him, I looked out on the stage. The Prophet turned back to Lamond. "Is he ready?"

"He's made great strides," said Lamond, "but no."

"I'd hoped . . ."

"I know," said Lamond and took The Prophet's head in his hands and cradled it to his chest. "Soon, maybe . . ."

Harold, Saul, and I were out scouting. Solomon Blue's drummer was drinking again. Augustine's playing was still smooth and crisp, but we were worried about his moods and what would happen if he started missing gigs.

That night we were at The Wail & Wine, a little club tucked away between North Beach and the Financial District that would close within a month and never be known for much of anything. That night featured a jazz quartet that included a pianist, a bassist, a female vocalist who tried whenever possible to imitate Billie Holiday, a dynamite R&B saxophonist who had difficulty improvising, and a promising drummer named Elmer Vanguard who went on to be a bodyguard for several prominent local politicians. The room was dimly lit by high spots, turned down as low as they could go, with candles placed on the tables.

Harold nudged me and I opened my eyes, unaware if I'd just started to nod off or if I had already fallen asleep. The singer was relating a story about her man tracking her down to Chinatown in the middle of an unsatisfying tryst. The drummer popped the drum snare to indicate the boyfriend knocking on the door.

I thanked Harold, but he shook his head and flashed a thumb toward two figures sitting at a back table beneath a pair of stag's head trophies. I looked over at them, but their table appeared even more dimly lit than ours, and the shadows cast by their table lights distorted their features.

Saul looked over at them and frowned. They hadn't seemed to have noticed us looking at them yet, but they certainly would if their presence upset Saul. He would make sure they noticed us.

Gradually I realized that, lighting aside, their faces were unnaturally sharp and their noses were thin and impossible long. They were at least seven feet tall and must have been incredibly uncomfortable with their legs tucked up against the table and their shoulders hunched over it. They were stick figures in sports jackets with little red caps on top of their heads with strange characters on them that could have been Chinese or Arabic but didn't appear to be either.

The singer was pacing back and forth onstage, lamenting the loss of her boyfriend and how she was no longer welcome down in Chinatown.

I looked back at the figures and realized that they were almost as bored as I was. They weren't watching the show even though their faces were directed toward the stage. I could see strangely large pupils moving slowly back and forth, taking in the entire room.

I whispered to Harold, "Let's go." Harold tapped Saul on the shoulder and we stood up as quietly as we could, collecting our coats and leaving through a side door.

We found ourselves outside in narrow alley lined with trash bins.

"What was that about?" Harold asked as walked toward the street.

"I don't know," I said, just as we heard a loud piercing shriek. Something hit us from above and we fell to the ground, knocking over one of the bins.

Saul got to his feet first and threw his shoulder into something that squawked in pain or surprise. A lone white feather fluttered by my head. I crouched on my hands and knees, looking for something I could either attack or ward off. Harold was still on the ground.

One of the figures from the club towered over me. I threw my hands up in front of my face, preparing for a blow. Saul grabbed the creature around the waist and drove it into me. Its legs crashed into my side and its upper torso folded over my shoulder and upthrust arms. It flipped over me and landed on top of the row of trash cans which miraculously held firm, supporting the beast.

Saul grabbed my hand and pulled me up. Harold was finally on his feet and the three of us dashed out to the street and ran until we came across a cable car and jumped onboard.

"You were lucky," said The Prophet, "they were overconfident. They often carry sickle-bladed knives which they manipulate quite dexterously."

"What are they?" asked Harold.

"Specifically," asked The Prophet. "I don't know. Some kind of bird-like creature from an ancient Egypt that never existed in our realm. They work for a Sorcerer there who would very much like to question me further. I took from him . . . a book—that told me how to walk through worlds.

"Perhaps they were merely meant as a warning." The Prophet thought for a minute, a concerned look creasing his brow. "I have something that might protect you."

He reached into his coat and pulled out several hand tied leather necklaces with a grey stone-carved wolf's head encased in a golden eye.

"These may provide some protection. Otherwise, Saul, you may want to take on your eagle form. They would have a hard time containing you then."

Saul nodded like this was a possibility, one he just hadn't thought of yet.

The Solomon Blue Band practiced most nights in the basement of a tiny church on Bernal Heights. Sometimes Saul and I would get there in the early evening just as the wind was picking up and I'd park my little Honda Accord on the narrow, winding streets near the church. We'd bundle up with jackets and scarves and walk down to Mission Street with all of its many shops and restaurants.

The night we saw the bird creatures again, we'd sauntered down Cortland Avenue, cutting down Winfield Street, a tiny road that ran down a steep hill. A flash of white caught the corner of my eye and I turned to see four or five figures, all white with short yellow beaks and golden claws, crouched on top of the same portion of roof belonging to a short house gated by a white picket fence.

One of the birds stood up and spread its wings, all but covering the other birds, showing an impressive span. Not knowing what else to do, I clutched at The Prophet's amulet under my shirt, sweater, and a jacket. The figure folded its wings back into its body and returned to its previous position. Several of the others started to slowly rise.

There was a deafening bang like that of a car backfiring and they scattered like so many large pigeons and flew away. I turned to Saul who had a pistol in his hand. He smiled roguishly.

"Knew that would come in handy," he said. He tucked the gun away beneath his coat. "Easier than becoming an eagle."

He winked at me.

I thought I'd be able to handle everything. Rumors of strange sorcerers (as if there were other sorcerers out there who were just normal everyday people), killer birds, oddball roommates, and God knew what else out there. But then my hair started to fall out in small clumps that collected in the shower drain.

Saul, meanwhile, took it all in stride. In fact, if nothing else, he seemed to be thriving, waking up to himself at last.

I started to think about moving out and getting a job. I wasn't sure how much longer Lamond and Egyptian Motherlode would find me useful. Certainly, if it were up to me, I'd have cut myself loose a long time ago.

But I couldn't think of much else to do. I had cards printed with my name that identified myself as the manager of the Solomon Blues Band. I'd had an artist turn the first letter into a drawing of a snake, which I thought looked rather sharp, but nobody seemed interested in being represented by the manager of a band that mostly opened for another band that was already considered unreliable. My only way out, I realized was to make Saul and the band successful—and I'd been trying to do that for months.

I decided that we needed to release a record and I began calling up local recording companies to make that happen. We recorded a demo tape of two heavy funk tracks in the men's bathroom of the church we rehearsed in where the acoustics were almost passable. A tune Saul had written, "Slouching Toward Bethlehem," an anti-war song, was straight hard driving funk. We paired it with a slightly more traditional cover of the T-Bone Walker classic, "Stormy Monday," which we retitled "The Eagle Flies on Friday." I think we recorded "Eagle" because Saul thought that it would be amusing to have a bird in the title of one of our songs.

"Birds don't buy 45s," I told him.

We got a lot of more interest in that tune than "Bethlehem," though, probably because of the implied religious content of the latter.

We played another gig with Motherlode in Golden Gate Park once they got back from a tour of the Pacific Northwest. The concert was illegal, although in the 1970s such things were not as strictly enforced as they'd been earlier. You couldn't perform in the park without a permit and you couldn't get a permit to perform in the park. But Motherlode set up their portable stage and went off clowning through the park in an effort to drum up business. Our role was to keep the audience until Motherlode got back. After the show, a hat would be passed around as a collection plate and we'd get a share of the take.

Clearly, I needed to find us better gigs.

The world throbbed, pounding in rhythm with my pulse. It stretched and pulled and I thought it would pull apart until I fell though the seams of my dreams to be lost forever.

I opened my eyes and I could still hear the throbbing, but my head no longer spun. The throbbing was coming from the door.

The door throbbed again, even though I was awake.

"Go away Saul," I mumbled. No more transformations, no more falling spacemen. *Go away.*

More knocking. At the *front* door.

"Fine," I shouted. "I'm coming."

I fell out of bed and threw on my robe and headed down the hallway, morning light draping through the windows. Dawn itself was still just a rumor. I opened the door and found The Prophet, his had hand still raised to knock again at the door. He looked at me curiously over thick, dark glasses.

"Solomon's asleep," I said. I didn't even know if he was there or not. Or alive. Or still in our dimension.

"I'm looking for you," The Prophet said.

He handed me a white Styrofoam cup lapping with black coffee and reached down to pick up another he had set down on the stoop so he could knock at the door. He wrapped the cup in his hands and blew steam off the top.

He looked up at me when I continued to stand stupidly, unsure what to do next.

"Get dressed," he said. "I need your help. Let's go find my notebook."

I stumbled back to my room like a zombie, put the coffee aside on my desk and rummaged on the floor for jeans that would be clean enough and a white T-shirt. I grabbed my jeans jacket off the back of a chair.

The notebook?

When he had fallen from the spaceship and I had rescued him from the sea, he had had a notebook, ruined by the saltwater. He'd said we'd get it—or a new one—later. I wanted to pretend he was just a crazy musician even when I knew, from my own experience, that it just wasn't so, not completely anyway. The music changed everything it touched, opened doors to other places, collapsed tough guys from other dimensions like turning off a television set, revealed starry skies inside night clubs. I pulled on socks and my white Converse.

When I stood and retrieved the still steaming coffee, I wondered if I could go back to bed, refuse to go with him. I stretched, arching my back and yawning, wanting nothing more than to close my eyes.

Saul's door was closed and I thought I could hear something behind it, but it sounded more like electronic bips and boops then someone sleeping. I ignored it. I took my first sip of coffee after locking the door. It was terrible. And with that bitter tang, I made a momentous decision: I would quit managing or doing anything with music, particularly if it involved The Prophet. I'd become a writer, clerk at Blockbuster Video, or sell newspapers on street corners.

"It's cold out here," was all I said, instead.

Damn.

"Come on," The Prophet said, and I followed. He took me by the wrist and led me toward the beach. He also wore a jeans jacket, but no shirt underneath. There was an old pre-Soviet-style Azerbaijan flag sewed on the back upside down, the crescent and eight-pointed star reversed. He had fringed jeans with beads tied at the ends of each strand and open-toed sandals. He had his fro teased out like a dark halo or a fuzzy space helmet. With every step the beads rattled and the sandals flapped.

We appeared to be reversing the half-mile walk from the sea I had led him on when I had first taken him home. I reflected that a million inexplicable things lay between that moment and this one.

Things I hadn't confronted since. Transformations and cracks in the cosmic egg and songs to raise the consciousness of the world. Bird people, servants of an ancient Sorcerer from Egypt—a different Egypt, one, The Prophet once revealed to me was on Nemesis, the planet circling in the exact opposite orbit from ours and so always hidden from us by the sun. But was anything weirder than the spaceship that had brought him to me?

"Are we going to board your spaceship?" I said, as the salt air grew more pungent.

"What?"

We turned when we arrived at the street running along the wall break that overlooked the shore. From here, we could hear the surf but not see it."

"The Mothership?"

He looked up, as if maybe the ship was back in view, silver flashing high up the light of the rising sun.

"Not yet," he said. "We're not ready yet. Besides it's really just a prop. Albeit one that can take you anywhere you like to go."

The sky was empty as my heart. The blue extended for miles out over into the whiteness of the rising sun. At that moment, the first tip of the sun itself beaded on the horizon. We continued to walk and, in a near panic, I realized I couldn't remember anything of my life that didn't include The Prophet. I tried to remember the street where I grew up? My parents' names? Did I have any brothers or sisters? My mind was full of blanks and I became frightened. Where was he leading me? What would happen to me if I lost him? Would I forget him too? Would I remember where I lived? How to feed myself.

"Let's see, now," he said. "Let's see. Let's see, I think I was over here."

We turned down an alley. It was clean with painted doors in green and blue on either side. The doors must have led to apartments, for window boxes above us hung with flowers and drooping vines. It was an idyll just off the beach drag that was quiet now, in early morning, but would be crowded and busy soon enough.

The Prophet began counting doorways on the right as he led us in. He stopped at five.

"Here," he said. "This looks right."

He stepped down three steps to a blue door, waiting ajar, with a hand-painted sign on it that said "Lothlorien." He pushed the door open, flipped on a string of dim lights, and walked down a long, narrow passage under the building, lined with pipes running over our heads, suddenly T-ing or shooting branches. At a dark alcove, he stopped to throw out his Styrofoam cup in a metal garbage can. Water dripped somewhere behind the can. My coffee had gone cold. When he held the lid up and motioned, I set my cup on top of clump of tied up bags inside. He continued on; I followed.

The passage went on longer than I expected, beyond the lights. The corridor opened irregularly on either side more and more often, other passages leading into darkness.

There was a new light ahead when The Prophet stopped at one of the dark openings, I stopped abruptly and heard, faintly, something behind me; I turned suddenly, glimpsing a spider the size of a large dog, silently backing up into the uncertain light until it disappeared. I froze with fear. Its legs had moved in a slow-motion creep; fur lined its body; two black orbs seemed to stare unblinking above a pair of mandibles the length of two curved hunting knives.

I trembled when I tried to speak. The Prophet took my wrist again.

"No way back," he said calmly. "Well, not anymore."

My hand trembled and he made a face.

"Just a guardian," he said.

He led me into the darkness of the side passage. The Prophet dropped my wrist in the darkness and I yelped.

"Ah, this one," he said, ignoring my mounting terror.

I heard him turn a handle and light spread out from an opening door. The doorway led to the back corridor of a restaurant: metal shelving holding cloth napkins, silverware, take out containers; steam condensing on an industrial dishwasher with a red light flashing; a workspace with a clipboard and stacks of invoices. Further in, a cook in a stained white apron carried a metal tray of food across the corridor; a waitress brought used dishes back and laid them on a back counter. We stepped in. No one seemed to notice us.

I watched The Prophet close the door and saw beyond him not a tunnel so much as a pathway through close growing trees under a thick canopy of green.

"No going back that way," he said. "Not after the trouble you caused."

He grinned at me, eyeing me over his dark glasses. How had he seen in the dimness with those on?

"What did I do?"

"You looked back," he said. "Twice now! Come on."

He hit me lightly with the back of his hand, like he was joking. I took hold of his shoulder.

"Why are we doing this?"

The worker in white passed back across the corridor. I couldn't tell if he was studiously ignoring us or couldn't see us. The Prophet took of his glasses and turned to me, staring directly into my face, closer than was comfortable.

"I had a vision," he said. "The people I love: Lamond, the other members of the band, are going to try to save me. They're going to get hurt."

"Your brother?"

"He's going to get in the way of a cosmic wind."

"That's sounds bad. Is that bad? That definitely sounds bad."

"He can't endure it. It may blast his mind into eternity, as easily as one of these dishwashers scours a plate clean. I need to change things. I need to take the encounter I must have sideways to . . . another place."

I didn't understand. "What encounter?" I said.

"'When the stars throw down their spears/And water heaven with their tears.'" I would learn much later that that was a quote from William Blake, a poet.

"You need to change things before they happen?" I said.

"Yes, exactly."

"So you've done this all before?"

"No. Time doesn't work like that. Nothing can be undone." He gestured, revolving his hands around one another. "But some things can be remade or made to seem as if they've happened a certain way—or you can change the venue in which they happened, you know. But not the absolute of the thing itself."

"So what exactly are we doing?"

"I need my notebook. But I can't get it. It's . . . like a book of spells or a book of ways." He motioned back at where we had been, the tunnels, the forest, the spider. "It's here."

He took my arm. He leaned in. "I need direction. This notebook changes things. It's like the difference between having a compass and having a map. Will you get this for me?"

I nodded. "What do I do?"

The restaurant worker passed across the corridor again carrying another metal tray. I could see sliced tomatoes covered in cheese and saran wrap.

"You go forward. Into *that* moment. You find me, eating. I'm having a sandwich. I'm looking at the notebook. You ask to take it, for a time."

He licked his lips. When I didn't let go or move, he motioned with his head for me to go to the front area.

"What happens then?" I asked.

"I give it to you and you come back here and give it to me."

"Huh? Why can't you do it?"

"I can't meet myself. That might be very . . . bad." He took a long breath. "Can you do this for me?"

I nodded again. But I was agitated.

"Did you really fall from the damn sky?" I asked.

"When the time comes," he said. "I will take you on the Mothership, if you really wish to go."

Again, I nodded as if we were sharing the same conversation, and he wasn't a lunatic and I wasn't a fool.

"I'm building a better ship," he told me. "We'll fly out past the asteroid belt, beyond the stars themselves. Out there, somewhere, there's a better place than this. I promise. But right now I need the notebook."

I let go of him and walked forward, in a daze. I felt a shift in the air, as if I suddenly had gone from the coolness of early morning to the heavier air of mid-afternoon. The place was empty except for The Prophet, sitting in a booth with a half-eaten pastrami on rye pushed back from him. He was perusing a notebook with a green cover. He had a second notebook, blue-covered, out and open in which he had copied symbols: some looked like hieroglyphics, some like runes, some just looked like squiggles. He took his Bic and, squinting first at the notebook, then at his copy, he adjusted a line he was drawing.

I walked up to him. The waitress behind the counter eyed me suspiciously as if she wondered where I'd come from. I ignored her.

"I—" My voice caught, and I had to stop and start over. "Can I borrow the notebook, for a bit?" I asked.

The Prophet did not look up. He just sighed, closed the green cover and slid it to the edge of the table.

"Thanks," was all he said. He reached out and took a drink from his coffee while gazing pointedly out the front window into the sun setting beyond the concrete barrier across the street which over-looked the beach and the ocean. We were not far in space, I thought. And The Prophet was dressed in the same clothes as he was . . . back behind me *then*, in the recesses of the diner's back passages.

"I thought I was going back into the past," I said. This is later today, isn't it? That's the notebook I am about to hand to you . . . back there . . . which you are giving to me now, a few hours later. But that doesn't make any sense?"

He put his cup down, leaned forward on his elbows, rubbing his nose with one hand. He did not look up at me.

"This isn't a science fiction time travel story," he said. "*You* are making this happen. You're dreaming this in, destabilizing . . . time itself, so you are also taking it out of our existence at the same time you're bringing it in. No paradox," he finished, with a shrug, "since there is only one notebook."

It was all paradox, actually. But I picked up the notebook, stuck it under my arm, and shuffled back to the other Prophet, waiting down the long corridor.

"Coffee?" the waitress said, but I shook my head. The busboys and cooks continued to work as I passed them as if I or they did not exist. I think they had it right.

"Excellent," The Prophet said, patting my arm.

"You're going to find a diner down the street," I said flatly, "where you can copy the contents."

"Yes," he said, "exactly so."

I turned to go back into the diner.

"Not that way," he said, taking my arm.

"But you said we can't go back."

"No," he said. "And it's dangerous to stay in the flow here, since we've created some turbulence. Best to, well . . . jump a little ahead, you see?"

I didn't.

"Well, you will. This changes things."

He gave me a smile that made me shiver. I smiled back anyway and he hugged me, putting his arm around my shoulder, he
moved me sideways, down a passage I hadn't quite seen before.
I wanted to look back, curious about the optical illusion, but he
held me close against him, and it felt good to have The Prophet
put all his attention on me like that.

"Saul is like a lighthouse in the storm," he said, as if continu-
ing an explanation I had asked for. "Between him and me and
Florence—I can find ways between worlds, entries, exits—that is,
if we get Saul up to speed. Then maybe I can close a gate I should
never have opened. The notebook shows me where to start; with
it, I can . . . triangulate . . . almost anything."

"Florence? The backup singer?" I had heard she and The
Prophet went back a long way, that they had a complicated rela-
tionship.

"She's got power," he said, frowning.

We passed out of the corridor we were in, out of a cool dimness, and found ourselves on the side of a stage. I could hear the
crowd out front, shouting for The Prophet. I thought, *when was
this show? Where and when? Was I already there somewhere?*

"Time to go on," he said. He let me go. I wanted to hold on to
him. I know he has that effect on everyone, but it was no less real
for that. I wanted him to smile at me again. I would have done
almost anything.

"Where's the notebook?" he asked just before he went on stage.

I had tucked it under my arm . . . but it was gone. I panicked
and looked back. Had I dropped it? But The Prophet reached behind his back and pulled out the blue notebook. It was the new
one he had been working on in the diner. He leafed through it,
touching the symbols. He looked pleased with himself, like a kid's
magician holding a bunch of flowers he had just made appear in a
trick he wasn't quite sure was going to work until he did it.

"There we go," he said. "Will you hold this until after the show?"

I took it and he strode away from me on to the stage.

"Like what?" I said, "Triangulate anything like what?"

"Entries," he said again, over his shoulder. "Exits." He continued moving away from me toward the members of his band who
greeted him warmly, never quite knowing when they might see
him again.

"Where have you been?" Lamond shouted, looking up from his bass.

"Don't try to save me," The Prophet called out to him, walking through gyrating dancers throwing glitter in the air. The crowd cheered, spotting The Prophet.

"Don't ever try to save me."

The Prophet put his arms around Lamond, but Lamond was busy trying to keep his bass line going.

"What are you talking about?" he shouted.

"Just let me be," said The Prophet. "When the time comes, just let me be."

"Nobody's going to hurt you as a long as I'm around."

"I can take care of myself."

The Prophet dipped his head and grimaced for just a second before turning toward the mic. He approached it slowly, a hum growing louder as he approached. The hum became a low thrumming, then a wail. He lurched forward and held the mic in both hands. He sang.

> *What if all of animated nature sings*
> *and we have never listened?*
> *What music in the spheres?*
> *What melody the stars?*
> *Can you hear?*

There was a smattering of applause, as crowd hushed to listen. The Prophet looked up into the lights and reached out with one hand, as if pointing to and warding off something.

> *I fear thee, Ancient Starfarer!*
> *With thy grey beard*
> *And glittering ship*
> *You sail the whirlwind of stars.*
>
> *Where do you take me?*
> *Where do you leave me?*
> *Alone and palely loitering.*

> *On an alien shore the spirts four*
> *dice for our souls,*
> *"I've won! I've won," cries Death-in-Life*
> *and whistles thrice.*
>
> *My companions drop lifeless*
> *And I awake to find me here*
> *On the cold hill's side*
> *Crying to the dark:*
>
> *What have you done?*
> *Why have you forsaken me?*
> *I fear thee*
> *I need thee, ancient Starfarer. . . .*

Clutching the notebook to my chest, I had fallen to my knees. I was weeping. The show was only beginning and every song seemed to take me out to distant places and strange dreams and leave me lost among a million million stars with no way home.

The next morning I woke up early, put a pot of coffee on to boil and made some phone calls to East Coast record executives who were already in meetings and would get back to me later as permitted by their busy schedules. I doodled ideas for band logos in a tiny notebook, spiral bound at the top, as I waited for calls that weren't coming. I tried to combine the words "Blues" and "Band" by using only a very large letter B to connect them. A couple of the logos were mildly interesting but rendering the word "Band" as the word "and" clearly didn't work and would leave anybody who looked at them to ask "and what?"

I leafed through the morning paper. President Jimmy Carter was moving to reconvene the Geneva Middle East Peace Conference, which sounded admirable if somewhat unlikely, perhaps a better news story for a future date if the talk progressed. In sports, the local baseball teams were preparing for another season of mediocrity.

I placed the newspaper back on the kitchen table mostly

unread. I thought about the day before when The Prophet had taken me on his back alley tour of other dimensions. I wondered if I could find my own paths by keeping my eyes open and looking for incongruities, folds in the fabric of the universe, and the dusty hidden corners where spiders the size of mastiffs lurked. The giant spiders gave me pause and I remembered The Prophet's warning about the need to keep moving when travelling on those planes of existence.

Perhaps there was something safer that I could try.

I stood up and paced. The coffee and the boredom had me on the edge, but I also now felt like I might be on the verge of . . . something I couldn't quite put my finger on. Clearly there were ways of connecting directly with the forces of universe if one knew how or, like The Prophet, had an innate talent that allowed a more direct connection.

The telephone rang.

"Solomon Blues Band," I answered.

I heard the crackling of a very bad connection and something else that sounded like the crinkling of sandpaper, as if the caller was calling from an outdoor cafe in the middle of a rain storm.

"Dyke?" whispered a gravelly voice.

"I'm sorry. What?"

"Arlester?" Neither word the voice said made any sense. Were they words? "Go home," said the voice. Those were words. "You're dead."

"I'm sorry," I said. "This is 555-2595. Area code 415."

"Remember," said the voice. "You're not supposed to be here."

And then the connection severed without so much as a click and the telephone began blaring in a loud, staccato.

I held the receiving end of the telephone up to my face to get a better look, not that that provided any insight.

I picked up my note book off the table and made a list.

> *Arlester*
> *Dike*
> *Dead*
> *Remember*

And then beneath that:

> *Are you dead, Arlester?*
> *Arlester died plugging the dike.*
>
> *Dam(n)*
> *Ditch*
> *Embankment*
> *Watercourse/Waterway*
> *Levee*

The call had obviously been a wrong number, but I'd always liked puzzles—the Sunday Jumble, Sherlock Holmes detective movies with Basil Rathbone, Colombo—and it bothered me that nothing about the call made any sense. "You're not supposed to be here," the voice had said. Could the call have been for Saul? Somebody else in the Band? Or somebody else someone thought was in the band. Perhaps somebody in a different band?

> *Don't forget you died Arlester*
> *Arlester overflowed with memories.*
> *The dead pouring through the busted dam*

I could feel my skin bunching up on my forehead.

> *You need to define your words.*
> *You need to ask better questions*
> *Who or what is Arlester?*
> *What sort of a dike?*
> *How could you forget you died?*
> *And who would want to remind you?*

I picked up the paper and flipped to the obituary page. Nobody named Arlester or Dike. No names of any consequence. Was that unusual? There was a prominent businessman who had died of a heart attack while playing racquetball, but the other six names listed were not famous people, just people whose families had taken out advertising to announce the time and place of their funerals.

Is Saul/Soloman also Arlester/Dike?
Could Arlester be a member of Egyptian Mother-
lode?
Do I need to find Arlester?
Do I need to avoid Arlester?

Crushed by roiling souls,
Pouring from the cave's dark mouth,
Overflowing the banks of purgatory.
Do any feel responsible?

I kept writing, a terrible free form poetry inspired by the telephone call and the recent events with eagles, birdmen, and spiders from other dimensions—dark stuff that led again and again to dismemberment and death. I was hoping that I could somehow wield some sort of power out of the creative process, but clearly I was not as gifted a writer as The Prophet was a musician, apparently I wasn't gifted at all. Or else the answer was hidden somewhere in my twisted writing as plain as day, lost in a mountain of gibberish.

I crossed out a line and turned to a new page in the notebook. I looked about the living room. Where could a rift into another dimension lie? Stark overhead lights left very little to shadow. A couple of books lay on the floor. The doors to my room and Saul's room were slightly ajar.

The bathroom door was closed. The light inside was off. Inside there was a built in shower/bath combo painted pink, a freestanding sink, toilet, medicine cabinet, laundry pail, and, most likely, one of Saul's towels on the floor.

But could there be something more?

I imagined the wall behind the shower gone, replaced by a long corridor made of large stone bricks the size of a man's head. The corridor would be dry with torches blazing in the distance, just close enough to light the way.

I stood up and walked to the bathroom door.

*

The bathroom was as it always was. I pulled the plastic shower curtain aside and reached for the back of the shower. My hand passed through the wall, about a foot before I felt cold stone. I wrenched my hand back in surprise as if I'd been burned. I reached my hand through the wall again and felt a corner made of stone.

I resisted the urge to stick my head through to get a better glimpse. I walked out, closing the door behind me, back to the living room where I grabbed my notebook. Time worked strangely in these places. Maybe I'd be able to take some notes and hand them back to myself before I started and save myself the struggle of writing them down.

I laughed, and felt the world tilt. I stumbled a bit and wondered for a second if it was the beginning of an earthquake? But nothing rattled; no walls creaked.

There was a knock at the door, but when I opened the front door, no one was there. The knock came again. It wasn't at the front door. The knock came from the bathroom door, which I had shut behind me when I came out. Puzzled and more than a little dazed, I didn't hesitate to head back into my bedroom and open the bathroom door.

The Prophet stood there in his space outfit, like I'd seen him in the beginning: mirrored thigh high boots and silver sparkle shorts, though he had on a white shirt this time, V-necked all the way down his hairy chest; he held his cheap looking bubble helmet, glued on plastic tubing hanging, under his arm. With the other hand, he took a last drag on a cigarette as he regarded me over dark sunglasses with intent, startled eyes, like he was seeing me for the first time. He was agitated, sweating.

"What's with the torches?" he said. "Can't you dream electric light?"

"I—I didn't—"

"You made a passageway, and I came through." He turned his hand with the cigarette out toward me. "Right?" It wasn't quite a question, actually. It was more an accusation. He entered the room, brushing past me.

"I tried—"

"All along I thought Saul was the key to help me unlock the

Sorcerer," he muttered more to himself than me. "But now it's you. You're the last trump I've got left."

Quietly, I said: "the triangulation?"

"Right." He stubbed the cigarette out in an ashtray on my nightstand.

"Look, Robert," The Prophet said, stepping toward me. No one called me Robert, only Bobby, when they bothered to use my name at all. I couldn't remember the last time anyone had called me that and I felt strangely exposed. I held my hands up. I tried to step back, put distance between us, but The Prophet took my arm, stepping so close that his beard touched my nose.

"Robert," he said, softly, "this is dangerous. We're out of time, like . . . *out* of it—in a place where time collapses." He paused, tried again. "Everything happens now. It's a nexus point. What I've been waiting for, planning for. Monstrous things are loose, on the hunt. What you did was like . . . opening a door from a lit room on to a midnight plain, it's a beacon to the monsters prowling the shadows."

"I, I didn't mean—"

"I know."

I shook, flushed; his hand on my arm, though slightly damp with cooling sweat, was steady. He squeezed my arm and looked at me like he had that first day when I fished him out of the sea and returned him to Saul. He looked like he wondered what he had missed, and how he had missed it. I felt my breathing slow, go shallow; he seemed to rummage in my heart, once again, and find it—*again*—wanting.

I would follow him into the stars. But I had no power, no way to help him.

"Are you the shaman . . .?" he said.

"I'm not anything," I said, but he wasn't listening. He had only been talking to himself. "I'm a manager for a band . . . not a very good manager, for not a very good band."

I dropped my head.

"You *have* power. I've seen it. What is . . .?"

The Prophet startled me by grabbing my face in both his hands, raising my eyes to look into his again. He leaned in close, wild eyed. He let me go as abruptly as he took hold of me. I stumbled back a half-step, as if he had held me up.

Circling in place, The Prophet began to shake his hands as if in an excess of nervous excitement. He stood in the bathroom, as if trying to find a way forward, a way out.

"The nexus is now. He'll be here soon. We have to get back."

"What going to happen. Where is Saul?"

"He's with Lamond right now, rehearsing. I was having *him* protected, while you were exposed here."

He shook his head ruefully. The Prophet entered the bathroom again; I hadn't moved so he ran back and pulled me in after him.

"We'll take your corridor. I can bend it to where we need to go."

"You said it was dangerous."

"I've got no choice," he said. "I've got people to protect. You, Lamond, Florence, Star Baby, Saul. None of you know how much I count on you, and what I've had to do to protect you all. The Sorcerer could rip the fabric of our universe without realizing what he was doing. He could destroy gravity, run time out of sequence, topple governments. He has more power than I do, but less control. He could blow all our souls into eternity where they may never be found again."

Did I really have a soul, or was The Prophet incorporating religious mumbo jumbo into his magic? Magic that worked, I reminded myself.

"I thought—"

"Where did you leave it?" He motioned to the dirty tiles of the bathroom wall. I saw tears in his eyes as he began to search frantically.

"Show me where you put it!"

I looked up, stupidly. There was nothing unexpected in the bathroom, no passage. Hadn't he just come through? Didn't he know where he came through? I pulled the shower curtain and touched the cool tile, tried to find where the wall fell away. The light began to flicker, but it wasn't magic—just a loose fuse that often went out like that.

"I didn't do anything," I said.

"There it is," he said, relieved. He pointed to the bare wall above the toilet.

He lowered the toilet seat and stepped up on it. I still couldn't see anything, but when he reached out, his arm blurred and *bent*, vanishing into the wall. It didn't seem to hurt him.

"Come on," he said, stepping up and through, bringing his leg up like going over a fence, somehow also sliding over and fading from view—he left me like a light going out on a dimmer switch.

I stepped up on the toilet seat. I reached my hand out. I was too slow. The Prophet reached back and pulled me into darkness. A light gust hit my face and a mist condensed on my cheeks like cold tears. I was on my hands and knees. The ground felt rough and loose, like packed dirt.

"Hurry," The Prophet said. "I need you close."

"What do I need to—how do I triangulate?" I asked.

"You just need to be there—you, me, and Florence. Like the witches in Macbeth, or the Fates, we have power together. We can bring help to us that way . . . when we are three . . . when we have a way to locate the break-in point, the way between . . ." He made a long sliding motion along my arm like the touch would show me what he meant. "We can plot the way between, the curve of the arc that slides between—we can triangulate a landing place for the traveler."

"I don't know what you're talking about," I confessed.

"Come on."

He pulled me up and we ran along, crouched down, through darkness. We moved quickly as shadows swirled around us, shapes becoming visible to me as my eyes adjusted. Other shadows seemed to gather out beyond them, in pools of deeper darkness; they moved back and forth, as if hunting for something. Like a terrible game of blind man's bluff with monsters. We zigged and zagged as The Prophet led us through. My breathing came shallow and my throat constricted. I stumbled. The Prophet grabbed my hand, dragged me close behind.

"Down," The Prophet said suddenly, and we dropped to all fours. Some *thing* flew above us, slow, inky black wings and a misshapen head against a dark grey sky. Then we crawled forward into a tunnel too low to stand; the ground inside the tunnel was dry, sandy to the touch. I heard a snarl not far behind us, just outside. We hurried on. I expected a claw to grab my ankle, or a sharp talon against my calf—but it never came.

"Hurry," The Prophet said, stopping for me to catch up. My knees had begun to ache and I was falling behind. "Please!"

I'd never known The Prophet to be frightened.

"I'm sorry," I said.

"You don't even play an instrument," he said forlornly.

I shook my head, not knowing if he could see me. We crawled on. My breathing became ragged with exertion; fear ebbed as time dragged, but not because there was anything less to fear.

"Do you sing?"

He still crawled forward. I shook my head again.

"Have you ever turned in to anything? An animal?"

I didn't even bother to respond, just tried to keep going. My hands hurt badly.

"If you don't change, you must have a familiar."

"I don't have a familiar," I said. "Do you still think I'm the . . . something to triangulate with?"

"God, I hope so," he said. I'd never heard him unsure, either. "Because here we are."

"What about Saul?" I said. "I thought he was being groomed for this, not me."

"I made a mistake with Saul," he said. "I tried to bring back an old friend."

"From where?"

"From the dead. I tried to bring back his spirit, but I was too late. All Saul got were my memories of my friend, not my friend's memories at all—see?" I didn't. "At least I think that's how it worked. There's still some of Dyke in there, I'm sure, but those memories are just an overlay, really. Saul is very much still Saul, except there's some extra stuff in there, too. I still hoped he'd be able to help, but I can't count on him. His development has been too slow. You're the one I need now, but in my rush I developed you too quickly. And now we're out of time."

The Prophet dropped away in front of me, his voice cutting off as he went. I swung my legs over the hole he'd fallen into, and let myself down to the end of my arms. My legs swung, touching nothing. I took a shuddering breath and let go. I landed, stumbling, in an open room, catching myself by holding a chair back that I'd careened into with my face. I rubbed my aching nose.

We were in the dressing room of a club: just a mirror with lights on it, a few chairs, an old worn couch with a sad, discolored kaftan thrown over the back cushions. Random jars of make-up and a bottle of hairspray were on the table before the mirrors.

I caught multiple glimpses of myself in the various mirrors. I looked like hell, strangely gaunt and very befuddled. The Prophet was already opening the door to the hall.

"Lamond," he shouted, running into the hallway.

"Wait," I said. I somehow got myself out the door, without knowing how. My knees cracked, and my legs ached. How long had we crawled through that dark, rocky land outside of time?

The Prophet sprinted down the corridor, toward the stage. I ran after him.

The corridor led to short steps that went up to an open area just off the stage. Two giant, sharp-beaked birdmen guarded the way; seven feet tall, carrying the short handles of sickle-bladed knives in each feathered hand. They were dressed in short Egyptian wraps, shirtless with muscled chests, metal armlets, just above the crook of their wings. Seeing us, they took deliberate warrior stances, one blade held out flat toward us, the other raised behind their heads, ready to strike.

Behind them, lights and sound filled the stage. The Motherlode members, as if in a stupor or a trance, were trying to play their instruments while chaos surrounded them. All I could hear were harsh dissonant squeaks and clangs that bore little resemblance to any music they had ever played, however odd. Beyond the warriors, above the band, I saw the impossible—a whirlwind of stars funneling down from an immeasurable distance, storm clouds lit by flashes of lightening circling in a terrible night sky.

Saul and Lamond stood together in the mix of players. Lamond appeared to be imploring Saul to sing, but I couldn't hear if he was or not, not over the discordant sounds all around us.

"We have to get to the stage," The Prophet shouted to me. He had stopped before the steps, before the giant guardians. He pulled out his notebook, the one I'd helped him find. "We have a way to call for help," he said. He looked back at me. "You gave that to me. This isn't the Sorcerer's—it's one I made; there's nothing for that bastard here. This is just revenge. I can end it. You get me on the stage and this will all be over. Call out!"

I put my hands up, pleading. "I—I don't have—"

He made a circling motion with one hand, meaning "hurry up." I shook my head,

He said, harshly, "Now!"

"I don't know how."

I thought: if he's counting on me to handle this, we're going to die. I began to cry. I wished I'd never tried to open that passage way in the bathroom. Beyond the birdmen guardians, cawing defiance, on the far side of the stage—beyond the overwhelmed Egyptian Motherlode playing like zombies beneath the threatening sky, I saw it: the inhuman Sorcerer, its head like a featherless bird's head, its eyes round and lidless and the sides with slits for ears. It held its arms out, gesticulating with sharp-clawed fingers, exhorting the darkness down—pulling it down.

Two more guardians towered over the Sorcerer, waiting with their sharp knives.

The Prophet touched my cheek. He looked at me over his dark glasses. How had he seen in the land of shadows with those damn things on? But, I realized, he hadn't seen at all, had he? Not like that. He looked without his eyes in ways I would never fathom.

His gaze held mine.

"We're at the nexus," he said. "We are at the gates of oblivion, the edge of time. We have come through heat and pain, to gardens dark with sinuous rills. Through peril to otherways—The Prophet's path. I can call down help through the Sorcerer's tear between dimensions . . . but only out there." He pointed. "Standing beneath it all."

I started as the guardians decided to come to us. They could not fit in the corridor together, and so one took the lead and stepped down toward us. It sliced the air with its forward blade, the other still high behind its head.

The Prophet squeezed my arm.

"Call," he implored.

The lead guardian stepped another step.

"Call!"

The Prophet turned in desperation to face what came to us, but he was too small to face this thing hand-to-hand. He had no weapon but his notebook, which he held up. He bellowed, but it was a cry of frustration. The leading birdman made a caw, weird and high-pitched in return. I held my hands up, palms out.

"Oh, spirit guide, ple—" I said, uncertain.

I felt like a fool, but before I even finished saying "please," a shadow descended rapidly from the darkness of the rafters. A giant spider landed on the back of the leading guardian; large, the size of a bull mastiff, it enveloped him in its long spindly legs, pulling it off the steps and up into the shadows, rising on a trailing strand of web.

"Holy crap," I said.

"That's so cool," The Prophet said.

The other guardian stepped back and looked up, clacking its beak, turning its head side to side, coal black eyes blinking rapidly. There was a cry in the rafters, suddenly cut short. Two sickle knives dropped, clanging loudly, then silence. A sticky glob of web spat out from above, landing on one of the reaming guardian's hands. When it reached over to remove the gob, its other hand became stuck. The guardian bent forward to bring its strength to bear and pull its hands apart; the spider landed on its back, enveloped it. My spirit guide paused a moment to look at me with hundreds of glittering eyes in two black orbs; I had seen it before, in the forest when The Prophet and I had gone to retrieve his notebook. It had not been stalking me then, I realized; it had been protecting me. The stage lights reflected in its many eyes like shattered stars. I could understand nothing about that long look it gave me.

Its front mandibles moved slowly, opened and shutting, as it held the giant birdman tighter into its embrace; the birdman seemed resigned. Without warning, the spider struck with a spike from its abdomen; the birdman shook in a sudden paralysis, dropping its sickle-knives; then they were both away into the rafters.

"Now," The Prophet called to me, running up the steps.

I followed, dazed. If I had a spirit guide, was I not a wizard? What else might I be capable of?

The Motherlode huddled together at the rear of the stage, with the drummers still beating a ragged beat, but the others no longer had the heart to play at all. Only Lamond still shouted, animated, cursing the Sorcerer, but he could not approach with the seven-foot guardians beside it. The Sorcerer had reached up and bodily pulled down the darkness in thick clumps, which pooled on the stage, as if two realties met and could not reconcile. It held great gobs of darkness to its chest.

As I stumbled onstage after The Prophet, under those encroaching stars, I could see, all at once, into new and impossible dimensions, bending out in all directions. I fell down to one knee, dizzy, disoriented. I threw up. The stars spun and stormed, and with a lurch I felt everything tip and then I was falling into them. The Motherlode, too, tumbled forward and *up*, toward the gaping, swirling night above us. We had set everything off kilter, The Prophet and I, running on stage. Gravity was losing hold as something else took us up.

A few of the band members, including Saul and Lamond, had managed to right themselves and were slowly staggering toward the Sorcerer, perhaps to make a last attempt to stop him. I caught myself with one hand. I thought I saw The Prophet fall, and so thought we were done for, but he only reached down to pick up a discarded mic. He stood, at ease as the world churned and tiled; he leaned forward as if supported by an imaginary wind that held him, stopping him from falling over.

"*The Time has come to speak of something far more deeply interfused*," The Prophet said, his voice reverberating into and out of the void.

Gravity seemed to right itself. I stood unsteadily.

I looked out from the stage and realized there was a small audience of no more than two dozen people who had come out to watch what must have been a rehearsal. They were relatives, sound crew, the lighting tech, and a few diehard fans. They stood listless and silent in shadow beyond spotlights glaring at us from above. They waited in a limbo for something to shake out—or maybe, for something to fit together and make sense at last, so they could know how to react. Faced with the impossible, they did nothing.

> *A Funk Sublime—a motion and a spirit that impels*
> *and rolls through all things—*
> *where every groove belonging to me*
> *as good belongs to you.*

The small crowd shuffled their feet, murmured. Two people applauded. Someone shouted, "about time!" The Prophet raised his open hand and brought everybody's attention back to him. Someone whistled from the back of the crowd; there was more clapping, feet stomping. The Sorcerer squawked angrily, gathering darkness in its claws, compressing it into a thickness, pin-pricked with stars.

Turning back, The Prophet said to Florence, "it's time. Make the call! It's time!"

The Prophet turned and dipped his head to the mic, falling back into his song's opening chant: "The time has come to speak of all unspoken things—why the darkness is boiling hot and whether pigs have wings."

I had heard the Motherlode rehearse the song before and wondered why they never played it. Now, the backing band should be coming in, but would they?

The Prophet vocalized low, pulsing hums, sometimes crying out, sometimes falling silent; he growled and the hair on the back of my neck stood up.

I glanced back toward the Motherlode. Lamond was urging them to play, and had begun to lay down a bass line; a drummer gave a tentative beat, realized the sound came true, then fell in line with Lamond's steady bass, driving a groove; other drum-mers, including, I saw, a great black bear, leaned over their up-right drums and beat out a complex rhythm between them. Ev-eryone else began to move, dancing around one another in their colorful dashikis, tie-dyed pants, mini-skirts with feather boas, and fringed leather vests. Lamond wore a fatigue jacket, ripped under one arm, pricey white chinos that seemed to be stained along one side with dark grease, and black steel-toed boots. He looked like he had slept in the gutter and dressed for the end of the world. He looked angry, and brought it all into a bass line to calm all those tumbling stars.

And they were slowing, and the storm clouds on the edge of that ragged tear in the world stormed less, and began to settle and even dissipate.

Florence, tall, and even taller with her platform shoes and long, frizzy hair, wearing spangled granny glasses, a multicolored T-shirt shirt adorned with sequins, an ankh necklace, and hip-hugger jeans, looked uncertain only a moment. Then she flicked a mic she still held on and stepped upstage.

"I think I hear the stars coming," she said, laying vocals be-hind The Prophet's lyrics. "I know I hear the stars coming," she said with more confidence. She closed her eyes. "I'm sure I see the stars coming—I see the stars coming," and on.

Far distant above our head from out of the deep starscape, something glinted, flames shooting forth. The disc-shaped spaceship that had dropped him into the sea now returned to claim its lost spaceman. It came fast but the distance was vast. As it approached, I could see it held lots of rectangular tanks connected together by metal piping, overlaying portholes, with an exhaust structure below. Parts of it looked a little lumpy, covered in sheets of tinfoil, possibly betraying that it had been added quickly using silver-painted papier mâché. Like everything I've seen connected to The Prophet, it didn't quite make sense. Real flames shot out below, with a spray of sparks and strobing light.

The Sorcerer paused, claws full of pulsing darkness, to watch the ship. It cawed orders to its guardians. The bird-men raised their knives, and moved toward Florence.

"Funk is the sweet voice," The Prophet said, earnest now, into it. "Funk the luminous cloud—all melodies the echoes of that voice—all colors a suffusion of that light."

The Prophet raised his hand, palm open, moving toward the middle of the stage; the storm clouds above continued to recede into the edges of the night above us.

The Sorcerer gathered itself, balling up the darkness it held to its chest with both claws, taking a long inhalation before pushing the dark outward in a violent motion at The Prophet. The darkness flowed across and struck, making him stagger and fall. It hit him with an arc of nothingness and vacuum. The crowd gasped. The Motherlode lost the beat, stopped playing. Florence screamed.

Lamond took off his bass and moved forward, toward his brother, blocking the flow of darkness with his body. Darkness enveloped him in waves, spinning him around like a top. I caught a brief glimpse of him, back arching like he'd been hit by an electric current, mouth open in a silent scream, before he disappeared like a swimmer beneath the waves of a tempest, his neck muscles bulging as he choked, skin turning ashen as he fell lifeless, limp. Then he was gone.

The guardians closed on Florence, but Saul stepped out of the Motherlode dancers to block their way, warding them off with his arms raised; they barely paused—one of them struck him on the head with the pommel of its knife and he crumpled to the stage.

Florence shouted and the black bear, the drummer, walking now on two legs, taller even than the birdmen, roared, stepping before her and smacking a birdman back where it lay, unmoving. The other birdmen quickly gave way, backing up. Saul lay deathly still, sprawled on the stage, red seeping from his head.

My spider guide dropped on me, holding me in its furred legs. I started, fearing, just a moment, the sting to follow, but I knew it had come to protect me.

The stage lit up brighter than the noon day sky as a ball of fire descended. We shielded our eyes and looked up as best we could; we could see far beyond the rafters into the illuminated night sky as all the stars seemed to supernova at once. Light everywhere.

The Mothership had landed.

The fire enveloped us all. We burned up. We died.

I can't explain the images and experiences I had in any coherent way. They do not make sense. I could lie and say: we didn't die. I feel asleep. I dreamed it. That would be true enough. But not the truth. I will have the truth, ragged and unprofitable as it is. I will stay with it and hold it in my heart. Because that is who I am, what I am . . . maybe that is what The Prophet saw in me that first time he looked into my eyes (and again, before he took me here through the tunnel I made to this moment) and judged my sorry soul. Maybe he saw I could not understand but that I would not turn away . . . and maybe that was enough for him to trust in me and bring the starship down. I like to think so, that it matters that I hold on.

We blasted off. I felt a churning in the pit of my stomach, my entire body had become an enormous weight pushing me down. I wanted to fall to the floor, but there was nowhere to fall to and so I never fell . . . or I never stopped falling.

The view out the porthole was breathtaking, stars twinkling brighter than I'd ever seen the before, darkness darker than my wildest nightmares.

*

I plucked the moon like a pearl out of the sky. I ate it and lay on my back with indigestion until even that ache left me, like the last thing I would ever remember.

The Prophet put his helmet on over his afro. He had on the mirrored, thigh high boots and silver sparkle shorts I had seen him wear when he was dropped into the sea. (How long ago? A million years?) The helmet was still just an upside down fishbowl with dangling corrugated tubing attached. Tufts of his beard stuck out below his helmet. He had some sort of silver headgear, a kind of diadem, about his head. He strode up a gangplank back into the spaceship.

"I'll be back," he shouted, waving goodbye. "I'll be back for all of you!"

Floating in the darkness beyond the stars, I had time to think. I thought about what The Prophet said once about where (and when) he went when he left us to travel through the music to the spheres: "I was in the time when the stars came down from their places and became gods." I contemplated what he meant for a million years of sadness.

We were joined by other spirit guides on that stage. A figure that was half man and half goat, a giant green and blue-scaled serpent, a wolverine, and a bunny rabbit.

My spider guide sent a filament into the impossible night above us. For an endless moment, it shot through sky before it landed on the underside of the departing Mothership. I felt myself lifted rapidly up into the rafters, into the stars. Distance in the small theater was not to scale, thousands of miles contracted into no space at all. I shouted, terrified. It was cold in space. We landed upside down on the undercarriage of the Mothership, flames shooting out around us. I gripped my spider's furry belly tight. For a moment we scurried along. The spider sent another filament out. I looked out at stars burning in the distance. I saw what seemed like planets, the hot gas clouds of Venus, red dusty Mars. Then the spider leapt again across the gulf of stars. I laughed in terror, overwhelmed. We swung back over the stage.

The spider set me down gently beside Saul where he lay unconscious, his head dripping blood. My spider disappeared into the rafters and was gone.

I saw Egyptian Motherlode's dancers moving in a circle around the moon. The drummers sat up on its dusty surface, laying down a deep and steady beat.

I heard Florence chanting. Her bear, one of its claws bloodied, prowled the stage, looking for another adversary. No birdmen guardians remained to be seen.

The ship was shooting steam and smoke out from its sides, hissing, as it came in to land; a door opened and a wolf-headed man peered down at us. He wore a white wrap around his waist, silver armbands, and a kind of coronet on his head. His arms and chest were powerful. His skin was dark and hairless, except for the wolf's hair beginning at the shoulders.

Lamond reappeared as the last wave of darkness crashed, then fell away, upward into the receding night; he lay like a mariner washed up on the waves after a storm; he still shuddered; he moaned.

Dragging himself toward his fallen brother, The Prophet cried out in anguish.

Slowly, the Mothership rose back into the night, flame cascading against the stage floor. Somehow the flames were not lighting the stage on fire, nor were they generating much heat.

"He's going away," somebody yelled.

"Thank God," someone else replied.

The ship rose above the rafters, continued on for some time, growing smaller and smaller.

There was a loud clap and a blinding flash of light. The night vanished.

Parts of the floor were smoldering, but nothing seemed to have caught fire.

Everybody screamed, panicked for the first time, pushing for the exits. Bodies were everywhere in motion.

The Prophet laughed, but he was crying, too. He helped his brother up, but Lamond did not seem to know where he was. The two began to move toward the back of the stage, passing through a door.

Florence cradled an injured rabbit in her hands.

Saul stood up suddenly. I reached out for him, remembering that my guide had brought me to him, that perhaps Saul needed me. He stumbled into me, but then clapped me on the back, smiling broadly. I held him up.

"What a wild ride!" he shouted. "Better than magic," he said. What was it, if not magic? I didn't bother to ask.

He sagged against me, suddenly tired. He held his head. There was blood, but the wound was only on the surface.

I found a side door and pushed Saul through it, into a side alley. We stood beside a row of garbage cans. I checked Saul's head more closely, then we laughed and shivered—for reasons we could not have explained to one another—gathering strength to move on again.

When the police and the medics arrived, they missed us among the garbage cans and I didn't care to alert them.

We left finally when the fire department showed up.

"Time to go home," I said.

Saul leaned on me and we staggered out a back way, though a maze of lonely alleys; slowly, stopping often, we made our way through empty streets. There was not a star in the sky, as if all the stars had been trapped inside that impossible night sky, spun like a web inside the theater, now lost forever.

*

I slept, on and off, for two weeks.

The Prophet, and the Sorcerer, were gone. I'd never see them again—or at least I haven't yet. I've never seen my spider again either. I am not so foolish anymore as to think this means such things do not exist, just that I've managed to stay out of enough danger that it would be necessary to summon it for my protection. That's what I like to think, anyway.

Lamond spent several weeks in the hospital for what was termed exhaustion. He came out of it physically after a month, but gradually lost his mental faculties. He was catatonic, like Saul when I first reconnected with him. Lamond was finally diagnosed with Huntington's Chorea, an inherited disease that results in the death of brain cells over time. It's the same disease that took the life and creativity of Woody Guthrie. Eventually, Lamond had to be moved to an institution. I would occasionally visit him there, though I never found much to say.

Florence gathered up many of the Motherlode that remained and headed North, first to Humboldt County in Northern California and later to Oregon, waiting for The Prophet to return, making music to soothe the savage stars. I thought Saul and I would go with them but Saul had other ideas. Two members of the Solomon Blues Band went with the Motherlode, the other stayed in the Bay Area and became a session musician who remains very high in demand.

I stayed with Saul, probably because we each felt responsible for each other in some strange way. We bought a duplex on Bernal Hill, not far from the church where we used to rehearse. Saul lives there still. He took some courses and became an actuary. He said he likes it—the certainty of it, at least—of death and numbers.

Dyke turned out to be "Dyke" Arlester Christian, who fronted the band Dyke and the Blazers from 1967 until his death in 1971. Christian had been preparing for a UK tour with Barry White when he was gunned down on the streets of Phoenix in what was determined to be a drug deal gone wrong. His killing was ruled self-defense. He is famously one of several prominent recording artists to have died suddenly at the age of 27. The list also includes Janis Joplin and Jimi Hendrix, both with their own Motherlode connections.

Dyke and the Blazers are best known for their recordings of the original versions of "Funky Broadway," later a hit recording by Wilson Picket, "We Got More Soul," and "Let a Woman Be a Woman, and a Man Be a Man," sampled on recordings by Tupac Shakur, Stetsasonic, and The Heavy. "Funky Broadway" was the first hit song to use the word "funky" in its title and was subsequently banned by many radio stations. Most of the band's singles were the result of lengthy jam sessions that were then edited down to fit the format of 45 rpm records. In recent years, the original versions have been released. Check out the expanded versions of "The Funky Bull," "Funky Walk," and "Moon" and you will hear a band in full throttle, unlike anything made by their contemporaries, pure gut-bucket soul.

I began to write down the stories of The Prophet, beginning with Florence. She encouraged me, and gave me what she had done, a story she'd gotten from Lamond about the early days. I interviewed Star Baby. I wrote my own story. And I found The Prophet's uncle living in Europe. For a time, that's as far as I got. I didn't know what to do with the manuscript. I left a copy with Florence and the Motherlode Collective and returned to San Francisco.

Like so many things with the Motherlode, like the strange rehearsals and communications with the dead, though almost nobody had been at the final show when the spaceship had landed, and many there remembered it faintly, with disbelief, or never saw what of some of us saw—still, everyone seemed to know about it, and to know what happened. They'd heard about it and it fired their imagination. Didn't you know about them, I'd be asked, didn't you used to work with them? I'd shake my head. I was willing to talk, but where do you start? Other bands landed the Mothership, sometimes fancy ones made out of fiberglass and silver laminae that landed on stage at the end of long jams. I would clap with the rest, feeling very little but a faint echo of what I had once experienced. These starships couldn't get more than fifty feet off the ground. But it was all right. It was fine.

I fell into writing about the Bay Area's music scene, which is, sad to say, a shell of its former glory. The punk scene briefly looked like it might revitalize The City's music scene after the dark days of disco, but high rents and corporate interests conspired to drive away many of the most talented artists.

After I ran my own music zine into the ground, following a brief rise in prominence, I headed East to work in New York.

When I discovered that Egyptian Motherlode were on tour again, with The Prophet, in California, I dropped everything to join them mid-tour. I was to travel with them as an embedded writer—at least, that's the plan I forced on my unhappy editor. By the time I got there, though, it was over. Egyptian Motherlode was gone again. All of them this time. I searched around, traced their route, went back to their haunts in California and Oregon, before finally returning with my tail between my legs.

More years passed before I thought to look up the band that played with Motherlode on their final tour. A short-lived, hardly remembered rap group called Crushed Ice which had disbanded after their first and only tour. It was not easy to track its members and I wondered sometimes if they, too, had gone up on the Mothership. Finally, I met Michael, then a graduate student in Anthropology, now Dr. Wiggins, who worked at a University not two hours by train from New York.

Michael gave me the last unbelievable piece of the story— which I have now given to you. He and I meet every few months for lunch at a sandwich shop near his well-manicured campus. We chat about our lives and music, but rarely The Prophet; still, we both like that someone else knows, that there's someone else who can appreciate and understand, someone who remembers. We keep an eye out for word that The Prophet will come again, that the music will start up. I imagine that this is how religions begin, even if this one is stunningly small. I long for the day when I will feel the electric current jolt me into dancing under the open night, when the mysteries of the universe will be explained, and when I will once again know what it means to see the world through the many faceted eyes of a spider. But I don't think it will ever happen quite that way again.

"Time like a bullet lodges in my heart," I say to myself, my head resting against the cool pane of the window on the train as I make my way to Michael. "The loneliness of an empty dream is memory."

I still don't know have much of an idea what those words mean, but I hold the opaqueness of them to me like rubbing a well-worn talisman to remind myself of my connection to a larger mystery.

For reasons I cannot explain, I feel certain we will meet again—The Prophet and I—at the most unlikely turn of the road. I do not wonder if, I only wonder when and where that will be.

I'm still waiting for another ride on the Mothership like The Prophet promised me. The real one, not the one I've seen land at the end of funked up music shows. The one that waits beyond the edges of our patched up, ragged world.

ABOUT THE AUTHORS

David Sandner is a member of SFWA and the HWA. His work has appeared in *Asimov's, Weird Tales, Realms of Fantasy, Pulphouse, Mythic Delirium*, and anthologies *Baseball Fantastic, The Mammoth Book of Black Magic*, and *Tails of Wonder and Imagination*. He is the author of *His Unburned Heart, The Afterlife of Frankenstein, The Fantastic Sublime*, Mythopoeic Award-nominated *Critical Discourses of the Fantastic, 1712-1831*, and editor of *Fantastic Literature: A Critical Reader and The Treasury of the Fantastic* (with Jacob Weisman) and *Philip K. Dick, Here and Now*. He is a Professor of Romanticism and Popular Literature at California State University, Fullerton.

Jacob Weisman is the publisher at Tachyon Publications, which he founded in 1995. He is a World Fantasy Award winner for the anthology *The New Voices of Fantasy*, which he co-edited with Peter S. Beagle, and is the series editor of Tachyon's critically acclaimed novella line, including the Hugo Award–winning *The Emperor's Soul*, by Brandon Sanderson, and the Nebula and Shirley Jackson award-winning *We Are All Completely Fine*, by Daryl Gregory. His writing has appeared in *The Nation, Realms of Fantasy, The Louisville Courier-Journal, The Seattle Weekly*, and *The Cooper Point Journal*.

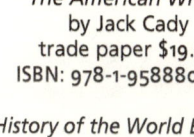

www.ingramcontent.com/pod-product-compliance
Lightning Source LLC
Chambersburg PA
CBHW020359030726
47496CB00007B/2217